A FAIR TO REMEMBER

The World's Fair Series

1901

A Fair to REMEMBER

SUZIE JOHNSON

AMHERST PUBLIC LIBRARY
221 SPRING STREET
AMHERST, OHIO 44001

DISCARD

WhiteFire Publishing

This is a work of fiction. All characters and events portrayed in this novel are either fictitious or used fictitiously.

A FAIR TO REMEMBER

Copyright © 2015, Suzie Johnson
All rights reserved. Reproduction in part or in whole is strictly forbidden without the express written consent of the publisher.

WhiteFire Publishing
13607 Bedford Rd NE
Cumberland, MD 21502

ISBN: 978-1-939023-49-0 (print)
       978-1-939023-50-6 (digital)

This book is dedicated to the memory my grandmother, Clara.
How I wish she were here to read it.
I found an old photograph of her from a picnic she went on with my
grandfather and some friends before they were married.
She was beautiful, and she is exactly how I pictured my Clara.

"If we confess our sins, He is faithful and just and will forgive us our sins and purify us from all unrighteousness." ~ 1 John 1:9

CHAPTER 1

Pan-American Exposition
Buffalo, New York
September 6, 1901

Joy sprang through Clara Lambert's veins like an exuberant child, out-rivaling even the most excited of voices shouting to be heard just outside the doors of the Temple of Music.

Like every other building and structure at the Pan-American Exposition, the Temple of Music was a carefully designed architectural work of art, teeming with color and light. Not the least of which rose overhead in a magnificent dome of stained glass. Backlit by the remainder of the day's sunshine, the shades of blue and yellow sparkled brilliantly. Clara marveled that mere men were capable of creating such beauty.

The camera she clutched under her arm would certainly never replicate what the naked eye could behold, and it definitely couldn't capture the color. But it would be a lovely reminder.

With both hands, she positioned the rectangular wooden box toward the dome. Angled such as it was, she was unable to look through the viewfinder. She'd just have to trust the photograph would record the image in a way that would do justice to the beauty overhead.

When she pressed the button, the now familiar whir and click of the camera indicated it had indeed performed its job with all of the ease her boss, Mr. Eastman, promised. Once processed, the film inside the camera would produce a permanent reminder of this most special of days.

The day she would meet President William McKinley. Not only was she,

Clara Lambert, standing right next to the platform where President McKinley would officially greet the men and women waiting to fill the giant auditorium, she would be one of the first to shake his hand. The opportunity to meet him before taking photographs as he shook hands with the public had been pre-arranged by Mr. Eastman.

She needed to be careful not to waste her film. Each spool held six exposures, and she only had one other unused spool in her bag. The others must have spilled out of her bag when she replaced the film in the camera after her visit to Niagara Falls. This was either the second or third photograph she'd taken on this spool. That left only a few for the president before she had to change the film—if she had the opportunity to sit down and do so. Not that she could do anything about it now. She glanced around the huge room. Once the auditorium filled up, there may not be a spot for her to reload the camera. The police officer who'd escorted her inside told her there were hundreds of people waiting in the heat so they could shake hands with the president. She'd been ever so fortunate not to be one of them.

Why had she been foolish enough to snap photos before she met the president? In case she couldn't change the film, she'd have to take extra care when she photographed him to ensure the pictures wouldn't be blurry.

Once again, like earlier today, Clara could scarcely believe her good fortune. This was most definitely a day to remember. Though she didn't get the opportunity then to meet him as she would this evening, Clara did get to photograph President McKinley and his wife earlier today as they took in the sights at Niagara Falls. Like many Buffalo residents who'd wanted to be at the Falls at the same time as the president, Clara had taken the train in hopes of seeing the president and Ida McKinley. They hadn't posed, and likely didn't even know she'd taken their photo. She'd definitely been blessed to have the opportunity to take more than one photograph of the couple who were so obviously devoted to each other.

Of the four photographers led inside the great room by one of

Buffalo's police officers, Clara was the only female. She stood where instructed, just to the left of center stage, which wasn't actually the stage in this enormous building. The elaborate stage was really in back of her. The entire middle section of seating had been removed, effectively creating a large center aisle, and at the back of the room was a slightly elevated platform draped with patriotic bunting. This struck her as odd since the music room's fancified stage was one of the most intricate she'd ever seen.

A small group of crisply-suited officers filed in. They wore uniforms that were specially designed for the Pan—the shortened nickname local people gave the Pan-American Exposition. Though their features were schooled to appear stern and official, she could tell by a faint lift to most of their mouths that they were proud to wear the uniform and to be here in this room while the public greeted the president. Clara wished she could spare the film to snap their photographs. Each man took a spot along the floor at the bottom of the platform and established themselves in pairs—six on each side.

One of the men, the one closest to her, glanced her way and her pulse sped up. From beneath the gold trimmed bill of his snug fitting black cap, the dark, inky depths of his eyes drew her gaze, and she couldn't look away. It had to be the excitement of the afternoon. Nothing more. Still Clara offered him a smile, shy at best, meant only to assure herself that the increase of her heartbeat was simply in response to the knowledge that the president was about to walk in.

When the officer didn't return Clara's smile, her heart pounded harder, its sound flooding her ears.

Well, then.

Drawing in a quick breath, she hoped the other photographers hadn't noticed. He might not put forth the friendliest demeanor, but the men protecting the president had to remain focused. True, the president wasn't in the room yet, but diligence was a must. She grew up hearing about President Lincoln and how devastated the country was by his assassination. Something like that could never be allowed to happen again.

Footsteps sounded behind her, and Clara turned. Three men were making their way toward the platform.

President McKinley.

The president wasn't a tall man. But the way he carried himself, the way he squared his broad shoulders as he walked forward, gave off an air of confidence—not in an imposing manner, though. At least not when he was greeting the public. Even now as he continued down the aisle with the organist playing "The Star Spangled Banner," President McKinley smiled with genuine warmth as he nodded to those inside the auditorium who stood at attention.

The two men flanking the president stopped as they neared the platform. The president stepped up, then turned and stepped back down.

"I'll just stand here. It's friendlier." He was closer now, and beneath his bushy eyebrows Clara could see joy radiating from his blue eyes. He truly enjoyed meeting people.

As his men stepped off to one side, they effectively edged aside the closest police officers. This seemed to cause upset among the officers as they looked at one another and whispered among themselves.

Finally, the president spoke up. "Gentlemen, don't be so concerned. There's no one here who wants to hurt me."

After a few more whispers, they finally stood silent.

The officer with the dark brown eyes had his lips pressed together. Annoyed? Concerned? Clara couldn't tell. But while she was watching him, he met her gaze once again.

She flushed.

Noise abruptly filled the auditorium then, as people began to stream from the four entrances of the Temple of Music. Thankfully that attracted the officer's attention, and he glanced at the president, then out toward the crowd. Fanning from either side of the platform, they were all corralled into a line that eventually wended its way down the center aisle, their backs to the beautiful stage, facing the president. The line stopped about twelve feet from where he stood. He merely stood there, seemingly unconcerned, hands clasped in front of him, smiling out at the people.

Clara rather liked that about him. From all she'd read about him, he had a true servant's heart. She considered it an honor to represent Mr. Eastman as she shook the president's hand and took an official photograph.

The president looked to the officer closest to him, the man with the brown eyes, and nodded.

The officer stepped toward Clara, never taking his eyes off her. Her pulse quickened as he stopped in front of her and held out his arm.

"Ladies first."

Now would be a good time for one of those souvenir fans she used to sell when she worked in one of the Pan's many gift stores. She fluttered her hand in front of her face, wishing it were possible to wave calmness into one's essence.

"Are you all right?"

"Just a little nervous," she whispered.

The officer bent close. "There's no need. I had the opportunity to meet him earlier. He really is the kindest of men."

One hand gripping the officer's elbow, the other clasping her camera close to her side, Clara stepped forward. When they stopped in front of President McKinley and the officer stepped away, her knees wobbled.

Should she curtsey? She hadn't given it much thought before now. How did one greet the president of the United States?

"Good afternoon, young lady." The president held out his hand to shake hers.

Instead of a quick handshake, as she'd expected, Mr. McKinley clasped her hand in both of his and covered it in warmth.

"Mr. President. It is such an honor to meet you." Nerves made her voice crack.

"Thank you, my dear. It is my own privilege and honor to be

here." He tilted his head toward her camera. "And you're here to take my photo as well? A lady photographer. I simply love it."

In spite of her nerves, she managed to tell him the reason she was photographing him. "Yes, sir. I'm a Kodak Girl. We take snapshots at different fairs and events for Mr. Eastman. He wanted me to be certain to take one of you."

"I would be delighted." The president stepped back and posed for her. At first his expression was stern, but then he raised the corners of his lips into a barely perceptible smile that softened his features. It was perfect.

Steadying her hands, Clara held the box at her waist and looked down at the viewfinder. She adjusted the height of the camera until she could clearly see Mr. McKinley. Then she pressed the button, comforted by the sound of the gears as they turned inside the camera box.

"Thank you, sir." She smiled at him and stepped back toward her designated spot so she could snap a couple more photos as he shook hands.

By now, people packed the enormous room. The line was long, winding all the way out the main doors, but no one made use of the seats. She would undoubtedly be able to sit down to change the film. She chided herself for her earlier worry. Her mother had always told her things had a way of working out.

After taking a couple more photographs, the counter on the top of the camera turned red. She sat down in one of the nearby aisle seats and slid the thin wooden plate off the back of the camera, revealing the inner workings. She carefully lifted out the wooden spool of wound film and placed it inside her bag. Then she threaded the sharp end of the smooth and shiny new film through the mechanism before replacing the cover.

She stood and brushed out the folds of her skirt. After straightening her hat, she adjusted the camera at her waist and stepped forward.

President McKinley was greeting a young gentleman with brown hair whose left hand was wrapped in some sort of bandage. As he reached out to shake the man's hand, the man shoved his injured hand toward the president.

A loud crack sounded in the air and the president's smile faded. He glanced around at the people nearby, seemingly bewildered.

Another crack filled the air, and this time the president staggered.

Officers from all directions sprang into motion, running toward the president at the same moment the man turned toward the crowd. Weak-kneed with horror, Clara realized his hand wasn't injured after all. He was using the bandage to hide a gun.

Several men from the crowd rushed forward and knocked the gunman to the ground. They jumped on top of him, shouting and pummeling their fists in an effort to actually strike the man. Women screamed as people rushed toward the exit doors only to find them blocked by armed officers and soldiers who had taken immediate action to secure the building.

Not far from where she stood, officers had helped the president to the ground. He lay with a folded jacket under his head, cushioning him from the hard floor. Several men were bent over him, and in one horrible moment, Clara knew at least one of the gunman's bullets had found its mark.

"Don't hurt him." The president's tone was weak, but Clara stood close enough to hear his voice as it drifted near. Was he actually begging mercy for the man who'd just shot him? Instead of worrying about himself? This was the kind of caring attitude that separated good men from great men. President McKinley was one of the great ones.

"Please, God, please let him be all right." Unable to look away as the men tended to him, she whispered the prayer over and over.

Finally a group of men rushed toward the president. Between them, they carried a white litter. Before long, they had President McKinley bundled on to it. With a swift gentleness, they lifted him from the floor.

He looked over at one of the men and reached out for his hand.

"Be careful how you tell my wife."

Tears filled Clara's eyes. She quickly dashed them away with the back of her hand, her heart aching for Ida McKinley and the news she was about to receive. But he was alive, and talking, and filled with concern for his wife. That had to be a good sign.

With expert care and practiced efficiency, the men hurried past dozens of armed men and through the doors as if they carried precious cargo. Once the president was on his way to a hospital, the soldiers, in uniforms of various styles and colors, no doubt representing different services, continued to block the exits. Stepping back toward the outer aisle of seats, she was struck with an overwhelming desire to collapse into a chair and process what she'd just witnessed.

Instead she did what Mr. Eastman hired her to do.

She took pictures.

"Please, everyone. Stay calm."

Clara had her camera aimed at the men piled haphazardly on top of the man who'd shot President McKinley. She was in the process of framing their image in the viewfinder for what would be her final photograph. Instead, she turned toward the platform, and to the man calling for attention.

It was him. The officer with the brown eyes. And he was slipping his arms into the sleeves of his jacket.

So he'd been the one to place his jacket on the floor for the president. In spite of the situation, her heart warmed as she watched him smooth his hands over the front of his jacket before fastening each shiny brass button.

"Gentlemen." The handsome officer's glance focused on Clara. "And ladies." His tone brought a sudden heat to her cheeks. "My name is James Brinton. I'm an officer with the Buffalo Police Department. We need you to be calm. The president is alive and, as you've just seen, has been taken to the hospital."

While he spoke he tugged on a pair of white gloves, taking great care to make sure the cuffs were tucked under the sleeves of his jacket. "We need your prayers for his recovery. But we also need to ask each of you some questions. So for now, no one can leave."

Much of the crowd groaned, but he ignored them, his gaze staying with Clara. "We just need to know what you saw and when you saw it, as well as if you are familiar with the man who shot the president. Do you know him? Do you recognize him?"

Clara looked over at the angry mob of men still piled on top of one another, their fists still hammering at whatever they met— usually each other since the man with the gun was underneath them all. More than one of them would come out of this with blackened eyes. Several policemen, all dressed in the same resplendent uniform as Officer Brinton, were in the process of pulling men out of the way in order to get to the man who shot the president.

"Please, gentlemen. Let us do our job. There's no need for more than one man to end up in jail tonight." Some of the men backed off, and Officer Brinton tipped his cap toward them in thanks. He started to step off the platform but stopped and turned back, his gaze sweeping over Clara once again.

"We'll try to be as fast and orderly as possible. After we've talked with you, you'll be free to go. Until then, please remain here in the auditorium. There are plenty of seats for the ladies among you."

He motioned to the rows of seats filling each aisle to the side of the platform. And as he did, dozens of women made their way in that direction.

"Thank you." Officer Brinton turned and left the podium. He headed toward one of several small groups of officers clustered about the room. Unlike the crowd, these men were calm as they spoke to one another, likely coming up with their plan to question the unruly men and women who shouted and tried to force their way past the military soldiers who lined the walls and barred the exits with their rifles.

So many men to watch over one president, and still someone managed to shoot him.

Clara's heart sank and once again she whispered a prayer for

President McKinley and his wife. Yesterday, after they'd toured the fair and the president had given a speech to thousands of the men and women eager to hear him, the first lady had been overcome with the heat. And again this morning, after their excursion to Niagara Falls, she'd been overcome and was unable to be here for the reception.

A blessing in disguise, perhaps?

It would be devastating for the frail woman to receive such news about her husband, but probably worse had she actually been witness to it. Thankfully he was alive and speaking, and Mrs. McKinley would be able to sit by his bedside as he recovered— instead of burying him.

The seats around her rapidly filled with women, many of them appearing faint. Either from the heat or the shock of what they'd just witnessed. Clara stepped back to be seated herself. She had yet to make eye contact with any other officer, so she sincerely hoped Officer Brinton would be the one to ask her questions.

Because the seats faced the elaborate stage at the front of the auditorium, Clara found herself turned sideways in her seat so she could watch the proceedings as the officers wrestled the shooter to his feet and hauled him toward the door. She stood, once again, and aimed her camera. As officers escorted him through the exit angry men struck out from all sides, pummeling him about the head and shoulders. They kicked at his legs, hitting more than one policeman in the process. When they were finally able to get the man through a wall of armed guards and out of the building, his ears burned a bright shade of red. Really, he would be lucky if that was the least that happened to him as a result of his despicable actions.

Satisfied that she'd captured the event for her final photograph, Clara sat back down. Around her, the women's conversations were filled with idle gossip and chit-chat. It seemed so out of place under these circumstances. She thought again of the first lady and the message she was about to receive. It should be delivered gently. Was it even possible to tell such news in a gentle manner?

Who was this man who'd shot the president? He looked young, about her age. What kind of anger would prompt him to perform such an evil act? It was hard to fathom. President McKinley was wildly popular, as evidenced by the number of people in this auditorium. One of the things that made people love him so much was his manner with the public. It was the way he would greet them, and go out of his way to shake hands and listen to what people had to say. He cared. He truly cared. And above it all, the gregarious, ever smiling man always tended lovingly to his wife. And after he was shot, his first concern was for his wife and how she would receive this news. Clara prayed Ida McKinley would not be stricken ill when she heard of the attack on her husband.

Vaguely, she became aware of someone standing in front of her. She blinked and shifted her focus to Officer Brinton. "I'm sorry." Clara looked up at him. Seated as she was, he towered over her. But his expression was gentle. "Did you say something?"

"I asked if you were all right."

Biting down on her lower lip, Clara nodded. "Thank you. Yes. I'm just—" She broke off and shook her head. "It's so sad. I don't understand why someone would do this."

Officer Brinton tipped his head, as if he agreed. As he did so, the cap he wore hid his brown eyes. "May I get you anything?"

"No. Thank you. But do you know how long it will be before I can leave?"

"We're conducting interviews as quickly as possible. In the meantime please let one of us know if you need anything."

Before Clara could thank him, he walked away.

Too late, she knew there was indeed something she needed.

"Excuse me, Officer Brinton?" She called out to him, but he continued to walk away, obviously having not heard her.

She sat for another minute, trying to appear calm on the outside. But the inside was a different matter altogether.

Why had she stopped by the refreshment stand on the Midway? Why had she been tempted by the icy cold bottle of Coca-Cola?

After walking around in the hot sun, it had seemed like the perfect idea.

Now, though, it was becoming a problem.

Finally, Clara stood and headed toward the exit of the auditorium, where both soldiers and policemen attempted to control a crowd of traumatized people who'd come to see the president. Instead they'd witnessed the unthinkable. Now they just wanted to leave. Beyond them, just outside of the auditorium, on the wall in the lobby of the Temple of Music, she saw what she was looking for.

A crush of people managed to force their way through the exit door on her right. And while the officers were duly distracted, Clara headed into the lobby and toward the sign depicting an arrow with three very simple, but relieving words:

Ladies' Comfort Stations.

CHAPTER 2

"I'm sorry, miss. No one gets back inside."

In one swift move, two soldiers dropped their rifles and extended them toward each other like an iron bar that would keep her from passing through. Did she really appear as a threat?

"I was in there waiting to be questioned, but I needed to…" She tipped her head back toward the sign on the wall so they'd understand where she'd been without having to actually say it. Heat climbed up her neck as they glanced at the sign.

The older of the two men looked back to her through narrowed eyes, the lines of his face hard. "It doesn't matter where you went. You weren't supposed to leave the auditorium. No one gets back in."

"But Officer Brinton said—"

"You'll have to wait here in the lobby."

There were a few benches, but they were already filled with men in suits and women in fancy afternoon dresses fanning themselves against the stuffiness of the air. In fact, men and women were seated on every available surface—including the window sills.

"But he won't know I'm out here."

The guard gave her a look of disdain then turned to the younger man. "Keep her out here. I'll see if I can find Brinton."

Once the gruff man disappeared inside the auditorium the young soldier turned to Clara. "He probably won't be long, miss."

"Thank you." Clara offered the man a smile. He didn't seem old enough to be a soldier in the army. She peered at his uniform. At least, she *thought* it was an army uniform. But it really could belong to some other service she didn't recognize.

The officer nodded then glanced around. "I'm sorry there's nowhere for you to sit while you wait." He looked pointedly at two gentlemen seated on a nearby bench.

Uncomfortable with the thought that he was about to shame the men into giving up their seat, Clara stepped toward the exit—which was also being protected by men in uniform. Soldiers, policemen, private guards. It was difficult to keep them all straight. She moved toward a tall, narrow window that had no ledge and leaned against it. "I'm happy to wait here."

"Very well. I'm sure your officer will be here as soon as possible." *Her officer.*

Clara flushed at the implication. "No he's just—"

Intent on controlling passage between the auditorium and lobby, the man was no longer listening. His gaze continuously shifted from the auditorium to the lobby and back to Clara. She turned back to the window, hoping no one around her was paying attention to the exchange.

Though it was growing late into the evening, tens of thousands of bulbs illuminated the buildings and walkways outside. It was bright enough to fool people into thinking it was daylight, were it not for the colors of the bulbs themselves. The ones shining down from the Temple of Music bathed the grounds below in a bright shade of yellow that couldn't begin to match the golden rays of the sun.

Lights of varying colors shined from all directions, the brightest coming from farther down the esplanade. Clara craned her head so she could see part of the Electric Tower. It rose beyond the scope of this tall window. But the light coming off it was brilliant, piercing, and one that was said could be seen all the way from Canada. She knew it was probably true, because she could see it from her bedroom window all the way across town. The newspaper said its nearly fifty-thousand lights paled in comparison to the tower's crowning masterpiece—an enormous searchlight.

The lights and color of the fair were specifically designed by the Pan-American Exposition's Board of Architects. Where the World's Columbian Exposition of 1893 was known as the White City because of its stucco buildings and electric lights, the Buffalo group wanted the buildings and grounds of the 1901 Expo bathed in exquisite color and to be known as the Rainbow City.

It was beautiful, that much was certain.

As Clara stared out the window, trying to identify which buildings were lit up with which color, a boy of ten or so tried to spill through the door from outside. He was stopped of course, by armed men.

"Sorry, son, you can't come in here."

"But the lady—" He shouted and squirmed against their resistance. "There's a man outside who wants to talk to her."

Clara turned to stare. Surely he didn't mean her?

Before she could ask, one of the men bent toward the boy. "You can give me the message and I'll tell her."

Sighing, the boy nodded. "Tell her Officer Brinton is out there waiting to talk to her."

Certain now that he did mean her, Clara stepped away from the window and closer to the doorway where the boy stood. "He's outside? Where?"

"Over there." The boy pointed and Clara stepped past the guards to get a better look. Air that was cooler than the stagnant discomfort of the music building brushed against her neck. Now that she was outside, she wouldn't be able to go back in.

However, once she spoke to Officer Brinton and he asked her his questions, there would be no need.

"Where is he?"

"Over there." The boy pointed toward one of the bandstands near the entrance of the esplanade.

A man stood off to the side of the bandstand. It wasn't Officer Brinton. He wasn't wearing a police uniform, or a uniform of any type. He wore a dark colored suit and a bowler hat. "That's not him."

"No." The boy shook his head. "He's the man who said you were looking for Officer Brinton. He said he knows where he is."

"Thank you. But I think I'll wait here."

"He said you'd say that."

"Did he?" That was a curious thing to say. And one that gave her caution. "Even so, I'm still waiting here."

The boy shrugged. "I gotta go find my parents." He turned and ran in the direction of the Electric Tower, which Clara knew was also the direction of the Midway where there were plenty of attractions for a young boy and his family.

People milled in every direction, and Clara watched as the boy disappeared into their midst. It was all very odd, and she couldn't help but wonder how the man knew she was looking for Officer Brinton. And why did he even care? No one patrolled the perimeter, so it made no sense for an officer to be outside when police were questioning people inside. Unless someone left before they were questioned. Considering how easily she'd slipped from the chaos of the auditorium, it could have happened. She leaned against the coolness of the building's outer wall, debating whether to try and convince the guards to let her back inside.

Unease gnawed at her when her gaze wandered back toward the man at the bandstand. If Officer Brinton wanted to talk to her, why would a different man send a boy to fetch her? This couldn't be right. She inched toward the door. If she told them she was concerned about a man outside, surely they would they let her back in. It couldn't hurt to try.

Even though they agreed that the situation was strange, they wouldn't let her back inside. But she did finally convince them to let Officer Brinton know she was outside. If he didn't come soon, she'd just leave. No one would know she hadn't answered any questions. They wouldn't even know her name unless they checked the list of photographers who had met the president prior to the reception.

Officer Brinton could track her down that way if he had any questions.

Before she started walking, she assured herself that her camera was secure inside the leather bag she held close to her side. As she looked up from securing the strap, a movement caught her eye.

The man in the bowler hat was waving at her. She furrowed her brow. Though she couldn't quite see his face, his size and stance didn't match anyone she knew. Prickles rose across the back of her neck.

She needed to leave.

Now.

Only one other time in his life had James Brinton felt this gut-twisting mixture of sorrow, horror, and guilt. If he didn't have an investigation to conduct, a crowd to control, the hollow numbness likely would have driven him to his knees.

"Brinton, there's a woman looking for you."

James looked up as one of the president's secret service agents approached. A woman? For some reason, he thought of the pretty photographer. He squeezed his eyes closed and huffed out a breath, wishing the action would dispel his guilt.

If only it were that easy. He lifted his cap and pushed a hand through his hair.

"Thank you, Agent Ireland. Did she say what she wanted?"

"No. She was trying to get back in from the lobby, and when we wouldn't let her through she asked for you. Said she stepped out there for something before she could be interviewed." Ireland shrugged as if he couldn't understand.

"Thanks. I'll go find her." James peered toward the lobby that teemed with people—men and women alike. "What did she look like?"

"Oh—you know her. That woman with the camera. The one who took the picture of the president."

Since he could so easily picture reddish-brown hair spilling out from under a tasteful but obviously expensive white hat, he didn't bother correcting Ireland's statement that he knew her. He didn't, of course, but he couldn't seem to get her off his mind. And he did know her name. Clara Lambert. Her name was the only female on the official list of those allowed to photograph the president this evening.

If he hadn't been watching her, he might have noticed that the man approaching the president wasn't really injured. If only. . . .

He shook his head. Now wasn't the time for *if only* and *what if.*

There was an investigation to conduct. Way too many people to interview, which was the reason he hadn't seen Miss Lambert again.

Not that he'd been looking for her.

"Thanks again, Ireland." James clapped the president's agent on the shoulder before he left. Of all of the men on the force, Ireland was the only one who regarded him with normalcy—as if nothing had ever happened to cost him the respect of his fellow officers.

Before he even approached the lobby, James was looking ahead, trying to spot a glimpse of her tasteful but obviously expensive white hat. He spotted several hats adorned with feathers, dead birds, and fur. But none were pure white with pearls and lace.

He approached the young army soldier who was standing watch at the entryway between the auditorium and the lobby. Some of his fellow officers resented the presence of army soldiers and guardsmen, but with nearly a hundred thousand people attending the fair each day, it was a necessity. They'd had to hire extra police officers as well. If not for the Pan, he probably wouldn't even have his job back.

"There's a woman waiting to talk to me. She has brown hair." He closed his eyes and tried to recall something more than her comely face. "She's wearing a white dress with pale blue pinstripes."

"I know the one you mean, sir. She was waiting right here for you."

"I don't see her."

"Yes, I know. She was waiting here until a boy told her you were outside waiting to speak to her."

"Are you sure?" It had to be a mistake. It didn't even make sense. Why would someone tell her that?

"I'm sure, sir. I heard it myself."

James rubbed at the whisper of discomfort that brushed along the back of his neck. "Did you see which way she went?"

The kid shook his head. "She was out by the big window for a little while, but then the next time I looked, she was gone."

Wherever she went, he would find her. These entire circumstances left him unsettled.

There wasn't very much about this night that made sense, but he couldn't help but believe the president being shot and someone pretending to be James were somehow connected.

Whether they were or not, what could the man possibly want with Miss Lambert?

Which way should she go? Trying to remain as unnoticeable as possible, Clara quickly took in her surroundings. She could step out onto the walkway and head toward the Electric Tower as the boy had. Or she could go straight ahead toward a large area of fountains. Either way, she'd eventually get to the train terminal at the opposite end of the fairground. And either way, the man at the bandstand would see the direction she went.

At the edge of the Temple of Music, flush with the building, was a colonnade that led to the Machinery and Transportation Building—an enormous building, at least three times the size of any other building at the Pan. If she could inch her way to the columns, she could slip through to the gardens behind the building and make her way to the Midway. Once she was there, even if the man happened to follow her for some reason, she could disappear in the throng of people and come out at the entrance of the train terminal.

A strong urge to hurry set her feet into motion even as logic told her she was being silly.

But was she really? This evening had been far from ordinary. The proof of that was the president who now lay in a hospital somewhere, quite possibly—most likely—fighting for his life. Simply walking away wouldn't be good enough.

With her camera bag tucked close to her side with one arm and her hat held firmly atop her head with the other, Clara increased her steps and began to run. Immediately, she stopped short. The flowing skirt of her afternoon dress wrapped about her legs in a weighty tangle. But if she lifted it while she ran, she'd lose her hat. She took the hat off and tucked it under her arm, resting it gently atop her bag. If she was careful, she wouldn't crush it.

"Miss! Wait!" The man in the bowler was shouting at her, waving, running toward her.

She raced toward the shadows of the colonnade.

"I said stop! In the name of the president, I order you to stop!"

Clara kept running. The man didn't work for the president. Of that much she was certain. If he did, he wasn't dressed like any of the other men she'd seen today. She'd had ample time this evening to study the different officers, soldiers, and guards. If he belonged to one of these services, wouldn't he be wearing a uniform? Believing as her mother did that one's instincts came from God and they came for a reason, she lifted the hem of her skirt even higher above her ankles and obeyed the urge to keep moving. As she grew closer to the colonnade, she drew on everything deep within her to go even faster. She needed to get to the Midway.

Though she was new to her job as a Kodak Girl, demonstrating how easy it was to take photographs—or snapshots, as Mr. Eastman liked to refer to them—Clara had spent the last few days familiarizing herself with the fairgrounds. Certainly she could disappear among the myriad of buildings and gardens. And if not, then in the midst of all the people who still wandered about in spite of the fact that the president had just been shot. How could they carry on as if nothing had happened? Was it possible they didn't know? Surely if they did, they would head home out of respect for their president. It struck her as obscene—not only that they were still here, but that she hoped to use their presence to her advantage.

"Miss, I said to wait!"

Bathed in the reflection of light from the surrounding buildings, Clara realized the colonnade wasn't as shadowy as she'd first thought. She wasn't sure how she could possibly hide, but still she ducked between the columns.

Hedges lined the gardens and were used artistically to create a courtyard effect. Clara dropped to her knees behind those closest to the back of the Machinery Building.

Footsteps drew closer.

Would this be the first place he'd look?

Scooting deeper into the shrubbery, she prayed the leaves wouldn't rustle enough to catch the man's notice. Lights weren't used in the gardens, so they could appear in their natural beauty. Clara considered this a blessing. Hopefully she was far enough back that after a cursory glance, he'd just move on.

Scarcely allowing herself to breathe, she listened for the sound of footsteps moving closer. Instead, sounds from all directions of the fairgrounds assaulted her ears. Shrieks of delight, music, barkers calling out to passersby. In stark contrast, the fresh scent of grass mingled with the fragrance of flowers and the dirt beneath her knees.

Closing her eyes, she breathed slowly in through her nose and tried to block out the periphery so she could focus only on what was nearby.

At the slight movement of nearby leaves brushing together, Clara held her breath and wished she could shrink farther back. She willed the man to give up and turn away. Between the branches, she could see him standing near the row of hedges. In the shadows, the tall, gaunt man appeared to have olive skin. It was difficult to be sure with the bowler hat casting his face in deeper shadows, but his eyes looked dark and close-set. His lips, pressed together as they were, formed an angry slash that marred a too-thin face.

After a moment where Clara feared her heart would beat out of her chest, the man turned and crossed back through the colonnade where he stood glancing in every direction. The lights from the Temple of Music emphasized a rage that seemed to radiate from his tense stare and clenched fists. Her decision to hide had been the right one.

When the man finally turned and headed toward the Electric Tower, Clara remained where she was until he disappeared from sight. Then she waited another few minutes that seemed an eternity to the cramping muscles in her legs. Finally she stood and brushed dirt and leaves from the front of her dress before scooping it up so she could run through the spongy grass. She didn't stop until she reached the opposite side of the gardens and a second colonnade that faced the canal and nearby Japanese Village. Only after she stood flush against the last column did she dare look over her shoulder to see if she'd been followed. Thankfully, the man was nowhere in sight. But to be certain, she stood statue-still for a moment longer.

The canal in front of her ran from the Fore Court of the esplanade, down the length of the fairgrounds, and to the Electric Tower. Both were widely visible, so taking a gondola wasn't an option. Her best bet would be to make her way along the Midway and eventually to the exit gate near the railroad platform where she could hopefully catch a streetcar across town.

Taking care that the man hadn't doubled back, Clara stepped out between the columns and ran toward a small bridge. Her footsteps echoed the pounding rhythm of her heart as she followed the bridge across the canal, where it opened into a garden that radiated an immediate sense of hushed peace.

Though she couldn't spare a moment to stop, she did look from left to right and took note of several hanging lanterns that cast a soft glow over perfectly pruned trees that struck her as dainty, lush grass, a waterfall, and flowering plants with delicate white blossoms. Somewhere nearby, someone played a soft tune on a flute. Women in pale pink kimonos served tea to a group of elegantly dressed women who barely glanced up as she ran past them.

Ahead of her, the lights were bright and the Midway swelled with crowds of people clamoring about, talking and shouting as they took in the many rides and attractions. She tried to adjust her pace to the people around her and willed herself not to panic at the assault on her senses. Surely she would draw more attention if she tried to shove past people. Hopefully there was some truth to *getting lost in a crowd.*

Though the sounds here were far louder than when she hid behind the hedges, her ears didn't take long to adjust. The aroma of sizzling meat reminded her that she'd missed her evening meal with the Martins. Eulalie Martin would forgive her, she knew, but Clara hated disappointing the older woman.

Keeping a watchful eye out for the man in the bowler, she wondered again why he was chasing her. And what did it have to do with Officer Brinton? She'd done absolutely nothing that would cause someone to track her down. Surely he'd mistaken her for someone else? Someone who'd obviously made him angry.

She could only hope that after tonight he wouldn't come back to the fair, since this was where she'd be spending most of her days. Other than the few mornings a week spent cleaning rooms at Nowak's Hotel, Clara would be here at the Pan taking pictures and demonstrating the camera for anyone interested. Mr. Eastman held to the belief that if women knew how easy it was to use his camera, they'd delight in taking snapshots to record memories for their families.

Glancing down to adjust the camera bag against her side, a sick realization enveloped her.

Her hat was gone.

She drew to a stop in spite of the crowd shuffling around her. Should she retrace her steps?

No. *He* might be waiting.

Not even the disappointment of losing something so precious would stop her. Above all, she had to get away from here and make her way to the railroad terminal. Later, when she was safely home, she could mourn the loss of her hat and all it meant to her.

Just as Clara stepped forward, a strong arm snaked around her waist. Before she could react or even scream, a rough sweaty hand clapped across her mouth. Alarm jolted her, and the smell of dirty skin made her gag.

CHAPTER 3

Clara struggled to get free of his grasp, but the man held her fast. Disgusting as it was, she attempted to bite the hand that covered her mouth. Rough fingers dug in to her cheek and chin as a reward. She kicked backward at his shin, but she merely lost her balance as he jerked her to the side. She fought the rising panic and tried to force herself to stay calm. The man had arms much like a trap one would use for defenseless animals.

"Don't. Scream." The man's voice rumbled low in her ear. "Make a sound and you'll live to regret it."

In spite of his warning, her mind fought against the urge to scream. It was an epic battle to keep silent.

Frantically glancing from one person to the next, not a single one so much as made eye contact with her. They simply kept up their steady stream of movement, swarming past, most with a clear destination in mind and blissfully unaware that someone amongst them was in need of help.

She really was lost in a crowd.

"Give me your camera, and you won't get hurt."

Her camera?

As she strained to get free of his grip, instinct had her reaching toward the camera bag at her side. As she touched it, its heavy weight gave her a moment of comfort.

She had no intention of giving it to him. But instead of fighting the man, she brought her other hand across her waist until she clutched the bag in both hands. Taking a deep breath, she jerked forward. While it didn't break the man's hold on her, it did catch him off guard. Before he could tighten his grip, Clara bit down hard against his disgusting hand.

He squealed and loosened his hold from her face. Clara whirled. With the camera steady in both hands, she slammed it against the side of his head.

He roared and reached out to grab her again, but someone stopped him.

"Go! Run. I have this."

Officer Brinton?

Momentarily stunned, Clara gaped at him. She was scarcely able to take in the sight of his black cap and white gloves before he shouted at her.

"Please, Miss Lambert, run!" His brown eyes were wide with warning.

She turned and did just as he said, urgency forcing her to ignore the sounds of scuffling and do everything in her power to get away.

Heavy footfall sounded behind her.

Don't get caught. Don't get caught.

A sign to her right declared *Battle of Missionary Ridge.* The cyclorama. It was a welcome relief. The round building housed a large war display. Several American flags stood sentinel along the edges of the circular roof. The enormous arched wooden doorway was framed with a false-front to create the illusion of a fortress. She could easily lose him in there. But as Clara approached the round building, she stopped short. It was closed.

Disappointment resonated deep inside. She had to come up with another plan.

"Slow down." The male voice sounded behind her, inciting her to run faster. The man in the bowler? Or Officer Brinton? There wasn't time to look over her shoulder. She had to keep moving and run as if her life depended on it. Because it very well could.

Hide in plain sight.

Frantic now, she glanced around. Like before, she needed to stick with the crowd. Maybe this time, with Officer Brinton in pursuit, it would work. But the crowd began to thin as people dispersed toward different attractions. Up ahead, she could see an oversized building shaped into a giant woman's face. Her wide-gaping mouth served as the entrance.

The sign said DREAMLAND, but to Clara it was more like Nightmareland.

Gruesome though it was, it could be an alternative. Beyond it was the Captive Balloon—a hot air balloon on a tether, towering far above the fairgrounds. Somewhere between the two was the exit she sought.

Also between the two stood a lone figure in a bowler hat.

Clara slowed her pace. She didn't want to get close enough to tell if it was *the* man, but the cold prickles crawling up her spine were all the indication she needed.

How had he gotten around her? And what had happened to Officer Brinton?

She wouldn't be taking the exit to the train platform any time soon.

After a couple of deep, steadying breaths she would step into the line for Dreamland. Or maybe even the Trip to the Moon. In there, she could try to hide behind the wall of Swiss Cheese. A quick glance around told her the lines for both were long and stagnant. Standing in one spot would leave her vulnerable. The only line that moved at a reasonable pace led to something that made her heart race all over again.

The aerio-cycle.

Like everything else at the fair, the aerio-cycle was illuminated with thousands of tiny bulbs. But to Clara, instead of making the ride attractive, the lights showcased something unpleasant. The aerio-cycle was a horrifying contraption, the likes of which she'd never seen. It appeared to be modeled, in some fashion, after Mr. Ferris's great wheel.

But the wheel was only a fraction of the ride. It was, in fact, two wheels that balanced on either end of a large steel beam and extended for what seemed like miles. Though logically, she knew that wasn't the case. It was much like a child's oversized seesaw—if one could overlook its height and the tiny little cars that dangled in the sky as the wheels turned.

While one wheel was up in the air, rotating at a height well above the Captive Balloon and Electric Tower, the other was near the ground slowly turning to disembark passengers and capture new ones. Once passengers were aboard the little gondola cars, one wheel dropped and the other rose until they were level and the beam rotated and one wheel swung out over the canal while the other extended across the Midway.

Sickly fascinated, Clara watched while the beam rotated again. After a minute, the wheel that had previously been in the air was now in front of her and the wheel with the newest passengers rose high above the fair.

Did she really need to get on this contraption?

The woman in front of her held a toddler by one hand. She shielded them both with a parasol. Clara wasn't sure why the mother still held the parasol open since the sun had set quite some time ago, but as she leaned over to peer around them she was thankful for the cover it provided.

The man still stood there.

Clara stepped slightly to the left, hoping to become invisible should he look this way. Heart hammering, she continued to shuffle toward the monstrosity.

"Mommy, I don't want to do this." The little boy in front of her wailed until his mother bent toward him.

"Hush, honey. It will be fun. You told daddy you would be a big boy and go on this with mommy since daddy was too scared. Remember?"

Wide-eyed, the toddler nodded.

"Please don't make mommy go on this by herself."

The boy kicked the ground with his toe and slowly nodded. But when it was their turn to climb into a passenger seat, the little boy shrieked and planted his legs so firmly on the ground, the child's mother couldn't budge him.

A quick glance toward the bandstand told Clara they'd caught the attention of the man in the bowler. That was all the impetus she needed. The instant the mother rested the parasol on her shoulder and bent down Clara scooted around the opposite side and stepped up onto the unsteady floor of the enclosed car that would surely lead to her death.

The metal car creaked and rocked as she stepped onto it, and she threw out a hand to steady herself. Her hand missed the metal support bar at the carriage's opening and she lost her balance. None too gracefully she tumbled onto a hard bench and continued falling backward, striking her shoulder on another bench behind her. This one was graduated enough in height to stop her from hitting her head on the third bench.

"Careful, miss." The young man who'd helped the previous passengers off the carriage held out his arm too late to stop her fall. But she reached out and allowed him to help her sit upright.

Dazed, Clara blinked and sat straighter. "Thank you." She attempted a smile but her lips seemed to stretch across her teeth in a grimace. She would have more than her share of bruises before this day came to an end.

"You'll be fine, miss. Just enjoy the view of the Niagara River. It's quite the sight with the reflection of the Pan's illuminations. If you sit up there, you'll have a better view."

With a glance over her shoulder, she saw he was right. But she was more interested in the view of the door and the rest of the gondola and her ability to monitor who came through the door and where they would sit.

Once again she took his arm and allowed him to help her up the tiny steps to the highest row. Then she scooted toward the window.

Soon the gondola would rise to heights no human should ever experience. Clara knew the river would be to her right and below her, the fairgrounds. She squeezed her eyes closed and wished she could stay that way for the duration.

Surely this was plain silliness. Hundreds, if not thousands, of people had gone on the aerio-cycle since the fair had opened in the spring. Thus far no one had been dashed to the ground, and she wouldn't be the first. She really should concentrate on mapping out an escape route, and she couldn't do that with her eyes closed. Slowly, she opened them again.

Two women boarded and seated themselves on the lower bench. They hadn't stumbled once. They were both smartly dressed in tea gowns, with their hair pinned neatly under their hats.

Self-conscious, Clara reached up to brush her hair from her face. It felt a tangled mess that wouldn't fall readily into place. She must look a fright after dashing in every direction without her hat to keep her curls neatly pinned. Was it possible she'd be able to see the hat from her perch in the sky? Likely not. And now that she had a moment to really think about it, her heart sank. Not because the hat came from the finest millinery in New York and not because it was made with hand-tatted lace and hand-beaded strands of pearls. Its loss saddened her because it was a gift from her father. And though he sent her things constantly, this one was special because it was from before.

"There you are." The male voice startled her out of her thoughts, and Clara bit back a scream. The carriage tipped forward, and Officer Brinton climbed up and seated himself next to her. "I didn't mean to frighten you."

Clara nodded, surprised no words came to her.

"I've been looking everywhere for you."

To her horror, tears sprang to her eyes and she blinked furiously, determined not to show weakness to him. She looked away, and down at her lap. The bottom half of her dress was covered with grass stains. Did he notice she was such a mess? She brushed at the stains while she regained her composure, finally asking, "Who was that man? Did you arrest him?"

He shook his head and tilted it slightly to the left. From beneath his cap, his eyes studied hers.

Clara sighed. "I was afraid of that."

"I'm sorry. I'll get him eventually. But right now it's more important that I keep you safe."

She hadn't expected that. "Thank you. There's a man in a bowler hat standing near the end of the Midway. I think it's him."

"So that's why you got on this ride. I wondered." He sounded less than enthusiastic. Could he possibly be afraid, too?

"Excuse me."

The attendant waved at them. "If you could slide down just a little, we can make room for one more." Officer Brinton did as asked, and by the time the gentleman was settled in place, Clara found herself smashed up against the window with the handsome officer snug against her side. The warmth radiating off him had a slightly calming effect.

Maybe this wouldn't be as frightening as she first thought. But Mrs. Martin would be far from pleased if she knew.

"Ladies and gentleman." The attendant pulled the gondola door closed before he continued. "Once all four of the gondolas are boarded, we will begin our journey. First we'll slide out over the canal before we rise to nearly three-hundred feet."

One of the women in the carriage gasped. Clara wanted to do the same, but she didn't want Officer Brinton to see her fear.

"After we're in the air, we will rotate for approximately ten minutes. You'll be able to see lights all over the beautiful city of Buffalo. And you should be able to see most of the Pan's attractions."

If she looked hard enough, she might be able to see if the man still stood near the gate to the train terminal. But would she be brave enough to look while suspended in the air?

The attendant pushed hard against the door to ensure it was secure. "You're all perfectly safe." He took his seat in the only remaining open spot on the first row. Clara hadn't thought he would actually accompany them on the ride. And while that should give her some measure of comfort, it really didn't.

Shifting as much as he could in the confined space, Officer Brinton twisted to face her. His brown eyes were dark with concern.

"Again, please accept my apologies for letting the man get away from me."

"How did you even know I needed help?"

"One of the president's men, Agent Ireland, sent me to find you. He said you were trying to get back in to the auditorium so you could answer some questions, but then for some reason you went outside."

Feeling suddenly defensive, Clara straightened. "I went outside because a boy said you were waiting to speak to me. But now I know it wasn't true."

"Did the man say what he wanted?"

"He intimated he was one of the president's agents."

"He's not."

"I know. Surely the president wouldn't employ a man who would behave in such a despicable manner. I could tell immediately he was lying. That's why I ran from him."

"You won't have any more trouble tonight. I plan to see you home and then I'll get all of our men to search for him."

Would he really see her home? Sweet relief washed over her, and she whispered a prayer of thanks. She was no longer alone in this nightmare. She wouldn't have to map out an escape plan after all.

"Thank you so much." She breathed in then slowly exhaled. "Now we can ask the attendant to get us off of here. Sir?"

The man was speaking to the woman seated next to him.

"Excuse me, sir?" Clara waved to try and get his attention. But before she could call out again, a high pitched groan pierced her ears, followed by the whirring sound of moving gears.

It was too late.

If he hadn't seen it for himself, James would have never thought it possible to fit so many people into one gondola car. Next to him, over the sound of machinery grinding its parts together, Miss Lambert gasped. Any other time he'd anticipate the view, but he could sense her fear and felt he had to do something to distract her.

"I found this for you, Miss Lambert."

Her eyes widened as she looked at the hat he held out to her. It was difficult to be certain in the poor lighting, but they appeared a soft shade of green that matched the Atlantic after a storm.

"My hat. I didn't even notice you holding it. Where did you—" She grabbed it from his hand and fixed it atop her head before he could even blink.

"Thank you." She offered him a wistful smile as she gazed up at him.

Green. Definitely green. With gold flecks made slightly brighter by a sheen of moisture. Between her eyes and her smile, she stole his breath.

His stomach dipped.

For a moment, the world spun out from under him.

In all his life, James couldn't remember a woman knocking him off kilter with just her smile.

Around him, women screamed. Shouts of terror mingled with shrieks of glee. Next to him, Miss Lambert gasped and reached out to clutch his arm.

She hadn't knocked him off kilter after all.

They were moving.

James tried to shrug off his disappointment. He placed his hand over Miss Lambert's where she still held onto his arm. Her eyes were squeezed closed, and beneath the shadow of her hat he could see tiny lines framing the corners.

"It'll be all right." As much as he tried to assure her, he also tried to assure himself. He hadn't thought he was such a coward. But their carriage, the carriage that now dangled from the giant wheel, rocked back and forth. Each time it moved it creaked and groaned, and his stomach lurched.

"We're just stopped so the gondola below us can pick up new passengers. We'll be stopped for just a moment. If you look to your right, you can see the canal. That's the direction we'll go once everyone has boarded."

After a moment the rocking stopped, and Miss Lambert finally opened her eyes. He watched, fascinated, while the tiny lines around them faded.

She let go of his arm and bent forward, effectively shielding her eyes from further view. Both of her hands flew straight to the leather bag in her lap. The bag he knew held her camera. After a moment, she looked up.

"Thank you for intervening when that awful man grabbed me."

"You're very welcome. We do need to talk about that."

Miss Lambert nodded. "I suppose we do."

"I'm James Brinton, by the way."

"Yes, I remember, Mr. Brinton, from your instructions to the crowd. Or should I call you Officer Brinton?"

"James. Just call me James."

She nodded. "I'm Clara Lambert. Please call me Clara."

"Clara." He knew her name, of course, but he rather liked the sound of it as it rolled off his tongue. "Your name was on the list of people to meet the president."

"I wonder how he is. Do you think he'll recover?"

"From what we heard the men say as they took him out of the building, it appears his wounds won't threaten his life."

Clara breathed out a sigh. "Thank you, God." Then she pressed her lips together, and the corners turned slightly downward. "I wonder how his wife took the news. He was so worried about her."

"I haven't heard anything about Mrs. McKinley yet. I'll probably receive an update in the morning. In the meantime, we need to find out what we can about the man who attacked you. Do you know who he is?"

"No, I don't." She hesitated, as if she wanted to tell him something else. But she remained silent, still carefully holding her bag.

"Why did you leave the music auditorium in the first place?" He didn't mean to sound confrontational, but he must have because she sat straighter before she answered.

"It wasn't intentional. I was stretching my legs because I needed to—" Her face flushed and she looked away. "Never mind. I was simply stretching my legs."

James had a fairly good idea what she needed. So as not to embarrass her, he remained silent and waited for her to continue.

"The guards wouldn't let me back in. Then a little boy told me you were waiting to speak to me outside. Obviously you know what happened next."

"Do you know what he wanted?" Even as he asked, James could tell the answer by her body language. Like a lioness protecting her cub, Clara's hands tightened on the bag in her lap. "When he grabbed me, before you intervened, he demanded I turn over my camera. Of course I refused."

James choked back his surprise. Most women he'd ever met would simply cower and hand it over. Not Clara. And yet this crazy aerio-cycle frightened her.

"Is that why he grabbed you?"

Fear flashed in her eyes. Slowly, lips pressed together, she nodded.

This wasn't good. His heart hammered.

Reaching over, James placed his hand on top of hers where they still clutched the leather straps of her bag. He would keep her safe. But any trust he might instill in her would surely fade and recrimination would fill her lovely eyes when he did what he knew he must. This time for him instead of the man who'd accosted her.

Because before this night was over he would also have to ask her for the one thing she didn't want to give up.

CHAPTER 4

Should she take a photograph while they were stopped? Dare she? Clara wasn't sure she could actually look out the window of the gondola. Thus far she'd been careful to keep her eyes trained on anything in the gondola's interior and successfully ignored her peripheral vision.

Yet there was an internal tug that was becoming increasingly more difficult to ignore than her peripheral vision. She fidgeted with the leather straps of her bag, drawing the camera only halfway out, not quite able to make a complete commitment.

The one thing that gave her comfort was James. The way he looked at her, having him here at her side. A warmth she hadn't felt before glowed in her heart, and she wasn't quite ready to let go of it. But there was something more. She felt…secure.

Secure enough to look out the window and take a few photos for Mr. Eastman?

Gears sounded, and the wheel began to move again. Clara winced as another set of shrieks pierced her ears. The gondola rose a quarter-turn into the air before it stopped again. This time they were at the top.

"How many more times do we have to do this?" James's low voice tickled her ear, and butterflies danced along her spine. Or could it really be the knowledge that they were now nearly three-hundred feet off the ground?

Her stomach leaped, and she pushed the camera back into the bag. She would not be taking any photographs from this height. Taking care not to catch a glimpse of any windows, she looked at James.

"We're at the top. They're loading passengers into another gondola." She didn't like the tremor she heard in her voice and glanced back down at her lap lest he see how unsettled she really was. "That means we'll rotate down and stop once more. Then when the last passengers are aboard, we're supposed to rotate slowly for ten minutes."

"Ten minutes?" Next to her, she felt James straighten. "That's a long time when you're, ah—"

"Afraid?" Clara glanced at him. His chin jutted out, his lips pressed together. He didn't blink as he stared at her. Was he deliberately keeping his face from showing any emotion? "James? Are you afraid?"

"I never said—"

"Nervous, then?"

He didn't answer.

Relieved that he was as frightened as she was, Clara couldn't help the grin spreading across her face. "Buffalo police officers can't show fear? Is that what this is?"

A muscle twitched near the bruised skin under his eye. The bruise he had because of her.

On impulse, she reached out and grabbed his hand. "It's all right. I keep thinking I need to take a picture while we're stopped, but I can't quite bring myself to even look out the window."

"Seriously? After running from that man, and then fighting him off, you're actually afraid of something?"

"I didn't say I was afraid. Maybe a little nervous, but not afraid." Clara gave him a measured look.

"So Kodak Girls can't show fear? Is that what this is?" He lifted the corner of one eye as if daring her to deny it.

"Touché, James."

His lips pressed together and he squeezed her hand. He opened his mouth to say something, but closed it again. Clara waited, curious to hear whatever was on his mind.

"Let's look together."

That wasn't what she expected. Her heartbeat kicked up. Could she do it? Slowly, she nodded. "I guess it wouldn't be good for a Buffalo police officer and a Kodak Girl to be afraid of anything, right?"

Surprise flickered across his face. Perhaps he didn't expect her to agree? He turned the hand she still held, until their palms touched. Then he laced his fingers through hers.

"And were you to use that camera of yours to take a picture, everyone would know of our bravery."

Clara rather liked the teasing that lilted in his tone, and she laughed. "Okay then. Do you want to count to three and then look?"

"How about we count to five instead?" A hint of mischief tugged at the corners of his mouth.

James Brinton most definitely knew how to turn a situation around.

Though he agreed that they would close their eyes while Clara counted to five, James couldn't take his eyes off her face long enough to close them.

When her hand squeezed his, he curled his fingers tighter around hers.

"One." She drew the word out slowly.

Her lips trembled.

"Two."

Dark lashes brushed the delicate skin just below her eyes, and he couldn't look away.

"Three."

The wariness began to ease from her face as her features softened. "Four."

She took in a slow breath then let it out again.

He waited.

Again her lips parted and she took a breath.

"Five!" She said it loud, with a hint of laughter. But…she didn't open her eyes.

"Clara." He tried to sound stern but knew he failed when she pressed her lips together and turned to him.

When she opened her eyes his stomach dipped, and this time he knew it had nothing to do with the wheel.

Her mouth spread into a grin and her green eyes widened as they met his. "You, James Brinton, cheated. You didn't close your eyes. Did you?"

"I have the right to remain silent."

"I can't believe a police officer wouldn't keep his word."

Those words stabbed at his deepest core. But he couldn't let her see that. She didn't mean them that way. He had to focus on the here and now and leave the past where it belonged.

Slowly extracting his hand from hers, he put his arm across her shoulders. He felt rather than heard her quick intake of breath.

"Well then." Her tone wasn't quite right. It was light and airy, but tremulous. As if she were nervous and trying to lighten the mood. "Why aren't you looking out at the view now?"

"What about you?" He tried to infuse the same lightness into his own voice.

"I'm waiting for you. That's all."

A smile bit at his lips and he couldn't hold it back. "You're afraid, aren't you?"

"No, I'm not."

"I'm a police officer, remember? I can tell when someone isn't being truthful."

"I'm not—I've never been this high into the air."

Neither had he, but he didn't tell her.

"Just the thought is dizzying."

"I agree. It is." He squeezed her shoulder. "Let's look together, Clara. Right now."

"I don't think—"

"You can close your eyes if you want, but I'm not going to." Drawing her closer, he twisted toward the window.

Close to her like this, a scent he couldn't identify wafted from her skin to tease his senses. Sweet, clean, fresh. Not overpowering like some of the women at church. He inhaled the calming fragrance and knew, in this instant, he could look out at Buffalo from this height without being afraid.

"Get ready, Clara." He leaned forward, pulling her with him, until they both were close enough to see outside.

The sensation of falling, of being pulled forward was strong. His stomach set sail. He blinked, but it wasn't enough to make the feeling go away.

He dropped his head forward and closed his eyes. But even so, his head swam.

"James, are you all right?"

He heard Clara, but he couldn't look at her.

The gondola moved then, taking his stomach with it as they plunged downward only to come to another grinding halt.

"I guess there really is a coward on the Buffalo Police Department." He tried to make it sound like he was teasing, but it wasn't easy since his head was still spinning. Now he knew why, in all of the months he'd been policing the Exposition, he'd never stepped foot onto the aerio-cycle.

"You're not a coward. It's vertigo." He felt Clara's hands on his shoulders as she shifted in her seat. "Let's turn away from the window. Come on. Just scoot back a bit more."

Eyes still closed, he did so without argument. Did he really have vertigo, or was he just afraid?

"Have *you* ever been that high before?"

"No," he admitted.

"But you didn't say anything when I said I hadn't."

"I didn't want you to be afraid." He slowly opened his eyes. The dizziness was fading, albeit not fast enough to suit him. "Your pictures. I kept you from taking them."

"No. You didn't. I didn't even have the camera ready." She was so sweet, so reassuring. "I'll have it ready when we're up there again."

He groaned and dropped his face into his palms.

"Ten minutes, James." This time it was Clara who put her arm around him. Correction. She put both of her arms around him, pulling him close as she murmured in his ear. "We can survive ten minutes."

It was the longest ten minutes of his life.

CHAPTER 5

From the moment they boarded the trolley, James's senses had been more heightened than usual. He was about as certain as one could get that they hadn't been followed. Still, as they walked the mile or so from the trolley stop near the library on Broadway, he felt the need to continuously look over his shoulder.

"Thank you, James. I can't tell you how much I appreciate this." Even as she said it, Clara glanced over her shoulder, affirming to James that his insistence on walking her home was the right one. Safety's sake aside, it was also important for her to feel comfortable and confident so she could sleep secure tonight. He planned to take steps to ensure that she would, but he'd save that argument until she was safely home.

"You're very welcome, Clara." She looked up at him, and even in the shadows, with her face illuminated only by streetlights, he could see a measure of trust. And that left him feeling full of deceit.

There was a battle he feared would be even larger, and it wasn't until they turned onto her street that he dared bring up the subject he'd dreaded since the moment she told him the attacker had been after her camera.

"Clara." James straightened and slowed his stride. He turned to look at her. "As much as I don't want to ask this of you, I must." Even before he said it, he knew what her reaction would be. "I need to confiscate your camera."

Clara sucked in a breath and whirled away from him before he could even blink. "You *are* with him. I knew it. You returned my hat as an excuse to get my camera."

She pulled the camera close to her side, her defensive stance telling him any trust he may have secured with her was gone. That was something he thought he'd gotten used to over the last year. But that same reaction from Clara—a woman he'd only known a few hours? It hurt more than the scrapes he'd received earlier this evening.

"No, Clara. I'm not with him. I promise. He's not one of the president's agents, and he's most definitely not a police officer. We don't chase innocent women and try to steal from them. We just ask nicely."

Eyes wide, she took a step back. "But you *are* just like him. You use innocent people, make them feel comfortable, get them to let their guard down, so you can swoop in and take what you want."

"I would never hurt you. And I definitely wouldn't steal from you. Even if I wasn't a police officer, I wouldn't do that."

She started walking then, away from him. He could follow her of course. But to chase her—that would make her believe she was right.

He called after her. "It's evidence, Clara. In a traitorous, heinous crime. We'll give it back to you. I promise we won't keep it."

"You most certainly will not, because you won't be getting it. It's not mine to give away." Clara shook her head. "I didn't photograph the man who shot the president. Someone knocked him to the ground and pinned him down. Then all of those men jumped on top of him before I could even get my camera aimed at him."

He well remembered, since he and Clara were in the middle of making eye contact when the shooting happened.

Guilt gnawed at him. Would he have realized the man was concealing a gun had he not been distracted by Clara?

"Besides," she continued. "You have him in custody. Why do you need the camera? And if my attacker wasn't one of your policemen, why did *he* want it?"

"Likely he's part of an anarchist group. We think there was more than one person involved in the assassination attempt."

"And you think I might have taken pictures of them?"

"I do. And I'm sure the man chasing you thought the same thing."

"Do you think he's one of them?"

"It's a very good possibility."

"Did you see him?"

Once again filled with a sense of inadequacy, James shook his head. "We struggled, I tried to restrain him, and then he hit me. For a minute, all I saw were stars. And then he was gone. I'm sorry. I tried."

She stopped walking then and turned to look back at him. Her lips were pressed together, and he could see her trying to process this. One hand covered the bag that held her camera, much like a mother would protect a baby.

"I'm not going to hurt you," he said softly. "And I'm not going to steal the camera from you. If I planned to, I could have done it before now. I wouldn't wait until we were on the street where you live. Would it make you feel better if you take it to the station on yourself? I won't even have anything to do with it except to make sure you get there safely."

After eyeing him cautiously to make sure he kept his distance, she finally relaxed enough to wait while he drew closer. "As I told you, it's not my camera to give away. It belongs to my employer. Mr. Eastman."

"I'm sure he would understand—if for no reason other than to help the president, and our country. I'm sorry if I came on too strong, Clara. Sorry I made you suspect my motives. We'll give the camera back after we've gone over the evidence. I promise."

She nodded. "Come on. Let's go." Turning, she began walking again. This time slowly, still maintaining a careful distance.

Adjusting his pace to hers, James stayed silent. Did this mean she would give it to him? He didn't want to push her. When she finally spoke again, her words took him by surprise.

"I don't even think you know what you're asking."

That was an odd thing to say. Was she questioning his abilities? The skill of his department? "What do you mean?" He tried to force defensiveness from his tone.

"It's not the camera you want. It's the film."

"Oh." Now he really did feel incompetent. "Right."

"And before you ask, you can't have the film."

"But—"

She was at his side so fast he had no time to react. What was happening to his skills of perception? It was such an important part of police work, and he was quickly failing.

Again.

"James, do you even know how your men would process the film?"

"We—" He shook his head. He didn't know for sure, and could tell by her stance that whatever he said would be wrong. It was obvious Clara knew something he did not.

"They wouldn't. It can only be processed at Mr. Eastman's offices in Rochester."

He should have known. He also knew by the way she fed him only a little information at a time that any trust he thought he saw in her eyes was merely an illusion. It would be difficult at this point to earn it back. And because of that, he needed to be firm—needed to be the police officer that he was. He held out his open palm.

"I'll go ahead and take it from you now, and I'll take it there first thing in the morning."

Staring at James's outstretched hand, Clara blinked back her surprise. "Excuse me, what?"

"The film. I'll take it to Rochester and have Mr. Eastman process it for the police department."

Though she'd drawn a certain comfort in having James accompany her home, she'd suspected all along that he had an ulterior motive.

And here it was.

"No." The dove gray two-story house where she lived with the Martins was in view now, and she headed toward it without a backward glance at James. But as she reached the wide sweeping porch, she knew he was right behind her. She turned.

"Thank you for seeing me home. I really do appreciate it."

He said nothing, only stared at her, determined. "The film, please, Clara. Don't make me have to confiscate it from you."

"You wouldn't!" She'd sensed she could trust him to a degree, and yet he threatened to confiscate her film—to forcibly take it from her? Disappointed, she turned back to the steps. Then she blinked and glanced over her shoulder, determined. "I thought you said police officers don't steal from innocent women?"

"Clara." He blew out a most exasperated breath that mimicked her feelings exactly. He dug his toe at a small rock near the steps. "Need I remind you that this is evidence?"

"Yes, you've made that perfectly clear. More than once." She tried to meet his gaze but looked down, focusing on the stains that marred the knees of her skirt. He had the most expressive eyes, and even in the shadowy evening light she found herself drawn to them.

If she wasn't careful, she'd find herself giving in to him. "And need I remind *you*, this camera and all of its film were entrusted to me by Mr. Eastman. I'll *not* let it out of my sight."

"Just what are you saying?"

Glancing up at him, she could see he knew exactly what she meant. His lips pressed together, and a small muscle twitched in his upper jaw. His eyes were bright with the reflection of the streetlight. She needed to stay firm, undistracted. "Exactly what you heard me say. The film doesn't leave my sight until I personally hand it to Mr. Eastman."

"Then I guess we'll leave first thing in the morning."

"I guess we will." She hadn't expected him to agree so quickly, but she wouldn't let him know that. "Good night, James. Thank you for coming to my rescue tonight and for seeing me safely home." She smiled to let him know she really did mean it. Then she turned and was halfway up the porch stairs when she heard his foot come down heavily on one step.

"I'm not going anywhere."

"What?" She turned and eyed him warily, not surprised that he stood right behind her. "Of course you are. I'll see you in the morning."

He stepped closer. "I can't leave you unprotected."

"The film, you mean." Even as she said it, a twinge of guilt bit at her.

"Clara, the film is evidence, yes. And I need to keep it safe. But it comes second only to you." His voice softened. "Your safety is far more important."

Touched, she blinked and softened her tone. "James. That's really not necessary."

"It really is." He folded his arms across his chest. "I'm not leaving here."

"But you can't—" She started to protest, but the door flew open and Mrs. Martin stood there.

Wisps of white hair fanned back from the older woman's face as she stepped outside. She immediately focused on the condition of Clara's dress. "What has happened to you, Clara?" The usual lilting tone of her German accent was gone, replaced with concern. "You look a fright!" She glanced at James and stepped closer to Clara in a protective mode.

"I'm all right, Mrs. Martin. Really." She reached out and patted the woman's arm to assure her that it was true.

"And who is this?" Her tone was sharp, unfriendly.

"This is Officer James Brinton."

Mrs. Martin gasped. "Officer?" She swept her gaze over his uniform and fear flickered across her face. "What is he doing here?"

"A terrible thing has happened, Mrs. Martin." Surprised that the woman hadn't already heard, Clara tried to form the words to tell her about the president, but found she couldn't get them out. Tears brimmed in her eyes and she looked to James for help. To her relief, he graciously stepped forward.

"It's President McKinley, ma'am. I'm afraid he's been shot."

"No!" Mrs. Martin gasped and clutched her chest. "Is he...? Will he...? He's not *dead* is he?"

"No." Clara pulled Mrs. Martin's hand into hers. She squeezed it and looked into her face. "Thank the good Lord for that. The president isn't dead. But he is hurt. The doctors are taking good care of him."

"Oh, thank you, God." The woman still held a hand to her chest as she searched Clara's face. "You were there then?"

Slowly, Clara nodded. "I wish it wasn't true but yes, I was."

Mrs. Martin pulled Clara into a hug, so gentle, so comforting, that for a moment it was as if she were in her own mother's arms. This brought a fresh round of tears to the surface, forcing the others to spill over. She reached up and brushed at them, even as she rested her cheek against Mrs. Martin's shoulder.

When she finally raised her head, she turned to James. He watched her with a softened gaze, not seeming the least bit put out at having to wait. Her heart warmed, and she silently mouthed her thanks before making introductions. "James, meet Eulalie Martin. She is my landlady and a longtime family friend."

"Though I'm sorry it's under these circumstances, I'm pleased to meet you." James extended his hand to Mrs. Martin, but she only scowled at him. Clara gave him a pleading look, hoping he wouldn't take Mrs. Martin's attitude personally. His return glance was so tender, it took her breath away.

"Mrs. Martin, Officer Brinton was one of the police officers guarding the president at the Temple of Music."

"Obviously he didn't do his job very well."

Clara gasped, unable to believe the woman could be so rude. "He saved me, Mrs. Martin. A man was trying to hurt me. Chasing me. James protected me."

Mrs. Martin's expression changed immediately. The protective, guarded scowl faded, softened. She put her hand on Clara's shoulder and studied her from head to toe. "You are all right, then?"

"Yes. Thanks to James."

"Forgive my rudeness." Mrs. Martin's broad face broke into a smile. "Thank you for protecting my Clara. She is special, this girl."

James looked at Clara. "Yes, she is."

Clara blushed under his stare, and for a moment she felt as if she were back on the aerio-cycle.

"Thank you for seeing her home." Mrs. Martin's tone was dismissive, and she tugged Clara toward the door.

"Excuse me, ma'am?"

Clara tensed, knowing what James was about to say.

"I'm not going anywhere."

Clara sighed, bracing herself. She should have expected this. Mrs. Martin turned and stepped toward James, piercing him with a sharp look and an equally sharp tone. "What exactly do you mean by that?"

"I'm going to make sure Clara is safe."

"Safe? She is in danger, then?" Mrs. Martin folded her arms across her chest and looked from Clara to James, and back at Clara again. "What is this about, my dear?"

Clara angled toward James, silently begging him to leave and not say a word. He ignored her.

"Mrs. Martin, Clara may not think she needs protection, but she does. The man who attacked her is still out there. I'm here to make certain he doesn't get to her again."

As Mrs. Martin gasped, James pressed his lips together and raised his eyes at Clara. To her, it was an answering look of victory. And while she simmered, he cleared his throat and proceeded to tell

Mrs. Martin everything that had transpired tonight and what they needed to do tomorrow. In a matter of seconds, she was ushered into the house with James right on her heel.

Obviously, he wasn't going anywhere.

And though part of her was relieved, the other part of her couldn't help but wonder if he was really here to protect her. The thought left her bereft, and oddly disappointed.

What if he was only here because he wanted the film?

CHAPTER 6

James felt the tension ease from his shoulders as they continued through a modestly decorated sitting room and into a large kitchen. Clara may not want his help, but now he had a most intriguing ally.

The German lady was as obstinate as she was protective, and he knew Clara wouldn't be able to win this argument. He only wished she wouldn't hold it against him.

As he followed them into the kitchen, James removed his cap and tugged off his gloves.

"Please have a seat, Officer Brinton." Mrs. Martin motioned toward a table in one corner of the small kitchen. A spicy aroma permeated the room, and his mouth watered.

"I hope you don't mind eating in here," Mrs. Martin said. "We have a dining room that is large enough for the guests. But I prefer this one when it is just family." He could tell by the way she looked at Clara that the woman considered her part of her family.

"Not at all." But he really should let Captain Green know where he was and what had transpired. "May I use your telephone to call my captain?"

Mrs. Martin shook her head. "I'm sorry, but we do not have

a telephone. My Emil—he always says we'll get one soon, but he never gets one installed."

He understood. In spite of the technology, not everyone had a telephone. His parents hadn't had one either. He would just have to get word to the captain once he was certain Clara was safe.

After tucking his gloves into the left inner pocket of his jacket, James pulled a chair away from the table for Clara. She gave him a frosty look, but he only smiled and held the chair while she sat. The detective in him knew it was important she trust him so he could get the film processed and take it back to the station. But as a man first and police officer second, he needed to gain her trust for more reasons than just the trip to Rochester.

The thought took him by surprise, and he brushed it aside as he moved to hold out a second chair for Mrs. Martin.

"No," she said. "You sit. I will get refreshments." She turned to Clara. "We must get those stains out of your dress before they set. But I suppose it can wait until after you have something to eat."

Before he sat, James unbuckled the yellow belt at his waist so he could remove his jacket. After placing his cap and belt on the chair across from Clara, he draped his jacket over the back of the one to her left. Then he sat down, leaving the chair across from him for Mrs. Martin.

After a moment of uncomfortable silence between the two of them, Mrs. Martin returned to the table with a pot of tea, three cups, and a plate of cookies so small he could polish one off with just a bite. She took one cup and poured from the steaming pot of tea before handing it to James. Of all the delicious smells surrounding him, James knew tea was not one of them.

"Thank you, ma'am." He accepted graciously, but his taste buds were disappointed.

Clara accepted her cup of tea with similar graciousness, though James had the sneaking suspicion that she was disappointed as well. He eyed the cookies, waiting for them to be offered, knowing he could devour the entire plate in a matter of seconds.

Should he take one? He could almost imagine getting his hand slapped gently if he did. Clara didn't seem inclined, and Mrs. Martin had turned away. His mother had always taught him that it was polite to wait until offered.

At the stove, Mrs. Martin lifted the lid off a pot and pushed a large ladle through the contents. James's stomach rumbled.

"You are hungry, Officer Brinton?"

Surely his stomach hadn't been that loud? Embarrassed, he stole a glance at Clara. She bit down on her lower lip, and her eyes glimmered with amusement. He turned toward Mrs. Martin. "Yes, ma'am, I am. And please, call me James."

Ignoring him, Mrs. Martin filled a bowl then bustled toward the table and placed it in front of him. It was filled with boiled potatoes, beans, and a spicy smelling beef in some kind of hunger-inducing broth. His stomach panged again, this time thankfully quiet. He looked from Clara to Mrs. Martin, wishing he could start eating before Clara was served and Mrs. Martin was seated at the table. Manners won out, and he waited while Mrs. Martin placed two more bowls and a plate of thick buttered bread on the table. Then he stood and held her chair, waiting until she was comfortable before he went back to his own seat.

Neither woman picked up their spoon.

James scarcely dared breathe lest his stomach growl again.

Mrs. Martin finally broke the silence. "Officer—I'm sorry, James. Will you say the grace for us?"

Clearing his throat, collar suddenly tight, he glanced from Clara to Mrs. Martin. He hadn't said much in the way of grace—or thanks—over the last year. In fact, he hadn't said much of anything in the way of a prayer. A pang edged its way over his heart. Trying to dispel its discomfort, he blew out a breath.

Mrs. Martin smiled in expectation. Angry and distrustful one minute, smiling the next, the woman confused him. Was she testing him?

Clara watched him as well, her green gaze one he could easily get lost in. When she arched one eyebrow, he realized he'd been staring too long.

"Of course," he finally said. "I'll be happy to ask the blessing." He bowed his head and waited a moment to gather his thoughts.

After giving thanks for the food, he added one thing. "And Lord, thank you for seeing Clara and me safely to this house. And please see us safely to Rochester in the morning."

To his ears it sounded almost as an afterthought, but he hadn't meant it that way. He glanced from Clara to Mrs. Martin. They both smiled and didn't seem upset by his words.

When they were finished eating, Mrs. Martin stood and turned to Clara. "You and James have some cookies. I'll be right back with a surprise to go with them."

James didn't need to be asked twice when Clara held out the plate. "Thank you." He said it before he reached for the cookies, relieved to have remembered his manners.

A repressed smile played at the corners of Clara's mouth as she watched him take the cookies, but broke fully into surprised joy when Mrs. Martin returned. There was no mistaking the delight rounding her cheeks and highlighting dimples at the corners of her mouth.

"This is for you, Clara." Something clanked heavily on the tabletop.

Curious, James angled to see around Mrs. Martin in time for Clara to take a long drink from a brown bottle that dripped with condensation. She set it on the table with a satisfied smile.

What was this?

"And I have one for you, too, James." Mrs. Martin placed a similar bottle in front of him. He peered at it, relieved when he saw the diamond-shaped label of bright gold with striking blue letters that spelled out the words Coca-Cola. Not that Clara or Mrs. Martin seemed the type to drink ale.

"Thank you, Mrs. Martin. I've not tried this before." He picked up the chilled, sweat-soaked bottle.

"Give it a try." Clara picked up her bottle again. "It's become my daily indulgence. Her eyes twinkled with joy as she watched him raise the bottle to his mouth.

As the cold liquid hit his tongue and then his throat, bubbles of effervescence filled his mouth and, though it defied logic, somehow managed to tickle his nose. Trying not to spit out the soft drink, he forced himself to swallow. The bottle hit the table with a thud as he set it down.

Across from him, the two women laughed.

The only answer he could give them was a little gasp of air followed by, "Ahh."

"It tastes pretty good, doesn't it?" Clara picked up her own bottle again.

Not to be outdone by Clara, or perhaps because he didn't really taste it on the first swallow, James picked up his Coca-Cola again.

This time he was prepared for the fizz and let it coalesce on his tongue until it was a smooth liquid. Then he swallowed with nary a tickle to his nose and flashed Clara a satisfied grin. "You're right." He tipped his head toward her and was rewarded with another instant of joy lighting on her face and in her eyes. He found himself quite fascinated with the expressiveness of her eyes. In that second, she gazed back.

Did she feel it, too?

Before he could give it further thought, she broke eye contact. As if suddenly remembering her Coca-Cola, she put the bottle to her lips and drained it.

James took another careful sip. "It really is delicious. I don't think I've ever tasted anything like it."

But even as he finished the drink, he wasn't sure he could describe the taste. He only knew he looked forward to trying it again.

As long as he could drink it with Clara.

"But why must you go up to Clara's rooms?" Mrs. Martin stood in the kitchen doorway, blocking James's exit.

Clara watched as the older woman pulled her shoulders back until she was as straight as the doorframe. With her hands balled into fists held close to chest level, her face a hard mask, Mrs. Martin challenged James with a fierce glare.

A rush of love wrapped around Clara like a blanket of comfort. Though she'd known she was welcome here, and Mrs. Martin doted on her, these months of grieving for her mother had been difficult. And without her father, lonely.

It was clear by James's stance that he wasn't about to back away. If anything, he also stood taller. "The man who attacked Clara wanted her camera. If he was involved with the man who shot the president, he must think there's evidence of it on the film. I'm certain he'll be back."

"He'll be back." Not, *"He might be back."* A chill seeped between Clara's shoulder blades and then spread up the back of her neck. She rolled her shoulders, trying not to feel unsettled.

"My Emil is afraid of no one. He is a fighter." Mrs. Martin shot a fist toward James. To his credit, he didn't flinch, or laugh. Clara bit her lip to keep it from betraying her own amusement. She rushed to stand by his side.

"But he isn't here, Mrs. Martin." Likely, Emil Martin was in one of the corner saloons drinking and showing his friends how strong he was by starting a fight. It was an almost nightly occurrence. "James just wants to make sure it's safe before I go inside."

"Then I will go as well." Dropping her protective stance, Mrs. Martin stepped out of the doorway and headed into the drawing room with the large bow on the back of her dress swishing behind her. "It's not proper for you to have a man in your rooms. Your father would be outraged."

A wave of longing washed over her at the mention of her father, but she effectively brushed it away. "My father isn't here." Her throat tightened in a painful squeeze. "If he was, then he'd be able to check the room for me." She followed the two of them out of the room, and although she didn't think either of them heard her, she added, "But of course you can come, Mrs. Martin."

Instead of climbing the large wooden staircase at the center of the room, James turned to the front door. "We should lock this door first. Will anyone else be coming in for the night?"

"Just my Emil. But he won't be here for quite some time. I will lock the door." Mrs. Martin retrieved a long slender key from a tall wood table next to the door. "We have only a few guests, and they are all settled in for the evening." She turned and looked pointedly at Clara. "That is why I was so worried about you when you weren't here for supper."

Before Clara could apologize, James interrupted. "How many rooms are downstairs?"

"Just my and Emil's room."

"And how many doors lead outside?"

"Two. This one and a back door."

"Is it locked as well?"

Mrs. Martin nodded. "I always keep it locked."

After James double-checked the lock on the front door, he stepped in front of them to lead the way up the stairs. Clara supposed it was meant to be protective, not rude.

Once he was at the top of the steps, James stopped and glanced from right to left. "How many rooms are up here?"

Ahead of Clara on the stairs, Mrs. Martin paused. "There are five guest rooms up here." Her tone had markedly cooled. "The one in front of you, two rooms on the right, and two on the left."

"My room is to the left, overlooking the street," Clara said.

James nodded and stepped aside so she could lead him to the door. "Is there a tree outside your window?"

"Yes, there is."

"Is there another room where you can stay for the night?"

Mrs. Martin edged in front of Clara and stared up at James. "Why are you so nosy?"

"I'm sorry to pry, Mrs. Martin. I need to know so I can make a plan to keep you all safe tonight."

"I told you before, my Emil can keep us perfectly safe. He has a very large gun. Clara will be quite safe here tonight."

This time James didn't back down. He moved closer to Clara, and to the door. "I don't doubt that at all. But he's not here yet. And don't you think the police department should do whatever we can to ensure Clara isn't attacked again?"

Dropping her head forward, Mrs. Martin drew in a breath before giving James a measured look. "Yes, you are right. I am sorry. I just want Clara to be safe as well."

They nodded at each other, and to Clara it seemed as if they were making a secret pact. Just as she was about to unlock her door, James closed his hand over hers. "Please, let me go first."

Warm and sincere, his eyes searched hers. Was it possible to get lost in someone's eyes?

"Clara?"

"What?" She looked down at their hands and pulled hers from the door handle—and effectively from under his.

"You both should wait out here while I check. Just in case."

She nodded, then stared as he opened the door to her room and stepped inside.

What was wrong with her? Surely she should be more concerned over the possibility of that dreadful man climbing through her window. Instead she was fixated on James and the way his eyes seemed to see right to her soul.

That and the rush of warmth that bathed her heart every time their hands made contact.

CHAPTER 7

Though he'd asked them to remain in the hall, Mrs. Martin had bustled her way into the room with Clara following right behind. And since no one jumped out to attack them, James was certain there was no one here. If there had been anyone in Clara's rooms, they'd likely been alerted by all of the noise and fled out the window.

From minute to minute with Clara, and now Mrs. Martin, James questioned his abilities as a police officer. Were they obstinate? Or was he just incompetent? He shook his head, certain it was the latter. And if that was the case, since the Martins didn't have a telephone, he should return to headquarters and ask that an officer be assigned to protect the two women.

Truthfully, there would be a lot of questions and he could be putting his job in jeopardy by not reporting this incident immediately—especially since he was already on precarious grounds.

But that would take time. While he reported in and explained the situation, and by the time his captain decided whether or not to assign someone to this case, Clara could be hurt—or worse.

James wasn't about to let that happen. Competent or not, job in jeopardy or not, he wasn't leaving Clara's side. At least not until the supposedly fierce and protective fighter named Emil returned. Even then, James had his doubts about leaving her at all until the film was processed in Rochester and he saw her safely home.

A warm glow bathed the room when Clara turned on a lamp. As James eyed it, he was struck by the expensive glass. He didn't know much about art or glass, but he was fairly certain it was designed by Tiffany. He'd once worked a case where a thief had made off with all of the Tiffany lamps in the fancy office of a lawyer downtown. If this wasn't the real thing, it was an expert replica. The beautifully carved table it sat on struck him as custom designed and was the perfect accent for the lamp as well as the rest of the furnishings.

In contrast to what he'd seen of Mrs. Martin's house so far, Clara's sitting room was far more tastefully furnished. As his eyes swept the small room, he could see there was nowhere anyone could hide. And if an intruder was here, they could only be in the bedroom. "Since you've insisted on coming inside, will you both have a seat while I make sure it's safe?"

"Do you really think the man followed us here, climbed the oak tree, and somehow broke in to my room?" Clara's eyes were wide with disbelief.

It did sound silly when she put it that way. "No," James admitted. "But I wouldn't be doing my job if I didn't make certain."

"Very well." Though she sounded reluctant, Clara sat in one of two chairs separated by another intricately carved table. Mrs. Martin eyed him with disapproval and sat as well.

It seemed as though the older woman wanted to trust him, but had a hard time letting go of her own protective instincts. And she probably leaned toward him being incompetent. But it didn't matter. The only thing that mattered was ensuring their safety. James eyed the door that he knew led to Clara's bedroom.

"I'll be right back."

Neither woman looked happy as he carefully opened the door. He turned back to them, his eyes locking on to Clara. "Look. You know I'm not trying to intrude on your privacy. But I have to be certain it's safe."

Understanding flickered across Clara's face, and he turned and stepped inside Clara's room, struck at once by the fresh clean scent.

It grew stronger as he stepped past the wardrobe to turn on another glass lamp. It was the same scent he'd noticed when they'd been on the aerio-cycle.

Her bed was neatly made, and he bent down to look underneath. Of course no one hid there.

He stood and tried to place the fragrance. He couldn't, but it was a sure bet his mother would have. An overwhelming longing sliced through him and almost brought him to his knees. Yes, he was an adult who missed his parents dearly. On the one hand, he was glad they weren't here to see his disgrace from the department. On the other hand, had they been there when it happened, they would have prayed him through it.

As always when he thought of them, guilt overtook him. It was his fault they weren't here. Heart heavy, he shook the thoughts away and forced himself on his reason for being in this room. Clara. He had to keep her safe.

The room was clean and orderly, with no clutter. There was a glass vase on her nightstand that looked suspiciously like the same glass in her Tiffany lamp. How could she afford the lamps and glass? Did taking pictures at the Pan really pay that well?

After switching off the lamp, he stepped over to the window and lifted the curtain. The window was latched tight, and there were no signs of anyone having attempted to enter her room. Nor were there signs of anyone on the street below. He turned the light back on then opened the small closet where he brushed aside several gowns to find at least six hat boxes stacked neatly one on top of the other.

There was no one hiding there, and as he stood and looked around he knew there was nowhere else a person could hide. He turned to leave the room so he could assure Clara her room was safe. As he did, his eyes scanned the small writing desk next to the closet.

A fresh stack of stationery and a pen lay across the desktop. Something about the first sheet of paper drew his eye. He stepped closer.

Father... The word was marred by a slash directly through it. Then, *I'm sorry, I can't*... Another slash. Something about the way they were written, the words themselves, seemed angry somehow.

Or sad. He glanced over his shoulder, feeling guilty. They were just words, crossed out, they didn't mean anything. And yet he felt like he'd just stepped into a corner of Clara's heart.

"So you think Clara should stay in my room tonight?" Mrs. Martin finally looked at him with approval.

"I do." James nodded at the woman. Clara could probably stay in her own room without incident, but he would rest far easier if she stayed with her overly-doting landlady. "I'll keep watch in your drawing room to be certain no one breaks into the house."

"Do you really think that's necessary?" Clara didn't look as approving as Mrs. Martin.

"I do, Clara. And in the morning we can leave for Rochester."

She straightened in the chair, as if drawing herself up would give her strength to argue. But then she nodded. "I suppose if you think it best. But how rested will you be tomorrow if you're awake all night?"

"I can sleep on the train. Besides, I won't get any sleep at all if I'm worried about you."

"All right then." She stood and headed toward her room. "I'll just gather some things together for tonight, and also for the trip to Rochester."

Surprised at her easy agreement, James sat in the chair.

Mrs. Martin stood and walked to Clara's door. "While you're in there, please change your dress so I can get those horrid stains out." She turned and glanced at James before she sat back down.

Since she didn't seem inclined to speak to him, he stared about the room in awkward silence.

A collection of ladies' hats, each adorned with lace and ribbons, each fancier than the last, decorated a wooden rack on one wall. Were these in addition to the ones in her closet? Or did these belong in those hat boxes?

Below the rack, on a lace covered table, fresh pink flowers stood neatly arranged in a vase.

On a shorter table in front of the chair where Mrs. Martin sat were two books and another pink flower sticking out of an empty amber Coca-Cola bottle. Perhaps Mrs. Martin was right about Clara's love for the fizzy drink.

James leaned forward and reached for one of the books.

Bicycling for Ladies, by M.E. Ward. The blue cover depicted a woman on a bicycle. Her skirts were gathered in front of her and a hat trailed behind in the wind. It was whimsical, and he could almost picture Clara as the woman in the illustration.

The other book was one with a gentleman illustrated in olive green. He, too, sat on a bicycle, but looked more reserved than joyous. That one didn't interest him as much. He flipped the cover of the book he held, and the pages fell open to one that was marked.

This time, it wasn't what was on the page that caught his interest as much as what marked it. He took out the card and studied it. The word *BOSTONS* was centered at the top, with a list down the left side and neat squares of tiny boxes across the card. Halfway down was a crease and the words *Official Score Card, Sold Only On The Grounds*. Under that, *CHICAGO*, also centered, followed by a list and small squares.

Scanning the list, James's eye caught the word *Nichols, p.* with a lot of scratch marks in the boxes to the left. This was a score card from last year, from a game between the Boston Beaneaters and the Chicago Orphans. Boston's pitcher, Kid Nichols, won his 300th game last year, against the Chicago Orphans.

Had Clara *been* at that particular game?

Peering closer, he saw the numbers 11-4 penciled into the top right corner. He couldn't help but grin.

Clearly there was more to Clara than pretty dresses and fancy hats. He'd learned a lot about her in these few minutes observing her room. She enjoyed Coca-Cola and flowers, and she clearly had an interest in bicycles. He could take or leave any of those things. But that she might actually enjoy the game of baseball set his heart tripping.

When she stepped back into the room, he smiled in spite of himself.

"What?"

"Nothing." He took in the white gown with pale blue pinstripes. It wasn't decked out with lace and pearls, but it was equally as striking. Or perhaps it was the woman in the gown? He stood and headed toward the door. "Shall we go back downstairs?"

More than just protecting her, James wanted to learn even more about Miss Clara Lambert.

"I'll be out here if you ladies need anything."

Clara watched as James tugged on his gloves. Once again in his jacket and cap, he looked every bit the Buffalo police officer. Had she noticed before how handsome he was in his uniform? She was sure she had, but right now, in this instance, it was as though seeing him for the first time. Especially standing this close to him. His gaze settled on hers and she flushed. Surely he couldn't read her thoughts.

"And don't open this door for anyone."

They stood just inside the doorway of Mrs. Martin's room. James had checked it as thoroughly as he had Clara's room. In fact, he'd gone through every unoccupied room in the house. Clara had no doubt she was safe. She smiled her thanks at him.

"I'll have to open it for Emil." Mrs. Martin held up the key.

"Only for him." James gave Mrs. Martin a stern look that she returned before she rushed him to the door. "Good night."

Before Clara could thank James, Mrs. Martin shut the door in his face. She ushered Clara through the sitting room and into the bedroom.

"You and I will sleep in the bed, and Emil can sleep in the chair." She pointed to the corner of the room at an oak and leather chair that reclined slightly. It didn't look very comfortable.

It was the first time she'd been in here, and Clara was surprised at how small it was. Surely in their own home the Martins would have kept the largest room for themselves? It only reinforced the generosity of the woman who put on such a tough front.

"I don't feel right taking his bed." She could only imagine what Emil Martin would have to say about that after a night in the saloon.

"Nonsense. He would insist. My Emil is nothing but a gentleman."

Knowing that to be true—at least in the light of day—Clara didn't argue. She hadn't really seen him after a night of drinking, but she'd heard him singing to the moon on more than one occasion.

Much later, when she awoke to sounds of scuffling and raised voices—one of which was unmistakably Emil Martin—Clara had to wonder again at the *gentleman* remark.

Alarmed, she carefully scooted to the foot of the bed. It was the only way she could get out of bed since Mrs. Martin had her wedged against the wall.

She scrambled through the bedroom door and tried to open the door to the hallway, but it was locked.

"What is it, dear?" Mrs. Martin was at her side in an instant.

"It's Mr. Martin. And James. I think they're fighting. Please unlock the door."

She muttered something in German that Clara didn't understand before pinning her with a firm look. "You stay here." Then she softened. "Just in case."

Though reluctant, Clara did as she was told and watched while Mrs. Martin unlocked the door and slipped into the hallway. The door was still opened just a crack, and she could hear Mrs. Martin scolding the two men.

Clara stepped toward the door and peeked out. There was a lot of blustering on Mr. Martin's part as the stout, bald man waved his arms back and forth, but eventually he shook James's hand. Then he turned to lock the outside door with his wife double-checking his work.

James looked up and caught her gaze. She put her finger to her lips, silently begging him not to draw attention toward her. His lips turned up in a slight smile and he nodded.

She mouthed a silent, *Thank you.*

The Martins were headed straight toward her, so Clara scooted back into the bedroom and disappeared under the covers just as Mrs. Martin burst through the door.

"Emil is going to sleep out there on the sofa. Your James is going to stay where he is in the drawing room. He's doing a fine job of keeping watch, so you should be able to sleep well."

Her James. It was the second time tonight he'd been referred to as hers. The thought warmed her.

Yes, she would sleep well knowing he was there.

CHAPTER 8

In spite of her hopes for a good night's sleep, Clara barely slept during the night. Both the anxiety of her own ordeal and her deep sorrow and fear for the president's condition had kept her tossing and turning all night long.

And Mrs. Martin's loud snoring hadn't helped much.

Because she hadn't slept well, and because she was eager to get to the train station, Clara was up and dressed early. She tiptoed past Mr. Martin, who still slept on the cameo-backed sofa that looked much too delicate for him. The man snored louder than his wife, and his oversized white mustache lifted slightly with each exhale of breath. It was difficult to imagine being in a room with the two of them as they slept.

Once in the main entry of the house, Clara was surprised that she didn't see James. She searched around, and her heart plummeted when he wasn't anywhere to be found. Based on yesterday, she'd thought him a man of his word.

Mrs. Martin, who had been up early as well cooking and preparing food for Clara and James to share on the train, came up behind her. "He left about an hour ago to go feed his cat, and then to let his captain know where you two are going. I assured him we would keep you safe until he returned."

He had a cat? Clara bit back a smile. A few minutes later, she spotted him coming up the walk—somehow managing to look neat and crisp in his uniform despite having slept in it all night. He held a small travel case at his side.

She raced outside and down the steps to greet him. "How is the president this morning? Have you heard?"

James gave her a quirky little smile. "Good morning to you, too." Then his smile faded a bit and looked uncomfortable, as if he'd said the wrong thing. "I went by my precinct to report in to my captain, and he said they've been issuing updated bulletins throughout the night. President McKinley is resting comfortably and is stated to be free of pain."

"Thank you, God," Clara whispered.

"They removed one bullet easily, but the other, in his abdomen, has not been found."

"That's good news, though, right?"

"It appears to be, yes."

"And what of Mrs. McKinley? He was so concerned for her. Have you heard any news in her regard?"

"Yes. She's holding up well and has barely left his side."

Clara felt a wave of compassion for the woman. "I wonder how her health is holding up. She must be exhausted."

"Undoubtedly," James agreed. "I'm told she took the news with strength, though she was already extremely anxious about his whereabouts."

"But wasn't he at the Exposition hospital?"

"Yes, but they didn't bring her there. And they apparently waited several hours to tell her what had happened."

Clara's stomach clenched. "How awful."

"Our police superintendent went straightaway to the Milburns' home where they're staying. He wanted to make certain no one from the outside could tell her. She was resting, so he broke the news to her family. They were reluctant to wake her, so he had guards placed outside the house. He even had the telephone system cut off so that no one could break the news until they decided how best to tell her."

"And so she slept while her husband's life was in the balance?"

James nodded, grim-faced. "Yes, and when she awoke they still didn't tell her. They waited until she grew anxious with worry that he'd not returned from the reception."

"That's unimaginable." Clara pressed her lips together at the harshness of her tone. "Sorry. I'm just—I feel angry on her behalf."

"I know. Me too. But she's with him now. She asked that they bring him to the Milburns'. The doctors agreed, and she's been with him ever since."

"Poor thing. She must be exhausted." She thought again of the beaming smiles of the president and his wife at Niagara Falls. A wave of sympathy washed through her. She remembered the president's command to his men when he realized he'd been shot. Even as he fell forward his first thought had been for her and how they would break the news. Not for himself. He was such a sweet and gentle man. She sent a prayer heavenward for his healing and for his wife's comfort.

A tender squeeze of her elbow caught her attention, and she looked up to find James staring at her intently. "Are you all right?"

Meeting his eyes, his unblinking and intensely brown eyes, she nodded. "Just thinking about what she must be going through. I hope she has someone to talk to. She's so far from home."

James shifted toward her, and before she realized his intent, he caught her hand in his, clasping it in a firm but surprisingly smooth grip. His touch did something funny to her insides.

"I'm sure she has plenty of support. If not, I feel certain the doctor's wife will see to it that she has everything she needs, as well as plenty of women to talk to."

"I'm so glad."

"Clara." At the sound of her name, she reluctantly pulled her gaze from James. Mrs. Martin stood in the doorway, Clara's travel bag and leather camera case in one hand and a cloth bag with refreshments in the other. "You'd better be on your way so you don't miss the train."

They both stepped back onto the porch and walked to the door. James took the bags from Mrs. Martin, then handed Clara the camera. "I'll carry these."

"Are you sure?"

He nodded and adjusted his own bag. It didn't take much to see this man had been raised right.

"Thank you, then."

"Good-bye, Clara, dear. You be careful now."

"Oh, Mrs. Martin." Clara wriggled free of the older woman's tight embrace. "I will. I have one of Buffalo's finest officers at my side." Clara slid a glance up at James then reached up to whisper in her landlady's ear. "Would you be able to let Vivie know I won't be at work for a couple of days?"

"I will, dear. Now you'd better hurry so you don't miss your train." Mrs. Martin ushered her down the porch steps. Mr. Martin appeared then, eyes bloodshot, clothes rumpled, and promptly stepped in front of James.

"You take good care of our Clara. Otherwise we'll be sending her father after you."

Clara said nothing, but she sincerely doubted her father would care enough to track James down.

No. That wasn't fair. He did care. She knew he did. It was just her mother, for some reason, that he hadn't bothered to be there for when she needed him the most.

"Yes, sir, I will." James shook Mr. Martin's hand and motioned for Clara to go down the steps ahead of him.

Still thinking of her father, she waved absently at the Martins and headed up the walk.

"Clara, is something wrong?"

She stopped and turned back, waiting while James caught up with her. Concern highlighted his brown eyes.

"No. I'm just thinking about my father."

"Is he far away?"

"New York City. Only a few hours by train."

She could tell James wanted to ask more questions—questions she didn't want to answer. "We'd better hurry, or we'll miss our trolley ride to the train station. Once we're on the train, we have some lovely German pastries Mrs. Martin baked fresh this morning."

He stared at her for another second before finally nodding. She should have been relieved that he didn't press her about her father. Instead, she was filled with an emptiness she couldn't explain.

As they walked down Sycamore, toward Broadway, James was quiet. Of course he had been awake most of the night watching out for her safety. Her heart warmed. Still, Clara had the feeling he wanted to ask her something. After they veered off the sidewalk and started through the park, she turned to look at him. "What are you thinking about?"

"While I was at the precinct this morning, I learned the man who shot President McKinley is named Leon Czolgosz."

Clara turned the name over in her mind several times before she tried to pronounce it. *Cholegaesh.* "Czolgosz," she finally said. "It's definitely a mouthful."

James nodded and opened his mouth to speak, but a movement behind him caught Clara's eyes.

"James!"

Before he could react, a man struck him on the back of the head. With what, Clara couldn't tell.

"James," she cried again.

"Run, Clara!" He staggered and fought to remain upright. Clara rushed to help him, but the man stepped in front of him.

Clara gasped. "You!" There was no mistaking the beady black

eyes and cruel mouth of the man who attacked her last night.

"Hand over the camera."

Caught between loyalty and self-preservation, loyalty won out. James helped her last night. She wasn't about to turn her back on him now. She struck out at the man.

"Clara, please." James sounded as if he were struggling to remain conscious.

"Help! Somebody help!" If she shrieked loud enough, the man was sure to leave. Besides, there was a precinct building at the end of the street. Hopefully a police officer would be alerted and come to their aid.

"Shut up, and give me the camera." His skin held a sallowness she hadn't noticed the evening before. But the sharp angles of his face reflected his evil intent.

"No." Even as she backed away, he advanced on her. "You can't have it." She knew she couldn't outrun him. Not when he was this close. But she could try.

Clara ran through the park, aware of the man behind her, aware that he was within a few steps of snatching her camera. She had to protect it at all costs. Mr. Eastman entrusted her with it and she couldn't, she *wouldn't* let him down.

Hadn't she screamed loud enough to attract attention? Why wasn't anyone coming? The man lunged toward her, reaching for the handle of her bag, and she screamed again as she dodged out of his reach. If James didn't have the other bag, she could swing it around and smack the man with it.

At that moment, Clara's foot caught something, and she tumbled forward. She tried to stop her fall, but there was nothing to grab on to. Her hip hit the ground first, a sharp pain jarring her. She was able to protect her head with her shoulder, which didn't take quite as hard an impact as her hip. Still, her shoulder felt as though it had shattered when she attempted to roll over so she could stand.

"Unfortunate for you, I'd say." The man stood over her, his mouth spread in a gloating sneer. He bent down to grab the bag but she managed to hold onto it. He jerked harder, and she felt it slipping from her grasp.

Drawing in a breath, Clara struggled to regain her hold.

"Enough of all this." The man made a low throaty sound and drew his foot back.

Pain exploded in Clara's ribs, stealing the breath from her lungs. She sucked at the air, but nothing happened. It was as if an invisible shield blocked it from entering her lungs. Frightened, she struggled once. Not even a gasp would move through her throat. Full-blown panic, unlike any she'd ever felt, overtook her as she tried to force her lungs to obey.

Seeing his advantage, her attacker gave a final jerk of the handle and wrenched the bag from her fingers. She was helpless to do anything about it except lay there like a fish in the bottom of a boat, watching as black dots floated before her eyes. Defeated, her eyes drifted closed just as a small bit of air whistled past her throat.

At the sound of flesh meeting flesh, she opened her eyes again and struggled to raise her head. Her vision was dim with patches of gray but, from where she lay on the ground, it appeared James had the man in his grip. Relieved, she closed her eyes again and let her head drop back to the ground. Drawing in one slim breath at a time, her heart pulsed in her throat as she listened to the sounds of the scuffle and wondered if her breathing would ever return to normal.

"Clara, are you all right?" She felt hands on her shoulder, then her face. "Open your eyes, Clara. Please? Just let me know you're all right."

She did as he asked, squinting to focus on his face. She blinked when the warmth of his brown eyes came into view.

"He's gone, Clara. He ran off like a coward." Strong gentle arms encircled her, carefully helping her to her feet. But he didn't leave her to stand on her own. Instead, he cradled her against him, holding her there.

After a few moments, he said, "Come on. Let's get you back

home."

Shaking her head, Clara struggled out of his arms and looked up at him. It hurt to gather enough breath to even speak, but this was important. "Camera," she managed to gasp. "He took my camera. I need to get it back."

"I've got it." James held up the familiar leather bag.

It was safe. Somehow, James managed to get her camera back.

"Thank you." She reached up and brushed her fingertips across his cheek, and he winced. Peering closer, she could see it was scraped up from the fight and the tender skin just below his eye was split. "I'm sorry. He hurt you because of me."

"No. He was bent on hurting anyone who got in his way."

He pulled her close again, wrapping his arms across her like a shield. She leaned her head against his chest, longing to rest here, to take refuge in the comfort he offered.

"Let's get you home now, and I'll go down to the precinct and file another report."

Planting her feet, still dazed and slightly off balance, she swayed forward but managed to stay upright. "We can't. I need to get this film to Rochester."

"We can do that later. Right now, we need to have you seen by a doctor." His soft tone and genuine concern spread warmth through her heart. Though her lungs still ached, she drew in a slow steady breath. "I can see a doctor later." She had to make him understand how important this was. "There's something on the film he doesn't want anyone to see. We need to get it processed so we can figure out what it is."

James looked away from her, his gaze roving the nearby trees. She tapped his arm.

"You know I'm right. You can forcibly take me back to the Martins', but I'll leave as soon as you're gone. I'll go to Rochester by myself."

"You'd do that, too, wouldn't you?"

Yes, she most definitely would. She'd do anything to make sure the film was processed. But instead of answering, she simply regarded him with a long, slow look. Finally, he huffed out a breath and afforded her a half-nod before he brushed his fingers under chin. "All right, then. Lean against me as we walk. I think we can still get to the train station on time."

CHAPTER 9

James looked down at Clara. Despite the jarring movement of the train, she somehow managed to fall asleep against him. Her hat lay in her lap and her head rested against his side. Dark hair curled against her forehead and brushed her cheeks. Sunlight streamed through the windows to highlight the luminescent streaks of reddish-gold that wound through her hair. He was tempted to reach out and touch it, to see if it was as warm as it appeared.

Instead, with his free arm he reached up to rub the back of his head. He winced as his fingers brushed over the tender knot. Unfortunately, it was the least painful of all his injuries. But he knew it didn't compare to the injuries Clara sustained.

Next to him, she stirred and sat upright. And as she did, a cool emptiness spread through his arm and across his chest. He longed to pull her close again, to try and regain the warmth.

"So what do you think he hit you with?" Her voice was soft and breathy from sleep. Did she always sound this way when she first awoke? "James?" She blinked and pinned him with her wide-eyed stare.

"Sorry." He pulled his gaze from hers and noticed the bright pink of her cheek where it had rested against his chest. "It may have been the butt of a pistol. Maybe even a rock. I don't know. But I'm much more concerned about you." He peered closer at her face and barely refrained from touching it. "What happened to your face, Clara? By tomorrow this will be a regal shade of purple."

Clara's hand flew up to touch her cheek. Like he had, she also winced. "I didn't even realize he hit me. I only remember him kicking me in the ribs after I fell."

"He kicked you?" Blood raced straight to James's head and roared in his ears like the ocean on a stormy day, effectively pushing aside the pain in his head. "After he knocked you down?"

"Shh, James. People are staring."

"My apologies, Clara. But I can't be quiet. It was disgraceful enough that he put his hands on you at all. And then he had the nerve to knock you to the ground."

"He didn't knock me to the ground. I fell."

Surely she wasn't defending the brute? "And then he kicked you, leaving you to struggle to regain your breath." James blinked. "I'm going to kill him."

James was fairly certain he could listen to the sound of Clara's laughter forever. It had taken him a while to calm down, but Clara hadn't given up. And now she had him laughing along with her.

"Try again," she said.

"Apeel-strudel." When he said it, she giggled once more.

"No, no. One more time. Like this." Speaking slowly, Clara enunciated the word. "Apfelstrudel."

"Ahh-pfill-strudel." James mimicked her perfectly. Or so he thought until she laughed again. He drew back, pretending to be hurt. "Go ahead and laugh. But can we eat it now?"

The artfully folded pastry lay on the cloth napkin spread out on the tiny table between them. The train rocked back and forth, but that wouldn't keep him from devouring the cinnamon and apple filling peeking through the golden-brown layers.

Tempted, James reached for it before Clara could respond. He bit into it and closed his eyes with an exaggerated sigh. When he opened them again, he found Clara watching with a slight lift at one corner of her mouth. He couldn't help but smile back at her.

Yesterday evening, when he realized he'd have to make a trip to Rochester, he'd been certain he was in for a day of boredom. He was pleased to have been wrong. And even after keeping watch at the Martins' all night, then going to feed Buttons before checking in at the precinct, James found he wasn't too tired to engage in conversation with Clara.

"Don't tell Mrs. Martin I couldn't pronounce the German name for her apple strudel."

"I won't. I promise." Clara put two fingers across her lips before she looked away with a smirk.

"So your entire job is to walk around the fair and take pictures?"

"Yes." Clara nodded, eyes widening. Her enthusiasm was palpable, quite like her personality. "Mostly of women and children. Although I haven't actually done that yet." She glanced out the window before turning back to him. "Photographing the president was my first assignment. Prior to that, I was practicing, just getting used to the camera. Today was going to be my first day at the fair photographing mothers with their children."

"Could I get a closer look at your camera?" This one looked different than the one they used at the station for photographing criminals. He'd never used that one before and didn't know how they processed the images. In truth, he'd never been interested.

Until now.

Clara looked from James to the camera, then to James again. She raised her left eyebrow then feigned reluctance. "Did you know that when I first saw you in the music auditorium, I thought you were kind of stuffy?"

If the quiver at the corners of her mouth were any indication, she was teasing him. James found himself smiling back. "And you don't any longer?"

She shook her head.

"What changed your mind?"

"One little thing. Any man who tries to pronounce 'apfelstrudel' is as far away from stuffy as one could possibly be." Then, laughing, she handed it over to him while flashing him a saucy smile.

The camera was solid, heavier than he figured it would be. He honestly wasn't sure he'd ever held the one at the precinct. He'd certainly never been the one to use it. He ran his hand over the square box and traced the brass ring outlining the lens.

"Don't touch the lens!" Clara grabbed for the camera, and James let her take it from him.

"Sorry. You have no idea how a fingerprint can mar a photograph." She glanced down, and her eyelashes fanned the curve of her cheeks. A striking image that had James fighting an impulse to reach out and trace the gentle lines with his finger.

The train jerked just then, and Clara's grip on the camera loosened. James grabbed for it, catching it just before it hit the floor. He placed it in her hands, covering them with his own. She didn't jerk away. Instead, she looked at their hands, then up into his face. For a moment, her smile was so bright that she appeared delighted.

Then she looked away.

When she did, he released her hands. But his gaze never left her face.

Her smile faded for just the briefest of moments before she schooled her features and the smile reappeared. If he hadn't been watching so closely, he might have missed it.

Carefully, she placed the camera in the leather bag and secured it on the seat next to her. Then she tucked her coat and travel bag around it.

"Don't you think it would be safer on the floor in case the train jerks again?"

"Probably. But imagine how many feet have been here. Where have those feet been? I don't want those germs on my camera case."

He bit back a smile. "So why women, specifically? Why not photograph men, as well?"

Clara straightened. "Well certainly, I can take pictures of men. It's just that Mr. Eastman believes the mother is the heart of the family. That if women could see how easy it is to take photographs— or snapshots as he likes to call them—with this camera, mothers would take dozens of photos documenting special moments in their children's lives. Moments you can never get back. Moments that will live on for generations."

"I see. So in a way you're selling cameras."

She was quiet for a moment, glancing down at the apple pastry before looking back up. Then she pressed her lips together and nodded. "I guess in a way, I am. I just didn't think of it in that way. I don't think Mr. Eastman does, either. He loves cameras and photographs and making people happy. When the women see how easy it is for me to operate the camera, and when they receive their photo from the fair, Mr. Eastman hopes they'll buy a camera for themselves and continue building on the memories."

James thought back through his childhood, of his parents who were no longer here, of his sister, Janine, who was living in New York City. She was technically only half a state away, a few hours by train—maybe a little longer—and yet he didn't get to see her often. He'd always been close to his sister. They'd been a happy family until the end.

What he wouldn't give to have a book of memories. And Janine would probably agree. "It's amazing, really. I'm going to buy one of those cameras for my sister. She deserves to collect memories for her and her daughter."

"Really, James? That's so wonderful." She grabbed his hand and squeezed while her lips twitched with a smile. When he trailed the tips of his fingers across her soft palm, she looked at his hand and immediately let go. "I'm sorry."

"Don't be." He smiled down at her then swept her hand back into his. It was warm and tiny, and fit perfectly in his. As he looked at his fingers wrapped around hers, he could almost imagine a memory book with their picture in it.

Though reluctant to do so, he slowly let go of her hand and reached for another piece of pastry. It stuck in his throat.

Memories were all he had, and he didn't even deserve those.

CHAPTER 10

"So what you're telling me is that our Clara is a hero." George Eastman's eyes were wide and serious behind the round rim of his spectacles. He sat behind a large oak desk in his office at the Eastman Kodak Company of New York, peering closely at Clara. Slightly older than her father, with short cropped hair the color of snow, he was a tall man and would have made an imposing figure even while seated if she hadn't already known he was extremely gentle and kind.

"No, sir, I'm no—"

Mr. Eastman shushed Clara with a wave. She stared at him, certain her eyeballs were about to pop out of her head. And though she made a concentrated effort to appear relaxed, it was a struggle. She and James were seated in matching oak chairs with tall slatted backs, each with a flat piece of dark leather padding the seat. There wasn't a speck of dust in sight, and the scent of wood soap hung in the air. And though it might seem strange to some, she rather liked the way it smelled.

"There's no use denying it, my dear. You risked your life to protect what could possibly be evidence in a most important event to our nation. And that dreadful bruise on your face—the man should be thrashed within an inch of his life."

"I'm all right, sir. I don't hurt as much as I did earlier. And really, I was only protecting your property. I wasn't trying to be a hero. I'm not sure I even risked my life. There's nothing on the film that's evidence. Not even a photo of Leon Czolgosz, the man who shot the president. As I told James, he was immediately assaulted and knocked to the ground. I think I took a picture of the men piled on top of him. But even as they took him away to jail, he was surrounded by men, and I couldn't really see him clearly enough to snap a photo."

"Well even so, Clara, a man attacked you, and you protected the film at great risk to yourself."

"Thank you, Mr. Eastman. But so did James. He's the real hero." Uncomfortable with the praise, Clara glanced around at the room. The walls were lined with framed photographs. Some were in sepia tones, and some appeared more modern. A tall glass display case in the corner behind Mr. Eastman's desk held several different types of cameras—some with bellows and brass fixings, some plain and boxy like hers. She knew some of them had lenses with stronger capabilities. They even used a different film process so one could take portraits.

Mr. Eastman leaned forward and steepled his hands. "I just can't believe someone would shoot the president." His voice was thick with emotion. "Why would this Czolgosz fellow want to hurt him? I can't quite get over it."

"We don't really know, sir." Sorrow pricked at Clara's heart. "It truly was a horrific act." At the thought of the president grasping his stomach and collapsing to the ground, Clara's voice faltered. "It was a terrible sight to see." Her eyes burned, and her nose tickled most unpleasantly. She sniffled, knowing there wasn't a handkerchief in her camera bag. She'd forgotten to pack one at all.

As if he sensed her need, James reached into his pocket and pulled out a white handkerchief. He pressed the crisp white square into her hand. "It's brand new, just for such an occasion."

"Thank you." She dabbed the corners of her eyes and then her nose. "Please forgive me."

"You have no reason to ask forgiveness." Brow furrowed, Mr. Eastman's eyes were drawn together in concern. He reached across the desk and clasped her hand in a warm squeeze. "If anything, I'm the one who needs to do so. I'm deeply sorry you had to witness the shooting. But even sorrier still that my camera appears to have put you in danger."

"Please don't think anything about that, Mr. Eastman. How could you know a man would do something so evil? Still, I think it's highly unlikely that there is anything on the film that will prove beneficial to the police and to the president's agents."

"You never know, Clara. Oftentimes the camera lens sees things we never even notice. We'll get the film processed as quickly as possible so we can figure out this other man's involvement."

The man's assault on her was still so fresh in her mind that a tiny shiver skittered across the back of her neck. She rolled her shoulders to shrug it away. "I'm still at a loss as to what this man thinks could be on the film. He seems so desperate."

Mr. Eastman sat back in his chair and glanced first at her and then at James. Finally, he tipped his head toward James. "Do you think he followed you here?"

James looked to Clara before he answered. "No sir, I don't think he did." He scooted closer to the outer edge of the desk. "It's hard to be entirely certain, and we must err on the side of caution. But I used every opportunity to watch as the train boarded. It's possible I missed him, but I feel fairly confident that he ran off after he attacked us."

A wave of gratitude bathed her heart. It was important for Mr. Eastman to know that without James, she wouldn't be sitting here with the camera.

"James has been very good about protecting the camera—and about protecting me. Without him—"

A movement of air brushed her arm as James shifted in his

seat. When she glanced over at him, he didn't make eye contact. Was he uncomfortable with the praise? Even so, she wasn't about to apologize.

"Officer Brinton." Mr. Eastman stood, towering over them, and reached out to clasp James's hand. James stood as well. "Thank you for protecting Clara."

"It was my pleasure, sir. And please call me James."

"Very well, James. And if you will, please call me George." Mr. Eastman nodded before he released his grip on James's hand. Then he turned to Clara. "My apologies that I won't have the film processed before the last train departs for Buffalo, but rest assured it is our top priority. And now, my dear, if you'll excuse me, I have some business to attend. I have an important meeting with one of my inventors regarding a patent we're working on."

Clara wondered what it could possibly be. She'd heard about his collaboration with Mr. Edison so they could make moving pictures. They'd even made a few moving films of some of the exhibits at the Expo. And she'd read about his work with a company that made something called an X-ray, where invisible beams could pass through tissue and illuminate the bones in one's body. It was all so exciting that when she read about it she immediately wished she could share it with her father. The newspaper article had said the rays could even detect if a bullet was lodged in a bone.

Had they used one of these to help President McKinley? She brushed her wrists along the bottom of her eyes.

"Clara?" Mr. Eastman tapped her on the forearm. "Don't look so serious. Everything will get sorted out."

Praying it would be sorted in the right way, she nodded.

"Now, my assistant has arranged for rooms for you at Della's Hotel. You two enjoy a leisurely lunch, and I will do my best to have the snapshots available for you later this evening. Hopefully by then there will be some positive news about the president."

"I hope so, too, Mr. Eastman." Clara didn't want to think about the news being anything but positive.

SUZIE JOHNSON

"And Clara, rest assured you will be fully compensated for all of your time today and tomorrow."

"That's very kind of you, sir. But it's not necessary. I'm just glad you aren't angry at me."

"Angry at you? My dear, whatever for?"

"For the extra work because of...well—" She looked at James. It wasn't his fault Mr. Eastman had to do extra work processing the film. It was Czolgosz and his horrific actions. "The trip here could have been a day spent taking pictures at the Exposition. Perhaps if I hadn't taken pictures at the president's reception, your camera and film would not have been put into jeopardy."

"Nonsense. What you did, what you experienced, it speaks to your integrity. If the snapshots turn out to contain evidence that could point to an anarchy group, it will all have been worth it."

As she listened to his words, her heart swelled with emotion and her eyes misted. Was it possible she could have actually made some difference in this world? Probably not in the scheme of things, but Mr. Eastman seemed to think so.

Not only did that touch her deeply, it brought an image of her father to mind. Or perhaps he was already there? Oftentimes he would give her a fond smile and tell her she made him proud.

In an attempt to keep her emotions at bay, she bit the inside of her lip.

Hard.

Next to her, James squeezed her hand. After a quick glance at Clara, he turned to Mr. Eastman. "I want you both to rest assured that after news of the photos and whatever they reveal is printed in the newspaper—and I'm sure it will spread to more than one newspaper—Clara should be safe. But I'll be by her side until we know for certain." His warm gaze swept over her, wrapping around her heart.

Mr. Eastman smiled at both of them. "James, it's been a pleasure. Now why don't you both head on over to the hotel and check in. Della knows that your rooms and all of your meals are to be charged

93

to me. She's a real darling, that one. She'll take good care of you."

"Thank you, sir."

After a quick hug, which was so fatherly Clara wanted to fall into its essence and remain just a few seconds longer, Mr. Eastman introduced them to one of his assistants, Mr. Spreckle, and excused himself.

Mr. Spreckle gave her several fresh spools of film. He even waited patiently while she inserted one of the cartridges onto the film-holding frame. Once she replaced the winding key, they stepped outside and Mr. Spreckle pointed down the block toward the hotel.

Before they started toward the hotel, Clara turned back and studied the six-story brick building that housed the Eastman Kodak Company.

"It wasn't at all what I expected," James said. "I never really thought about it, but Mr. Eastman has a lot more going on here than just developing film."

"I know." It had been beyond her expectations as well.

"The way Eastman is marketing these cameras, it's almost like he plans to see a camera in every home."

She thought about this for a moment. "Imagine it, James. If you do buy a camera for your sister, when her little girl is all grown-up, she can have an entire book of memories."

Was Mr. Eastman on the cusp of something that could prove revolutionary?

Excited at the thought of being a part of it, she grabbed James's hand. He didn't let go, and when he squeezed her hand she pictured a memory book with photographs of little brown-eyed tots that looked just like him.

The hotel was an easy walk from the Eastman Kodak office building. The air was warm and pleasant, and Clara was thankful James stayed next to her side. Not because she was worried about being attacked again, but because having him at her side gave her a sense of closeness she hadn't ever felt before.

There was something about him—perhaps his dedication to his

job, to protecting her...no, that wasn't quite right.

She glanced up at him, and his gaze caught hers. The intensity in his brown eyes softened with warmth, and she felt certain these new feelings weren't about his work ethic.

As they walked past the window of a nearby jeweler's, a flash of gold caught Clara's eye. She stopped to peer closer.

Nestled on a bed of pink velvet, the ladies' pin in the window was crafted of delicate gold and twisted into a circle. In the center of the circle, also made of fine gold, was a small bird perched on a branch. At each point connecting the branch to the golden circle was a tiny pearl.

Nearly pressing her face to the glass wasn't good enough. She needed to go inside, needed to examine it, to touch it. She edged toward the door only to find it locked.

"Clara, what is it?"

"This pin. My–my mother. It reminds me of her. It looks—" She stepped back to the window and stared at it again, hoping her voice didn't betray the sudden swell of sadness.

The intricate workmanship of the bird seemed so familiar. Was it possible this pin was her father's work? The thought was ridiculous. And yet it really wasn't. It was...possible.

James drew nearer and looked at the pin. "Do you think it belongs to her? Was it stolen?"

"No. Not at all. But it's so delicate and lovely, it reminds me of something she would wear." Clara swallowed hard before correcting herself. "Would have worn, I mean."

"Did she have one like this?"

"No. But my father was designing a pin very similar to this for her birthday. He'd taken it from a sketch she'd drawn."

"He's a jeweler?"

"Yes." She nodded. "Looking at this, I can *see* her. For a minute, I wondered if—"

"Clara?" Concern shone down at her from James's eyes. "You wondered what?"

Did she really want to discuss this now? Her mother's illness? Her father's betrayal? She shook her head. "It's not important."

"I'm not sure I believe you."

Before she could answer, a boy with tousled dark hair called to her from across the street. "Hey lady." He waved as if to be sure she'd see him. "Is that some kind of camera you have there?"

Since the style of the camera was fairly new, especially compared to those Mr. Eastman had in the case at his office, she wasn't surprised the boy was curious. She couldn't help but smile in his direction. "Yes, it is." He was holding on to a bicycle, and a little blond boy stood next to him.

"Can I see it?"

"Of course." Eager to take a photograph or two, she hadn't put it back in the bag after loading it with new film. Now she was glad. She glanced up at James, surprised to see him grinning.

The boy leaned his bicycle against the side of the wooden building. "We'll come across the street." The smaller boy followed suit and they both crossed the dirt road. As they walked toward her, Clara kept a wistful eye on their bicycles.

James must have noticed. "Do you ride?"

"It's been a long time, but one of my friends in New York City taught me to ride." She'd always wanted one for herself. "Surely you are the luckiest boys in the world to each have your own bicycle. Perhaps we should go over there so no one will bother them."

"Oh, no, lady. No one will bother them. I promise."

"All right then. Let me show you how this works." Clara glanced around for a place to sit down. She didn't see one, so she walked over to a nearby fence and leaned against it.

The boys exclaimed over the camera as she showed them where the lens was. "After you aim it at your target, you look down at this little circle. It's called the viewfinder." She glanced at the boys. Their little faces were scrunched in concentration—the older boy's face, especially. It was as if he inhaled each of her words.

"Once you see the image in the viewfinder, you just snap and click, and the camera takes a photograph. Or—you could call it a snapshot. I call them photographs, but Mr. Eastman calls them snapshots because he wants people to realize how easy it is to take the picture."

"Wow!" The dark-haired boy looked up at Clara. "Do you think you could take our picture?"

"Of course." The boys stood near James and posed for her, grinning all the while. Their boyish eagerness and youthful innocence tugged at the edges of her heart—as did James's willingness to indulge them.

"When the film is printed, I will be sure and have Mr. Eastman send you your photos. I just need you to tell me your names and where he can send them."

"The Kodak man?"

So they knew Mr. Eastman branded his film as Kodak. How interesting. "Yes, if you want to call him that. He sells cameras and processes film. I work for him taking pictures."

"You do?" The older boy's eyes widened. "I want to do that. Do you think I could work for him when I grow up?"

"Me, too!" The younger boy stepped closer to his brother.

Clara hesitated. She wanted to tell the boys they could do just about anything when they grew up, but she didn't want to interfere in anything of the hopes and dreams their parents might have for them. "You might want to talk to your family about it, but I'm sure being a photographer is something you could do."

"Is that what a picture taker is called? You're a photographer?"

The boy didn't even stumble over the word, and Clara smiled, impressed. "Yes. I'm a photographer." She didn't think she could explain the term *Kodak Girl* to them. And even though she hadn't done anything but practice taking pictures, she was a photographer.

A photographer.

In all seriousness she hadn't yet thought of herself in those terms, but she rather liked the way it sounded.

"I'm Robbie, and my brother is Bert," the older boy said. "We live at the hotel here on the corner. You can have the Kodak man deliver our snapshots there."

"At Della's Hotel? That's where we're headed right now. We're staying there while Mr. Eastman processes some film."

"Della is our mother. So it won't be hard for them to find us."

"Very well then." Clara nodded. "We'll make sure you get them."

"Thanks! We have to do an errand for our mother."

Before Clara could even respond, both boys were across the street and on their bicycles.

"Eager little guys, aren't they?" James peered at her, one eyebrow raise. "Robbie and Bert?"

That was all it took for Clara to burst into laughter. "Their father's name must be Robert."

James's laughter echoed hers. "That was so nice of you to take the time with them."

"I was happy to. They're adorable. But I wonder what their mother will say when they tell her they want to be photographers?"

"If she's anything like you, I'm sure she'll encourage them to follow their dream."

There was a definite sadness in his tone, and Clara couldn't help but wonder at the reason.

CHAPTER 11

"I just need a few minutes in my room, and then I'll meet you down here so we can go eat some lunch." Clara turned toward the stairs to follow the young man carrying her bags, but before she could even put one toe onto the first step, James cleared his throat.

She angled toward him, knowing what he was about to say. "Really, James?"

"I need to check the room before you go inside."

"But he's not here. And if he were, I doubt he'd even know where we would be staying tonight."

James shot a glance at the clerk, then back to her. His voice lowered to a whisper as they followed the man up the stairs. "I need to make sure that *if* we were followed, there's no way anyone could get into your room."

If she was alone and the man followed her, Clara doubted she would be able to fight him off a second time. Thankful James was here to look out for her, she nodded. "Thank you."

James turned to the clerk, who was looking at them both with open curiosity. "Please wait with Miss Lambert while I check the room."

While she waited, Clara glanced around the hallway. Though larger, the layout was similar to the upstairs at the Martins' house. Here there were four rooms on either side of the staircase and two directly in front of the landing.

Which room was James in?

"You can go in now."

"James." Startled, she hoped he didn't realize she'd just been thinking about him. "Thank you."

"The only way anyone can get in is through your door. But they'll have to come through me to do it."

Was he planning to sit outside her door all night long?

As if reading her thoughts, he said, "I'm going to keep you safe, Clara. It's my job."

The way he said it, his tone warm and full of reassurance while his eyes softened as he gave her a sweeping glance, felt like there was more behind the words than just a job. Even if that wasn't true, it was still comforting to have him there.

"Thank you, James. I'll hurry and get ready so we can eat."

He gave her a long, measured look then motioned for her to go into the room. "Take your time getting settled. I might need more than a few minutes myself."

She nodded then turned to step into the room.

"But Clara?"

She stopped and looked over her shoulder.

"Wait for me here. I don't want you to leave the room without me." He pressed his lips together as if forming an answer for her anticipated protest. When she didn't do so, he said, "I'm sure it's perfectly safe, but I don't want to take any chances."

"I promise." She stepped into the room to find the young clerk pulling at the pink and white curtains that were haphazardly smashed between the window and a dark wooden chest of drawers—pushed against the window by James, no doubt.

She helped straighten the curtains, as well as the lace cloth on top of the dresser. A framed portrait had been knocked over. When Clara picked it up, she saw that it was of a woman speaking into the mouthpiece of a telephone. Curious, she studied it. It was a photograph, not a painting. And yet somehow the picture had a wash of green, brown, and rich mauve tones running through it.

Would any of her photographs come out this nicely? Whatever process was used for the picture, it was something she would like to learn. She'd have to remember to ask Mr. Eastman about it.

"Everything is ready for you, and your bags are right here on the bed." She'd been so taken with the photo, she'd forgotten about the young man. He was already headed out the door.

"Thank you so much." She reached for her bag. "If you'll wait just a moment, I'd like to compensate you."

"No need, Miss Lambert. Mr. Eastman has already taken care of it." The boy beamed, and Clara was certain Mr. Eastman was as generous with these hotel arrangements as he'd been with her. She didn't know if he had a family, but if he did, they were blessed to have such a wonderful man in their lives.

As she freshened up she thought of her own father. He was generous as well. Kind and loving, and always there for her and her mother. Or so she'd thought. He'd had the entire world fooled. She prayed it wasn't the same for Mr. Eastman and his family.

By the time she put her bags in the wardrobe, combed her hair and pinned her hat back into place, James still hadn't knocked on the door. Clara's gaze wandered back to the portrait. Was this something she could learn to do? The thought excited her, and she found herself smiling as she went back to the wardrobe and retrieved the bag that held her camera.

What if the man broke in here while they were gone? Even though Mr. Eastman had the film, the man wouldn't necessarily know that.

She had to keep the camera with her no matter what.

When James did finally knock at the door, Clara was surprised to see he'd changed out of his uniform. He wore indigo blue trousers and a cotton shirt of pale yellow. He looked different out of uniform. More relaxed.

And he was just as handsome as ever.

He descended the stairs ahead of her, and she didn't catch up with him until she reached the bottom. His lips were pressed together, but their edges quivered just enough that it was obvious he was trying not to smile.

He was hiding something.

"Where are we going?"

"Downstairs and out the front door."

"We're not eating in the hotel restaurant?"

"No. I have something better planned. I hope you don't mind."

That was interesting. Had he gone wandering around while she'd changed her clothes? Surely it hadn't taken her that long. "How could you have found something better when neither of us has been here before?"

"You'll find out soon enough." When they reached the open doorway, James let Clara pass first. He graced her with a smile she readily returned, and for the first time she realized he held a large cloth sack that was weighted down with its contents. She suspected it had something to do with his surprise, so she refrained from asking about it.

Once they were outside she glanced around. "Which way?"

"To your right."

Curious about what he could be up to, she followed him as he rounded the corner behind the hotel. She came up short as he stopped at the entrance to an alley. Just as she was about to quiz him she noticed Robbie and Bert standing there with smirks on their freckled faces, dirt-smudged hands stretched out toward James.

"Pay up, mister. We done what you asked."

Clara shot a glance at James. What kind of business could he have with them? She hadn't pictured him as the type to interact with kids. Though truthfully, it fit well with the memory book she'd imagined earlier. She watched as he dug in his pocket and pulled out a few shiny coins.

He grinned as he filled their palms, and Clara felt an unexpected tug at her heart. Not only had he really engaged them in some as yet unknown activity, he obviously delighted in dealing with them. This was a side of James she wanted to know more about.

Before she could say anything, the boys turned and ran the

opposite direction. She watched in amusement, and one called over his shoulder, "See you soon, mister!"

"What was that all about?"

"Oh, you know how little boys are. They always have a secret."

As she watched James press his lips together and struggle not to smile, she nodded. She knew exactly how boys were and James, she was certain, was trying to keep a secret.

Clara rather liked this playful side of him. She shook her head. They hadn't known each other long enough for her to even be thinking like this.

Besides, once the photographs were turned over to James's superiors, their lives would go on as before and she'd likely never see him again.

That thought left her feeling almost as empty as she felt the night she first arrived in Buffalo after her mother died.

"Turn right, Clara." James walked a few steps behind her, anticipating her expression when she saw what he had planned.

Clara did as instructed, but she turned and her gaze strayed across the street and to the left toward the jeweler's shop. No doubt longing after the pin that reminded her of her mother. Since the shop was closed, he'd have to make a concerted effort to distract her.

"Cute boys, aren't they?" It only took two strides to catch up with her.

"They are." Her eyes practically sparkled as she said it. She had obviously enjoyed their earlier exchange. He hoped she would enjoy the next one as much.

"Remember what they were doing before they came over to ask about your camera?"

"No, but I do remember they each had a bicycle."

"Right over there." James pointed across the street to a wooden fence where the boys stood wearing enormous grins.

Clara smiled at the sight of the boys, but her eyes widened when she noticed the two bicycles resting there.

"We beat-cha here, mister!"

"James?" Her green gaze was questioning, and when he nodded, her face broke into an eager grin—not at all unlike the one the boys had worn when she showed them the camera. On her, the grin did funny things to his insides. She smiled at him once more before she ran toward the bicycles without once looking back.

Would she be upset if he mentioned her impulsiveness? Or would it be better if he said nothing at all and just vowed not to let her out of his sight?

"So." Clara clasped her hands behind her back as she looked at them. "Are you really letting us ride your bicycles?"

"We are." Robbie nodded, his dark curls bouncing with the movement, then glanced sideways at James.

"You kids are so sweet." She planted a kiss atop each of their heads then turned back to James. "They're letting us ride their bicycles!"

More like he was paying them to be able to ride the bicycles for the afternoon. But because of the splash of red spreading across Robbie's face, James didn't bother correcting him. He had the feeling Clara wouldn't approve of him embarrassing the boy.

When James first joined the police department, they'd taught him how to ride a bicycle. But he hadn't been assigned to the bike patrol and he'd never been on one since. He walked over and put the bag containing their lunch into the wire basket of the second bicycle.

When he turned, Clara was struggling to rearrange her skirt so she could get on the other bike. He looked away and motioned for the boys to do the same so she could have some privacy until she was ready. He should have warned her of his plans in advance so she could dress accordingly. Although, how did a woman dress to ride a bicycle?

Had this been a mistake? He'd wanted to surprise her, but here she struggled with her clothes while he wondered if he could even remember how to ride. "Perhaps we should just eat in the restaurant after all."

"No, James." Clara's protest was urgent. "I want to ride."

Both of the boys looked up at him with scrunched up expressions. Perhaps concerned James would cancel the ride and take back his money? He wouldn't do that to the little guys. "We'll be back in a couple of hours. Shall I meet you boys here in the same spot?"

"Yes, sir. We'll be right here."

They were polite young men, and no doubt good kids.

"We'll see you boys later." At the sound of Clara's voice, James looked over to see her balancing the bicycle perfectly while he talked with the boys. She had both hands wrapped around the handlebars, with her hat clutched in her right hand.

Not only had she taken her hat off, she'd taken the pins out of her hair. Her thick brown curls framed her face and brushed her shoulders, the red highlights flashing in the sunlight. Swallowing past the sudden lump in his throat, he went over and took the hat from her and tucked it into the basket on his bicycle. Finally, with Clara watching intently, he threw his leg over the bicycle and sat. "See you boys in a couple of hours."

"Have fun with yer lady." With that, the boys disappeared around the corner.

Though he was fairly decent at reading the expressions of others, Clara watched him with one he couldn't read. Surprised at his conversation with the boys? Or perhaps curious over whether or not he could ride a bicycle?

"Shall we?" Though his smile was glib, his heart tripped as his foot found the pedal.

Why did he have the sudden sinking feeling he was about to make a huge mistake?

CHAPTER 12

Clara's heart tripped as James turned and flashed her a grin over his shoulder. His bicycle wheel wobbled dangerously and her breath caught.

"Look out!"

He whipped back around and gripped the handlebars in an obvious attempt to control the bicycle. As he struggled, Clara sucked in a quick breath and watched while James fought to keep the bicycle upright. She didn't breathe easy again until he won the battle.

"This is a mode of travel I suggest you avoid in the future."

"I don't know." He glanced back over his shoulder, and Clara's heart nearly stopped.

"James! Turn back around and pay attention." She knew she sounded like an old fishwife, but she didn't want to see him hurt. "Please?"

"Yes, ma'am." Though he immediately did as she asked, she could hear the amusement in his tone. "But you have to admit, it is kind of fun. And I'm sure I'll only get better with practice."

"It is, and you will." Clara smiled at him, even though he obviously couldn't see her. "I'm loving it." She pedaled faster to catch up with him so they could ride side-by-side. He may not be experienced, but his legs were longer and he could cover more ground with one push of the pedal.

When she caught up with him, he turned to her and grinned. "I think when we get back I may just have to purchase one. That would be the best way to practice, don't you think?"

Though it surprised her, it was news that also delighted her since she was actually saving for her own bicycle. They could go on rides together through the gardens near the Midway where he'd rescued her hat. And after that, they could sip tea at the Japanese Village that she'd run through last night. Was it really only last night? It seemed like days ago.

"Why are you so quiet, Clara?"

"Sorry." She turned back to him. "I was just thinking. I've actually been saving for a bicycle myself."

"Really?" It didn't sound like a question. In fact, he sounded rather amused.

"Yes, really. I've been saving for quite some time now. I'm hoping I'll earn more money from Mr. Eastman than—" She broke off, pretending to be distracted by the sight of children playing in a nearby field.

How would he react if she told him about her other job? Clara cleaned rooms in a downtown hotel. Would he think less of her like some of the people she encountered while doing her job?

"You could ride to and from the fairgrounds every day instead of taking the trolley."

Surprised, Clara kept her eyes trained on the path in front of them instead of looking over at him. Was he thinking about the man who'd attacked her? "I could," she agreed. "It would be nice to ride around the fair, too, looking for people to photograph. Although at times, there are so many people at the fair, a person riding a bicycle might cause too much confusion. And if I wasn't riding while working, I'd need a place to store it."

"The grounds at the Exposition are huge. I'm sure they could find a place to store a bicycle."

"And you, James—if you keep practicing, perhaps you can become a bicycle patrol officer."

James chose that moment to get off the bicycle and start pushing it alongside her as he walked. The path they rode on was beginning to incline, but she didn't think it was all that steep. Though she didn't want to, Clara knew the polite thing was to get off and walk with him.

"Aren't there bicycle officers at your precinct? Do you think your captain would let you ride around town on patrol?"

He didn't answer, and when she looked over at him, he didn't make eye contact. What did that mean? Should she change the subject?

"I'd think you'd be able to cover a larger area that way. That would probably make your captain happy."

"Plus false secret service agents wouldn't outrun me quite so easily."

Relieved at the teasing in his tone, Clara laughed. "True." Then she pointed at the bicycle. "Do you want to try again?"

"I'm ready whenever you are."

Clara got back on the bike. Now the hill really was steep, and she had to practically stand to pump the pedals hard enough to get going on the hill. But she still managed to get ahead of James as he struggled to get his bike moving again.

"It gets easier each time," she called over her shoulder. "How far are we going?"

"I don't know. The hotel clerk said to keep going this way and we'd run into it before long. And he said we'd recognize it when we see it."

"Very well." The muscles in Clara's legs trembled and burned as the grassy slope steepened. She wondered how James's legs felt. It also grew more difficult to breathe, so she didn't waste her air asking him.

As they pedaled up the well-worn dirt path, both of them breathing a little harder than they were a few minutes ago, the sweet scent of wildflowers drifted from the fields to tickle her nose. The strain on her muscles was worth it, and she couldn't imagine anything more pleasant than riding a bicycle to a picnic spot with a beau.

Not that it was happening now. James wasn't her beau. But it wasn't a bad thought.

One of the boys had told him to have fun with his lady. Heat rose on her cheeks. Was it brazen of her to want to be the girl he courted?

When he caught up with her, she was happy to see his face was flushed as well. Likely he would think hers was from exertion, and not from her daydream about his handsome face and infectious smile—his smile that at the moment seemed forced.

"This is a pretty tough hill." James sounded as out of breath as she felt. "If you'd have asked me an hour ago if I was physically fit enough to ride a bicycle up a hill, I would have easily said yes. Now I find myself questioning my judgement."

"Me, too." Clara hopped off the bike again. Her legs needed a rest. James followed suit, and she bit back a smile. "You'll think different once we conquer this hill. After this you'll be a better bicyclist than any of your fellow officers could dream of being."

No longer breathless, James laughed and the sound lifted her heart.

They were nearly to the top. Up ahead, at the crest of the hill, she could see the perfect picnic spot under a giant maple tree. Leaves dotted the lush grass, and she couldn't wait to reach it. Clara glanced back over her shoulder.

"James. The view. Look at how far we've come."

Behind them, blades of grass covered the sloping hill that led down to the street where they started. It seemed so far away, and they'd climbed so high, they could see rooftops. Oaks, maples, and sycamores were scattered here and there, and they were high enough to see over the tops of the lower ones.

The sound of James's laughter lifted her heart, and Clara was thankful they could take a little time out of their crazy journey to have some fun. For whatever reason James came up with the idea of a bicycle ride, she was glad.

But she still couldn't help studying the hill behind them to make sure no one followed.

From her spot under the maple tree, Clara finger-combed her hair and watched as James pulled buttered bread and slices of cheese from the wire basket attached to his bicycle. She marveled at all he'd done in so little time. The bicycles, blanket, and food—why had he gone to so much trouble?

Did he feel sorry for her? The thought didn't sit right. She tucked the pins back in her hair and arranged it under the hat. It was something of an unruly mess, but it would have been worse if the tangles were wrapped around the pins—as would have happened while riding. Besides, her hat would have been ruined if it had flown off her head.

Once her hat was firmly back in place, she glanced up at the branches overhead. Though half of its leaves were on the ground, the large maple shaded the midday sun, making this a lovely spot for relaxing. For whatever reason he'd brought her here, she was glad.

The faint tinkling of glass hitting glass caught her attention.

"Would you like something to drink?"

Clara looked up as James turned away from the bike and came to sit next to her.

"Coca-Cola?" He handed her a brown bottle dripping with condensation.

"James. Thank you so much." Suddenly thirsty, she reached for the icy bottle of deliciousness.

"This is so—" She stopped to take a nice long swallow before she finished. "—refreshing. You'll never know how much I appreciate it. Especially after riding up this hill."

"You're welcome." His smile, quirky and lopsided, grew wide and drew her in as he held out his other hand. He held a few sprigs of lavender tied together with a delicate cream-colored ribbon.

"James! This is so sweet." She took the tiny posy and waved it beneath her nose, closing her eyes as she inhaled its fresh, unmistakable scent.

Maybe this wasn't because he felt sorry for her, after all. Maybe he really wanted to spend time with her. The thought quickened her heart.

She watched him for a moment longer before reaching for a piece of cheese. It was less than a second before James followed suit. The food was delicious, but it couldn't compare to the Coca-Cola. It wasn't long before she savored a second bottle, sipping slowly so it would last longer.

"This was perfect, James. Really."

"I'm glad. You deserve a nice afternoon out after the duress of the last couple of days." He shifted on the blanket, and something in his tone made her look up at him. "I'm really eager to see these pictures, to see if we can figure out why this man tried to hurt you and steal your camera."

"Do you really think he had something to do with Leon Czolgosz?"

"I hope not." Something flickered across his face. It was gone before she could even think of what it might mean. But she thought she knew anyway.

"You think he was part of a larger group, don't you? Anarchists."

He nodded. "Pretty certain, yes."

"Me too." A shiver whispered across the back of her neck, and she glanced around. "Do you think he followed us?"

"I don't think so. I've tried to keep a close watch. I haven't seen anyone suspicious. But now that you've brought him up, let's try and go over what we know about him."

When they'd tried earlier, Clara couldn't really come up with a good description. Neither could James, for that matter. Although he'd apologized for not taking better notice, he said he'd been more focused on protecting her.

"Dark eyes, brown hair. Taller than me."

After running a hand through his hair, James speared her with a brown-eyed glance. He lifted an eyebrow and a smile played at one corner of his mouth. "Know anyone else who fits that description?"

"You're right. That was dumb." At least half the men in Buffalo fit that description.

"No, Clara. Not dumb. Human. I told you before, he was chasing you. He attacked you. You were traumatized. It's normal not to remember when you're first questioned."

"Still, I should have noticed *something* about him."

"And as the officer protecting you from an attacker, I should have noticed more, too."

"But you said you couldn't get a really good look at him because of the shadows. And this morning, he hit you in the head before you could even react."

Was it really only this morning that they'd walked through the park? In spite of her myriad of aches and bruises, it really did seem like the morning events were the distant past.

"I appreciate your sticking up for me, Clara. But I really am beginning to doubt—"

"What?"

James was quiet, too quiet. Clara could picture the tiny gears at work inside his brain.

"What are you thinking?"

Some unpleasant emotion tugged down on the corners of his mouth. "Nothing, really." He shook his head and looked away. "I really should have noticed more details. I used to be a detective."

Used to be? Wasn't a patrol officer a step below the rank of detective? Maybe he'd wanted to take a demotion. Given the storm that played out on his face, she decided not to question him. He'd tell her when he wanted to—*if* he wanted.

"I used to be very good at my job."

Again, *used to be*. What did he mean by that? And why did he sound so melancholy when he said it? "James," she protested. "You're a wonderful police officer."

He blew out a breath and gave a cynical laugh. "I wish you were right. Last night was different because of the shadows. Not picking up on details could almost be forgivable. But this morning…" He shook his head. "I've come across a lot of criminals, and I don't usually forget a face. Even if I didn't get a good look at him when he attacked us, one thing keeps coming back to me."

"What's that?"

"It's a feeling, really. Something about our encounter this morning—I felt as if I should know him."

"Do you think if I could give you a better description, it would help?"

"It might."

Unease shuddered through her. "I don't want to think about him ever again. I keep hoping he will show up in one of the pictures, and I'll recognize him immediately so I don't have to ever think about him again."

"Me, too. But if we know ahead of time some of the characteristics we're looking for, we'll be more apt to recognize him."

Of course he was right. And Clara was willing to do whatever she could to help.

Something must have shown in her expression because James gave her hand a quick squeeze. "Let's try something that might help you remember."

When she nodded, James scooted around until he sat cross-legged directly in front of her. Then he reached out and took both of her hands in his. Without thinking she curled her fingers against hands that were warm, smooth, with a strength that made her feel as delicate and lovely as the spray of lavender he'd given her. Was that how he saw her? Or did he see her as a weak-spirited female who needed a police officer to look out for her?

"Stop thinking so hard."

Not wanting him to know what she was really thinking, she

pretended like she was thinking about last night. "I just hope whatever you're planning will work."

"It will." He pressed her hands with a gentle touch. "Now, close your eyes and concentrate on my voice."

She did as he asked, but the only thing she could concentrate on were their hands nestled together.

"I just want you to relax, Clara, put all other thoughts out of your mind. When you do, I think you'll be able to get a clearer picture of your attacker's face. Do you think you can do that?"

"Yes." She focused on his voice as he asked her questions—some related to the events leading up to the president's reception at the Temple of Music, and some related to pictures she'd taken before she arrived at the auditorium. Eventually they covered the shooting of the president, and finally the moment she first saw her attacker.

"Before you try to picture him, I want you to shift your focus to your surroundings now. What do you hear? What do you smell?"

That was easy. She heard the laughter of children playing along the hillside. And after a second or two, she noticed the sound of birds chirping overhead. But that wasn't all. She breathed in the fragrance of fresh grass and of the lavender sitting in her lap. And then she caught the sweetness of the cherry pie sitting in front of her in a tin on the blanket just waiting for her to take a bite.

It was then that she pictured him. More than just his eye or hair color. A shiver ran across the back of her neck. How could she have not remembered? "His eyes are dark, like I said before—but it could have been because of his hat. There's no warmth there. They're cold and hard. Angry." James could say all he wanted about being traumatized, but these weren't details she should have forgotten.

"That's good."

"They're set close together, too. Like a rat."

In front of her, James laughed. As much as she didn't want to, she tried to block out the sound and concentrate on the image of the man. "It was hard to tell in the artificial light from the Electric Tower, but I think he has a dark complexion—as if he's been working in the sun all summer long. He was wearing a bowler hat. But you remember that, right?"

When he said nothing, she continued. "It cast more shadows over his face, making it even harder to see his features. But he definitely has darker skin."

"Beady eyes, bowler hat, and skin that is either due to an olive complexion or too much time in the sun. You're doing great, Clara."

"But I'm not sure how helpful that is. Lots of men wear bowler hats. And you remembered it, too."

"That's true, but you're picking up details. And your details are helping me to remember things, too. We can't really look for angry eyes in the photographs, but darker skin tones shouldn't be too difficult to spot when we look over the photographs and compare the men to each other."

Clara wanted to keep her eyes closed longer, just so she could listen to his rich, warm tone. She felt encouraged to keep trying, without the same pressure as the night before.

"It was hard to see because of the long coat he wore, but I think he was thin."

"What made you think he was thin?"

"I'm not sure." She thought for a moment before she remembered. "His face was long and narrow, with hollow cheeks. As if he'd missed one too many a meal."

"You could tell that in spite of the shadow from his hat?"

She nodded. "I could. There were times when he was close to me, that his face was too near mine. I don't know why I didn't remember it sooner. Especially after this morning." She shuddered. "How could I forget such an important detail?"

"It's easy to do under those circumstances. Don't be so hard on yourself. I do remember that he was taller than me, and though I didn't get a good look at his face, I should have noticed he was thin. But you did, and now you've remembered."

Still, she couldn't help but feel there was something else she hadn't remembered.

"You did really well, Clara. Now open your eyes."

When she did it was to see James staring at her intensely with wonderful brown eyes that weren't close-set or cold. They were warm and smooth, like liquid chocolate. Her heart did a funny dance in her chest. James's eyes probably never harbored a bit of the cruelty she'd seen in those other eyes.

"I think when we look at the photos we can look at every darker complexioned man and search out thin faces. And we'll be sure to look for hollow cheekbones." He picked up a slice of pie and handed her a fork. "Now eat so you don't end up with your own hollow cheeks."

Forcing back a smile, Clara took the pie. She couldn't help but moan in pleasure as the flavor burst in her mouth. "This is amazingly scrumptious!"

"I agree."

Clara smiled at him, only then realizing he hadn't taken a single bite of pie. It wasn't until she playfully reached to take his pie from him that he looked away and busied himself eating.

CHAPTER 13

James could tell Clara was nervous as they waited inside the large meeting room at the Kodak building. Earlier, on the walk here, she'd confessed that she was half-afraid her photographs would be blurry, and half-afraid her attacker wouldn't be in any of the pictures. He'd tried to reassure her, but her anxiousness wasn't so easily banished.

Before long, Mr. Spreckle entered the room. As the gangly man spread the photographs across the table, Clara shot James a sharp glance. When she raised her eyebrows and tilted her head toward Spreckle, James knew exactly what she was thinking.

If not for his lack of olive skin tone, even Mr. Eastman's assistant would fit the description of her attacker. Skinny men with dark hair and dark eyes were everywhere. James bit back a smile.

As she watched Mr. Spreckle place the photographs across the table, Clara's green eyes were wide. James wasn't even tempted to look at the pictures—he would have a hard time seeing anything but her.

"Mr. Eastman will be right with you."

"Thank you, Mr. Spreckle."

By the absent way she murmured, James could tell she was

already focusing in on one of the photographs. He really needed to do the same thing.

The fresh scent of furniture wax hung in the air, reminding him of his mother—which reminded him of the current situation and how disappointed she would have been with him if she'd been here to see his disgrace. Still, he couldn't say he was glad she wasn't here, because he'd give anything to have her back.

"James."

At her breathy whisper, he shook his head to clear his mind. "What did you find?"

The wistful serenity on her face drew him, and he stepped closer. But as her gaze met his, her eyes were bright.

Slowly, she lifted a photo off the table. "Hold it this way."

Taking great care to hold it by the corners the way she demonstrated, James took the picture. He immediately noticed why she was so touched by the photograph.

President McKinley and his wife, Ida, were standing as close as two people could stand. The president wore a top hat with the brim curled just so. The first lady's hat was small, fitted to her head with a narrow brim. It wasn't fancy and ornate like the one Clara wore. Mrs. McKinley clutched at her hat as if to keep it from blowing off her head and into the raging waterfalls behind them. Clara had framed them in such a way that the falls were a beautiful and perfect backdrop for the photograph. And unlike his usual posed photographs, the president gazed at his wife in such a way that it was clear he adored her.

Clara tapped the bottom edge of the picture, right beneath the president. "You can see how much he loves her."

"I know. I was just thinking the same thing. It's a beautiful photo, Clara. You've captured them so very well."

"Thank you." She smiled up at him, and for the briefest of moments he remembered that instant on the aerio-cycle when his stomach had dipped.

"You are very gifted at photography. It is clearly something you should focus on. Mr. Eastman taught you well, and he'd be smart to keep you in his employ."

"Quite right, Mr. Brinton." Mr. Eastman walked over to Clara. "I'll say, Clara, you did a fine job with your camera. I do hope you stay with me for a long time. Clearly your talent goes beyond teaching women to snap pictures to record family memories. You have an excellent eye for lighting. And for composition as well. Why, I'd even go so far as to say you have the making of a professional photographer."

Almost as wide as it had been as they'd ridden the bicycles through town, Clara's smile brightened her face, and it warmed a long forgotten part of James's heart. It surprised him to realize there was a feeling, an emotion he'd been lacking for quite some time. And though he would likely never get to explore it, were he given the opportunity he knew Clara was probably the only person who could evoke the unfamiliar emotion.

"Thank you, Mr. Eastman." James heard the mixture of surprised pleasure in her voice.

"There's no need for formality, Clara. You're part of the Kodak family now. Please, dear, call me George."

"Thank you, Mr. Eastman." Clara stopped and flushed. "I'll try."

James couldn't help but laugh since he was having the same problem. Mr. Eastman followed suit before pointing at the photo James still held. "You captured the joy on their faces. A snapshot, a moment of innocence where the two of them had no inkling of what that dastardly Czolgosz was planning."

As they all studied the photo, James tried to view the photo without bias. Not sure if he succeeded, he found it wasn't difficult to agree with Mr. Eastman. The moment between the couple was perfectly imaged and would undoubtedly live on. It really drove home the truth that one never knew what the morrow held.

Beside him, Clara blinked rapidly. When she finally looked up from the photograph, her eyes glistened and her lashes were damp.

"You know, Clara," Mr. Eastman said. "This photograph of the president is so well done that we might be able to enlarge it. Maybe even give it to the president for his office at the White House." He paused for a moment before lowering his voice to a near whisper. "That is, if he survives this dreadful shooting."

The brightness in Clara's eyes brimmed to full-fledged tears, and she blinked once more.

"I'm sorry to bring up such an unpleasant subject, my dear." Mr. Eastman reached into the breast pocket of his suit coat and handed Clara a crisply pressed linen handkerchief. "It's a terrible thing, but good that the scoundrel didn't get away." He turned to James. "Do you think he acted alone?"

"He said he did. But he's a follower of anarchist Emma Goldman. I'm really hoping we'll be able to use Clara's photos to pick out some kind of signal, eye contact, anything that will lead us to a larger group of anarchists."

"Now that the snapshots are developed, do you suppose she's safe?"

"I hope so, because now that we have the photos, there would be no reason for anyone to go after her."

"Yes, that would be the best outcome of all. But if someone is still after her, I trust you'll protect her." Mr. Eastman's eyes were wide, reflecting his concern.

The glimpse of fear that Clara so valiantly fought to keep from showing now pinched her face. Glancing back to Mr. Eastman, James nodded. "Of course. I won't leave her side until I'm certain she's safe."

"Thank you, James." Mr. Eastman reached for his hand and pumped it once. "We can't let anything happen to our Clara."

A sharp knock sounded at the door, and Mr. Spreckle let himself in. "Excuse my interruption." He turned to Mr. Eastman. "There's a problem that needs your attention, sir."

"Thank you, Spreckle. I'll be right there."

Interesting that Mr. Eastman had taken his assistant's words at face value instead of questioning him. There had been so many times James had wished for the same courtesy from his own boss. But then, when he finally did get it, he'd ruined everything.

"Clara, James." Mr. Eastman nodded to both of them. "I hope you'll forgive me for abandoning you. But before I go, I was planning to ask if you would so kindly consider delaying your return home by a day. Or at least consider taking the afternoon train tomorrow, instead of the early morning one. There is a matter I was hoping to discuss with you, and my mother would relish the opportunity to meet you."

"We don't want you or your mother to go to any trouble on our account," Clara said.

"Nonsense. You and James are the ones who have been inconvenienced by a day of travel and a stay in a hotel. It would be wonderful if we could at least feed you a nice meal before you head back home."

It was hard to miss the hopeful expression on Clara's face as she turned to look at James. Clearly she didn't want to disappoint Eastman.

If they didn't return to Buffalo tomorrow, James wasn't sure how he'd explain it to the captain. But intensity darkened the green of Clara's eyes, and he knew he couldn't say no.

"We can't stay an extra night, but we don't have to take the first train. We'll be happy to take the later train, sir." He could only hope he wasn't making a huge mistake by not showing up on the first train of the morning. He was already in jeopardy at work.

"Wonderful." Mr. Eastman's smile was instant. "Mr. Spreckle will pick you up in front of the hotel at ten sharp. He'll bring you to our home where my mother will serve a late breakfast. And then Clara and I will talk."

Mr. Eastman stepped toward the door, but stopped and turned back once more. "Please, Clara, take your time looking these over. And be sure to ask for Bernice before you leave. She's at the front desk. She'll get you a clothing voucher so you can replace the gown that was ruined when you were attacked."

"But Mr. Eastman, you've been more than generous."

James's eyes widened in surprise. One mystery solved. Clara could afford the beautiful gowns, and probably the hats as well, because Eastman paid for them. The man had seemed so fatherly. Suddenly he wasn't as inclined to go to the man's home tomorrow morning.

Moments later, James was ashamed of himself.

"Nonsense," Mr. Eastman said. "It's not every day one of our young Kodak Girls suffer an attack. I'd rather you didn't go to the extra trouble of trying to salvage the gown. Besides, my accountant will consider it a business expense."

"Is it a uniform?" James couldn't help himself.

"In a manner of speaking, yes it is. The Kodak Girl is your average woman, showing other women how simple it is to use my camera. I want the image of the Kodak Girl to be fashionable and yet approachable."

That made perfect sense, and by the time Mr. Eastman left, James put aside the unwelcome emotion he now recognized as jealousy.

"Thank you, James." Clara reached for a photograph as soon as the door closed behind her boss. "Now where should we start looking for clues about the man in the bowler hat?"

"The best place is always the beginning—your first photos when the McKinleys were at Niagara Falls, all the way up to yesterday."

Clara nodded. "And hopefully tomorrow there will be some further news about the president's condition."

"I hope so, too. We need to keep our thoughts focused on the doctor and the good work he's doing to—"

"Pray," Clara interrupted. "We need to pray. I agree about focusing our thoughts, but they need to be on the good Lord above, not on the doctor. I mean, of course pray for the doctor and his associates as they tend to the president, but God is the one we need to turn to right now. We need to be praying constantly."

James wasn't sure he agreed. But he certainly didn't want to argue or start a debate. Not when their concern for the president was so great. So even though his heart wasn't in agreement, he merely nodded and glanced over the assortment of photographs.

When he did, his heart nearly stopped.

"Clara? Would you care to explain this picture to me?"

James's tone turned her blood to ice. His jaw was set in a determined manner. What could he possibly see? A chill spread out from the center of her chest and seemed to cover the entirety of her body as she approached and he merely stared at her through narrowed eyes.

Uncertainty washed through her.

"Who is the man in this picture?" James held up the photo and her first thought was of the smears he was leaving behind since he held it clumsily, covering one corner with the pads of his thumb instead of protecting it.

As she drew closer to the photo, her unease grew like a widening pit in the center of her belly.

"Is that—"

"Apparently so. But the question is, why is he in one of your photos, in the hallway of what appears to be a hotel or boarding house? Clara, what were you doing there? Why is Czolgosz in one of your pictures?"

Why was James accusing her? Gone was the gentle, caring protectiveness. Now he spoke as if she were the criminal, not Leon Czolgosz.

It was as if the afternoon spent riding bicycles and enjoying the picnic lunch were all but forgotten. And though she'd originally thought he'd been trying to take her mind off the terrible events at the Temple of Music, his expression and his tone left her to wonder. Had it all been a plot to get her to let her guard down? To trick her into revealing something because he really thought she was a criminal?

This was absolutely unfathomable.

Straightening, she whirled to tell him exactly that. But when she stared him directly in the face, her eyes wavered to the soft lines of his mouth. It gave no hint of the tone he'd just used. Her gaze lifted to his. It was tender. Concerned. The same expression he wore after they'd been attacked on the way to the train station. The attack that seemed like days ago had really only been this morning.

"I don't know him, James. And I don't know why he's in this photo. Honestly, I don't."

"Then how do you explain this?"

She followed his glance to the table and to a photo that sat alone— separated from all the others as if it was of utmost importance.

Bile rose in her throat, and she had to force herself to keep from being sick. Czolgosz was in that one as well. She squinted at it and shook her head.

The evil man had somehow made it into her photos. How? She was at a loss to explain it. Prior to the shooting at the Temple of Music, she'd never seen Czolgosz in her life. She had to make James believe her.

"Where were these taken?" His gaze hardened as he drilled her with a glare. "I know it's not at the Martins'. But it *is* at a hotel or boardinghouse."

For more than one reason, Clara's heart sank a little as an extra layer of frost edged over it. She shivered and swallowed hard.

"Mr. Eastman isn't the only person I work for." Her voice sounded tinny to her ears. She kept her eyes focused on James and tried to still her trembling hands. What would he think of her when she told him?

He nodded. "Go on."

"That picture was taken at my other place of employment. I recognize the sideboard in the hallway. And the vase that's sitting on it. I put it there. It was a gift from my father." She hated the watery sound that edged her voice.

Did his expression soften? Or had she imagined it?

No matter, it was time to tell him. Any softness he might feel toward her was about to disappear. She took a deep breath and steeled herself.

"I work at Nowak's Hotel and Saloon." She paused. Even to her, knowing the truth, it sounded seedy and unscrupulous. "Well technically I work at the hotel above the saloon. But they're owned by the same man." And as much as she needed the employment, she probably wouldn't have a job when they returned to Buffalo. But she left that part unsaid.

"And you met Czolgosz there?"

"Yes. I mean, no!" Did it really appear to James as if she knew the man? This was growing worse by the moment. She leaned forward and picked up the photograph. How *had* Czolgosz ended up in her picture? "I don't know him. I've never met him. Until just now, I thought I'd never even seen him before. If you look at the numbers Mr. Eastman's processors marked on the prints, you'll see it was one of the first photos I took."

Clara held her breath while James squinted and looked closer at the corner of the picture he held. Her heart stuttered against her breastbone. Finally, he nodded. She allowed herself to breathe.

"I was so excited when Mr. Eastman gave me the camera. I couldn't wait to take pictures with it—to practice so I'd know what I was doing when it came time for me to demonstrate it at the Exposition. I didn't want to appear incompetent."

"I can't imagine you as incompetent, Clara." His tone changed. Softened. All authoritativeness disappeared. He certainly didn't appear judgmental that she worked above a saloon.

He probably thought she was there for far more unpleasant reasons than the truth, but he didn't even ask her what kind of work she did.

Not wanting him to consider it further, she rushed to tell him. "I clean rooms. It's certainly not what I envisioned myself doing when my mother died and I came to live with the Martins. But there you have it. And the day I met Mr. Eastman, I was actually working at a second job." She watched as his mouth fell open, but didn't miss a beat. "When he hired me, I was able to quit that one, and it gave me hopes of eventually quitting the job at the hotel above the saloon—which is really working *for* the owner of the saloon. My mother would have been mortified."

"Because you clean rooms?"

"No. Never that. My mother believed in hard work and making an honest living. She would have been horrified at me working above a saloon."

James nodded. "Are you aware that Nowak's is a Raines law hotel?"

Raines law? It wasn't anything she'd heard of before. But his tone had taken on a slight edge, so she knew it couldn't be good. "I'm not sure what that means, but I can assure you that there is nothing unseemly going on in Mr. Nowak's hotel."

"Does he serve liquor?"

"Yes. He does. But I don't have anything to do with that. I just clean the guest rooms."

When James looked down at her, his warm expression held no condemnation. She let out a slow breath.

"I'm sure you have nothing to worry about. It's just that some saloon owners get fancy in their attempt to skirt the law and serve liquor on Sundays. They have to be attached to a hotel. Saloon owners get creative in what they try to pass off as a hotel, and well…" He looked away. "Sometimes the combination of hotel and saloon turns into something more…unseemly."

"Oh." Though he still wasn't looking at her, Clara glanced away. She knew exactly what he meant. Did he think she worked in such a place? The thought sickened her. "I can assure you, nothing like that goes on there."

Perhaps her tone was a bit too indignant. But it was enough for James to reach out and gently touch her shoulder.

"I believe you, Clara."

Relieved, she offered him a tentative smile. "If there is anything like that going on, I know nothing about it. And the girls I work with are good, decent young women."

James offered her a soft smile. "I'm sure your mother would agree with your judgement and wouldn't be mortified."

"Thank you." She hoped it was true.

"You came to live with the Martins' when she died. But your father lives in New York City. Why didn't you stay with him?"

Pain lanced her heart, and she bit her lip in an attempt to keep the pain at bay. "I don't want to discuss him."

"We don't have to."

James amazed her. He didn't push. Most people would dig, trying to extract details, even when it was clear the subject pained her. Even Mrs. Martin, as much as Clara loved her, continually brought up the topic of her father.

Before she could continue, he opened his mouth. "What did you envision?"

Clara blinked at the sudden change in subject. The question surprised her. And she didn't have a clear answer for him.

"For your life," James prompted. "You said this wasn't what you'd envisioned."

"Oh. Well, I'm not really sure. I never envisioned anything more than being a wife and mother. Although—" She broke off. Did she really want to bring up her father?

"Although what?"

"My father traveled a lot for his work and some of the places he described—London, Paris…. I always dreamed of going to Europe. But those big cities, while they'd be nice to see—no, a *dream* to see—there were other places I'd hoped to see someday." She tried to shake the melancholy thoughts from her mind. This wasn't the time to think of things like that. "After my mother died, I knew I had to get away. And I hoped to find one job that would support me. Something I would enjoy, and that would allow me to save enough money to open my own business."

"What about Czolgosz?"

Again, he surprised her by not pushing and asking what had changed about her hopes and dreams. But—she wrinkled her nose—did they really have to discuss Czolgosz?

"Why was he in your photo, Clara?" James's tone became more business-like. More police interrogator-like. "Perhaps if he were in a snapshot of a crowd, but by himself? In a hotel hallway? You must have seen him."

"James, I honestly don't know. I don't know him. He must have been a guest at the hotel, but I wasn't paying any attention to the man himself when I took this photograph, I was focused on the camera. How can I make you believe me?" She closed her eyes and turned away.

When she felt his warm hand on her shoulder, she wanted to melt into his touch. Then he tugged her around to face him.

"I believe you, Clara."

Surprised, she blinked back tears. "You do?" Maybe she wouldn't go to jail after all.

"I do." He took her hand in his.

The relief she felt nearly brought her to her knees, and he wrapped his arms around her.

"Hey. It will be all right. We're going to get you through this. I promise."

Something about the certainty as he spoke, and the strength of his arms around her, infused her with hope. With everything in her she prayed he was right.

CHAPTER 14

The following morning, James stood with Clara outside of the hotel before the specified time, waiting for Mr. Spreckle. They had their bags with them because they would go straight to the train station from the Eastmans' house.

"Hey, mister. Wait!"

James turned to see Robbie and Bert running up behind him. "Is something wrong? Did we damage one of the bicycles?"

"No," Robbie said. "We wanted to ask you something." He pointed at James's chest. "Is that a real policeman's badge?"

Biting back a smile, James nodded. "It sure is."

"It's pretty neat looking." Both boys stepped forward for a closer look at the badge that was specially designed for the Pan-American Exposition.

"Wow." Little Bert looked up at him, blue eyes bright, freckles dotting his nose. "Are you a policeman, mister?"

"I sure am."

Robbie's eyes widened with enthusiasm. "When I grow up I wanna be a policeman."

"Me, too." Bert bobbed his head.

"Hey there. I thought you boys wanted to be photographers."

Clara sounded perturbed, but James knew she was only teasing.

Bert scrunched his little nose as he squinted up at Clara. "What if we wanna do both?"

"I'm sure you can each grow up to do whatever you want to do as long as it's good honest work." When she smiled at the little boy, James found himself willing to do anything he could to get her to smile at him that way. "And if you find yourselves wanting to do two jobs, I'm sure that will be perfectly acceptable."

Something about the way she spoke to the boys tugged at him. It had yesterday, too, when she was showing them her camera. He could imagine her with her own little boys, laughing, taking their pictures, passing out hugs.

"I suggest you boys stop in at your local police department from time to time to let them know of your interest." He knew mentoring young kids was important to their future. Most officers he knew were more than happy to do so.

The clippety-clop of horse hooves clattered on the street, and James looked up to see Mr. Spreckle approaching. "It looks like our ride is here."

"Bye, kids. It's been lovely to know you." Clara stooped down to kiss each boy on the cheek. "I hope to see you again soon."

They both beamed up at her. Then when Spreckle helped her into the wagon, they turned their attention to James and each gave him their interpretation of a salute.

James tried to listen while Mr. Eastman's mother went on about the breakfast they'd just eaten. He nodded at all the appropriate times—he hoped. He didn't want to hurt the woman's feelings. Her food *was* delicious. But his mind was on Clara and the large oak door that separated him from both her and Mr. Eastman.

He'd spent a restless night, worrying over the photographs. As far as both he and Clara had been able to tell yesterday, there was no sign of the man in the bowler hat in any of the pictures. They'd looked at the pictures what seemed dozens of times.

There were the photos taken at Nowak's that she'd said were for practice—the ones with Czolgosz, and one of a man hugging a woman with blond hair. Then there were the ones she took of the McKinleys at Niagara Falls, and one taken in her rooms at the Martins'. On the Expo fairgrounds, there were photos of John Phillip Sousa with a group of Hawaiian musicians, John Phillip Sousa at the president's speech, the president at the reception, the dome inside the Temple of Music, and finally the photographs of the shooting aftermath—a group of men piled on top of Czolgosz, and few taken of different clusters of people throughout the room.

There was also a picture of himself that he'd been surprised to see. She'd taken it without him realizing it, sometime after they first made eye contact, before Czolgosz shot President McKinley.

But as far as he could tell from looking at the group photos, there wasn't a single image of the man they were looking for.

And that begged the question—why had he been after the camera? Did he merely *think* he might be in a photo and therefore implicated in something sinister?

"Clara's photographs are simply stunning," Mrs. Eastman said. "Don't you agree?" She tapped the edge of a photograph that sat on the table.

"Yes, she has a natural ability for photography." James leaned toward one last picture as he spoke. It was something about this shot that prompted this meeting with Clara. In the photo, President McKinley sat behind the wheel of a car, smiling as he entered the grounds of the Pan-American Exposition. It was taken the day before he was shot. The same day as the photo of the McKinleys at Niagara Falls.

How Clara had found the time to take so many pictures that day, James didn't know. But when she'd taken that photograph, she had no idea it might be the last time he waved to the people who admired and trusted him enough to re-elect him to lead their country.

A dull dread seeped into his belly, clawing at him. James surprised himself by offering up a silent prayer that it wasn't true. He prayed the president would recover so he could hold his loving wife once more. If he didn't…James shook his head. As unthinkable as it was to have witnessed the shooting, it was more so to think the president might not survive his wounds.

"I think my son wants to use it in his advertising. I think that's what he's talking to Clara about."

The man was happy with her photographs. That much was clear. But to James, a gray cloud hovered somewhere in the vicinity of the ceiling, waiting for the most inappropriate time to burst its gloom over everyone—especially Clara. Because there was something in one of those pictures that nagged at him as it hovered at one corner of his mind—just out of his reach.

James glanced toward the oak door again.

"And she has lovely taste."

James followed the direction of Mrs. Eastman's slender finger as it tapped the edge of a photograph that had not been taken at Nowak's. Nor had it been taken at Niagara Falls or the Exposition fairgrounds. This was the picture taken in Clara's sitting room in the Martin house. And the item Mrs. Eastman pointed out turned his blood to cold sludge.

"This Tiffany lamp must have set her back more than a month's wages."

Just as he had suspected before.

James didn't know much about the glass business, but he knew expensive when he saw it. And yet something didn't make sense. Clara was working two jobs. Why, if her father was a successful jeweler? And if he wasn't successful, where was the money coming from for all of these expensive items?

Inside his study, Clara waited nervously for whatever it was

Mr. Eastman wanted to talk to her about. She prayed he wasn't planning to fire her after all. Yesterday evening he'd seemed pleased with her work. But perhaps he really believed she was a liability and couldn't quite bring himself to tell her yesterday because he'd been so concerned over her bruises. After all, he'd said it himself. It wasn't every day that a Kodak Girl was accosted.

Her heart sank. The trip to Rochester had most likely already lost her the job at Nowak's. She wasn't sure what she'd do for income if she didn't have this job. The Martins were kind enough to let her live with them, but she couldn't rely on them forever. And she wasn't about to take money from her father.

A steel band squeezed her heart. The less her father knew about her situation, the better. She looked back at Mr. Eastman and tried to focus on what he was saying. "Clara, my dear. As you know, I've been very impressed with your photographs."

"Thank you, Mr. Eastman."

Mr. Eastman peered at her over the top of his glasses. In her nervousness, she'd forgotten something she really wasn't comfortable with anyway. "I thought you were going to call me George."

"Sorry, sir. G–George."

He laughed. "That's better. Now. Let's get down to business."

She clasped her hands in front of her and tried to still her quaking knees.

"You've done far more than just demonstrate how easy it is to use the Brownie camera. I believe you have a keen eye for proper lighting, for the heart of the subject—you capture things that require more than a passing glance."

"Thank you, sir." Perhaps he wouldn't notice that she hadn't called him by his given name. She'd been brought up to respect her elders, and most especially those who were her employers. Her grandmother would have been scandalized to hear her call her boss by his first name.

"You've done excellent work, Clara. I'd like to hire you to do more than demonstrate the camera at the fair. I'd like to hire you to take photos with a different type of camera—one that takes portraits. I'd like to display them here in my studio. Not only here, but also in my offices in Toronto and France."

France? Had she heard him correctly? Would it be possible for her to go there? She wanted to ask, but held back since he clearly wasn't finished explaining the job.

"I'll train you, of course. I'm planning a major expansion of my business, Clara. I think that after you have some more experience, you could eventually run your own photography studio. And there's a very good possibility that I could help you get started. I could sponsor you, and in return you could let me use some of your photographs in my advertising."

Clara's heart leaped, and she tried to keep her mouth from gaping open. "I'm flattered, Mr. Eastman."

"It's more than flattery, Clara. I'm sincere."

She could hear the truth in his tone, and she smiled. "I'd love the opportunity to learn from you, sir. I sincerely hope I can live up to your expectations."

"You will. I've no doubt. Now your first assignment is for an event that is a few weeks away. Have you heard of Annie Edson Taylor?"

Surprised, Clara could only stare at Mr. Eastman. Of course she'd heard of Annie Edson Taylor. She couldn't believe Mr. Eastman had heard of her as well.

Mrs. Taylor was a woman with a plan—a plan she told anyone and everyone. A plan that excited most people who heard about it. If Clara was going to be assigned to photograph an upcoming event, then photographing the woman who planned to ride over Niagara Falls while sealed inside a barrel would be the perfect assignment. She tried to tamp down her excitement while Mr. Eastman gave her all of the details.

"So in the meantime, you will continue to demonstrate the camera at the fair. And you can expect a raise in your next paycheck."

As much as she wanted to know, Clara didn't ask him how much the raise would be. Her mother taught her never to discuss money.

It was in poor taste, she always said. Her father, on the other hand, would have been disappointed in her for not asking. She could only hope it would be enough to make up for the job at the hotel. It would be lovely to work only for Mr. Eastman. Perhaps one day she really could move out of the Martins' and even buy her own house—a house that she would someday hope to fill with children.

"And in a couple of weeks, you can come back here for some training with the new camera. I'll have it ready for you."

As Mr. Eastman said it, a stray thought leaped to her mind. Now she really would be able to see the sweet little boys again.

When they said their good-byes to Mr. Eastman and his mother she was in somewhat of a daze.

"I've thoroughly enjoyed getting to know you, James." Mrs. Eastman's face flushed a rosy shade of pink as she spoke to James. "I do hope you'll come back and visit sometime."

"I enjoyed it as well, Mrs. Eastman. And thank you for the delicious brunch."

"And I sincerely hope you'll be able to take some of the suspicion off of Clara." Mr. Eastman stepped forward and shook James's hand. "If you need any help from me, please let me know."

"Thank you, sir."

And just like that, Clara's bubble burst.

Suspicion? Had she missed some part of the conversation? She thought James had believed her about Czolgosz and the photographs. Was he back to suspecting her again?

Surely he couldn't suspect her of the attempt on President McKinley's life?

Something was wrong with Clara. They sat on the train in the lounge car, facing each other, with a small table between them. Try as he might, James was having a difficult time lifting her out of her melancholy. Had something gone wrong in the meeting with Mr.

Eastman? She'd yet to say one word about it.

"Clara, please talk to me. Did something go wrong with Mr. Eastman?"

Biting her lip, she shook her head and looked out the window. "No."

"Then what happened to upset you?"

Slowly, she lifted her gaze to meet his. She swallowed hard and appeared to struggle with her words. Finally, she said, "Are you going to arrest me?"

"Arrest you? No, of course not." How could she think that of him? "Whatever gave you such an idea?"

"The pictures." When she glanced away, he understood.

"The ones from Nowak's?"

Clara still couldn't seem to look at him. James reached out and cupped her chin. Then he gently turned her head until he looked into her eyes. "I'm not going to arrest you, Clara. I believe what you told me."

"Really?"

"Yes, really. And I'm going to make sure my captain believes you as well."

She looked away from him again. Why?

"Clara? Don't you trust me?"

As if in answer, Clara bent down and picked up her camera bag. After rummaging through it, she held something out to him. An uneasy feeling gnawed at his belly, and he reached for the pictures in her hand.

"I'm so sorry, James. You trusted me, and I didn't trust you. Something Mr. Eastman said made me think you might be planning to arrest me."

"I don't understand." Although as he thumbed through the pictures, it became glaringly clear. Before they'd arrived at Mr. Eastman's house this morning, she'd given him the photographs to give to his police captain. But obviously, sometime since then, she'd managed to go through his bag and retrieve the pictures of

Czolgosz. He pressed his lips together and turned away from her wide, unblinking expression.

"I'm sorry, James."

"Are you, Clara?" He shoved the pictures into the inner pocket of his jacket and turned back to face her. "Do you know what you could have cost me by taking evidence? My job."

Clara shrank back from him, but he couldn't seem to stop himself.

"Yes. You could have cost me my job. I thought you were a good Christian girl. But you didn't stop to think about anyone but yourself. I guess with your Tiffany vases and Tiffany lamps and your fancy hats, you never really considered anyone else's job, did you?"

"But I did consider your job, and I gave them back to you before anyone knew. And I don't expect you to believe me, but I really am sorry. I just—I got scared."

And he'd just compounded her fear. Overcome with guilt at the words he'd let flow unchecked, James puffed out a long sigh then turned away from her.

Silence echoed around them in spite of the fact that they were on a moving train. For a brief moment, James had to wonder at the other passengers in the rail car. Had they overheard the conversation? Undoubtedly he'd not only frightened Clara and attacked her integrity, he'd also humiliated her.

"You're right, you know."

Her soft words, uttered before he could apologize, took him by surprise. Surely she didn't mean about Czolgosz. "What am I right about?"

"You didn't exactly say it, but you questioned my faith."

"I did?" James shook his head. "No. I didn't."

"It was implied."

"But Clara, I didn't m—"

She reached out and covered his hands with her own. "You were right. I didn't put my full trust in God. I always claim I trust Him, but when it came down to it, I let my fear over those pictures get in the way of my faith. I was afraid you were planning to have me arrested. I wondered if you were only being nice to me, protecting me, as part of your job. And I thought maybe the picnic was a trick to get me to let my guard down."

A groan welled up inside him. Had he treated her as if he only considered her a job? He'd been intrigued by her from the moment he first set eyes on her. But had he seen those photos of Czolgosz without knowing her, wouldn't he have brought her in for interrogation on the spot, assuming a connection between them? What were the chances of her taking such a photograph without either of them realizing it?

But then, someone must have. Perhaps that's why the mysterious man was after the camera.

Would his captain believe that though, with only her word and his own that such a man existed?

He pulled his hands from hers and ran them through his hair. His cap sat on the seat next to him, its gold braid bright and mocking. The jacket he wore suddenly felt heavy—especially where the inside pocket brushed against his chest. He tugged at the collar.

"I'm sorry you thought I was questioning your faith. I'm the last person on earth who should doubt someone's integrity."

"What do you mean?"

Did he really want to tell her?

As she watched him, it was as if she'd pushed any thoughts for herself aside. Concern pinched her features, and he was certain the concern was for him.

And that was the reason he found himself telling her of his shame. "I did something that was so horrible, Clara, so unforgiveable, it's a wonder they let me back on the force."

"Nothing you could ever do is unforgiveable, James."

"You're wrong."

Clara shook her head, but he didn't argue. He just explained. "My grandfather was a police officer. And so was my father. My entire life, I looked up to them. I wanted to be just like them."

"And so you are."

"And so I'm not. I'm as far removed from them as it's possible for a son and grandson to be."

"Somehow I find that difficult to believe." Her tone was soft, and he tried to breathe in its soothing effect. As if it would somehow settle over his spirit and act as a balm for his heart.

"Years ago my father arrested a man suspected to run with Butch Cassidy."

Across from him, Clara sucked in a sharp breath.

"Jones was his name. Milton Jones. It wasn't long after Jones got out of prison that my father was accused of murder. The body of a young woman was found in my mother's garden. There was evidence to suggest my father did it. But my mother and I both knew better. The woman kept company with Jones, and after he blackened both of her eyes she decided to become my father's informant while he was trying to build a case. But then she turned up dead."

For a moment, remembering the image of the bloodied young woman half-buried in his mother's vegetable garden, James could only listen to the clickety-clack of the wheels as the train steamed toward Buffalo. Clara, to her credit, didn't push him. She merely waited with patience until he was ready to speak again.

"My father was framed out of retaliation," he finally said. "But the captain didn't believe it. In spite of an entire life spent serving on the police force, my father was arrested for murder."

Clara's gentle expression fell and her eyes widened. "James." She gasped as she said his name. "I'm so sorry."

He gave a curt nod, not sure he really wanted to continue. But then she reached out and touched his arm. Was it pity? Or encouragement? He studied her expression and saw empathy. She cared, and for some reason that gave him strength. "I did the only thing I could do. I made the evidence go away."

Indecision rippled through him as soon as he said it. He tried to gauge her reaction. She stared, unblinking, but he thought maybe her respiration had increased. It had been a mistake. She was no doubt disgusted by him. Still, now that he'd said this much, he had to finish telling her.

"It backfired. After they were forced to let my father go for lack of evidence, Jones decided he was going to have his revenge one way or the other. He killed both of my parents. And it was my fault. If I hadn't tampered with the evidence, my father would be in jail, but he'd be alive. So would my mother."

"But James—"

"No." His harsh tone silenced her, and she stared up at him with wide, unblinking eyes. He didn't need her defending him, didn't want her feeling sorry for him. He didn't deserve it. "It shouldn't come as a surprise that I lost my job." He thought back to the day he'd spewed his guilt-ridden confession to the captain as they'd stood next to his parents' graves after the burial. It was something he couldn't keep bottled up. And though the captain said he would have done the same thing, he still had to take him off the force. "They've only recently let me come back to work. But they're watching my every move to make sure I don't mess it all up again. It's horrible to be under such scrutiny, but in spite of it, I'd gladly give up the job if I could have one more minute with them."

Clara opened her mouth only to close it again. She bit her lip, shook her head, then after another moment of hesitation, took his hand and laced her fingers through his. "I just don't understand how someone could take another person's life." Her tone was filled with some of the same shock and disbelief it held after Czolgosz shot President McKinley.

"I know." He looked down at their clasped hands and wished he could shield her from the harsh realities of life. "But they do."

"And you do your best to capture them." She gazed at him with a soft smile.

Too exhausted to say anything more, he only nodded.

Clara stood and walked around the small table, weaving with the train as she did. Then she squeezed into the small space next to him. Before he could guess her intent, she pressed her lips to his in the sweetest kiss he'd ever known. Then she wrapped both of her arms around him and leaned her head against his shoulder.

They rode the rest of the way in silence, and it wasn't until the train was pulling in to the Buffalo station that she broke the stillness. "I'm sorry, James. It's a terrible thing that you and your family suffered. All you've been trying to do is recover, and here I've gone and made things even more difficult."

"No, you haven't, Clara. And even if it might have been true at the beginning—which I'm not saying it was—it's definitely not true now. Somehow in these past few days, you've managed to steal a little piece of my heart."

"So now I'm a thief?"

She said it with the proper amount of outrage, but the gleam in her eyes belied the inflection of her tone. They stared at each other for a moment. Her lips twitched as if she was trying not to laugh.

But James's breath caught in his throat as he realized the truth. If it came right down to it, he would have done the exact same thing she did. He would have hidden the photographs from his captain.

Because no matter that it was his lifelong dream and he was only just now starting to gain it back, he would give up his job in a heartbeat in order to protect Clara.

CHAPTER 15

"Good morning, Mrs. Martin. I trust you slept well last night?" Clara took the last step before she planted a kiss on the older woman's cheek.

Mrs. Martin finished adjusting the drapes before turning toward Clara. "I didn't hear you come in last night, dear."

"It was late when James and I returned, and I didn't want to wake you or Mr. Martin."

Mrs. Martin wrung her hands together and tilted her head in a way that reminded Clara of her mother. "I'm so sorry, dear. I'm afraid I've made a terrible mistake."

"Mrs. Martin, what do you mean? Surely it can't be that bad."

"Mr. Nowak's assistant was here yesterday. You know, the pretty girl with the black hair?"

"Vivienne?"

Mrs. Martin nodded. "Yes, that was her name. I'm so sorry. I never did get over there to tell her you wouldn't be in to work. I meant to ask Emil to go around and deliver your message, but, well, we had a new couple come in right after you left. Before they could even get settled, they asked if I'd care for their children while they did an errand."

"It's all right, Mrs. Martin."

"I don't know about that, Clara. I don't think it's all right."

Clara didn't know either, but she didn't want Mrs. Martin to be more upset than she was already. In truth, she didn't earn enough from Mr. Eastman just yet, in order to get by on that job alone. She desperately needed the income from Mr. Nowak for just a little while longer, and she prayed her position hadn't been terminated.

Though she tried not to show her distress over possibly losing her job, she must have failed because Mrs. Martin came over and pulled her into a hug.

"Oh, I hope I haven't ruined things for you."

In a wave of longing for her mother, Clara melted into the woman who had been her mother's childhood playmate. And try as she might, she couldn't help but wish it was her own mother she hugged, instead of Mrs. Martin. Even so, she was thankful God had placed the woman in her life at a time when she truly needed it.

"You haven't, Mrs. Martin. I'm certain of it."

Mrs. Martin hugged her harder, until Clara finally whispered her thanks in the woman's ear.

"That's what I'm here for, sweetie. Now why don't you go and let Mr. Nowak know you're all right. And please give him my apologies. I'll never forgive myself if you lose that job because of me."

"Yes, of course. I'll go at once." Even if she was most probably terminated from her position, she needed to do the proper thing and explain. She went to the mirror in the hallway and adjusted the pins in her hair. Then she put on her hat and turned it until the decorative flower on the brim, made of beaded pearls, sat at a jaunty angle.

James had called it a fancy hat, but his tone sounded like he didn't approve. She hoped that wasn't the case because she liked the hat and didn't think she'd stop wearing it just to win his approval. Besides, Mr. Eastman expected her to look nice for her job.

She paused at the doorway and gave Mrs. Martin another hug. "I'll be back to get my camera before I go to the fairgrounds."

"The fairgrounds? Don't you think you should rest a bit? Surely it can wait another day?"

"I'm rested, Mrs. Martin." Clara smiled brightly in hopes of proving it was true. "I promise."

"Do you think I should send for Emil to accompany you?"

"No. That won't be necessary, but thank you for thinking of it. James should be on his way to the police station right now, turning over the photographs to his captain. There's no longer any reason for the man to come after me."

Even as she said the words, she prayed they were true.

"Officer Brinton. You made it back with the photographs, I presume." Captain Green rose to greet James as he walked through the door.

"Yes, sir. I have the photographs right here." He patted his jacket pocket where the photographs were and drew in a breath. *The jacket pocket above his heart.* The weight of the photos in that particular pocket weighed heavily on him last night after he'd been sharp with Clara. But it was the lack of weight that bit at him now, and he forced himself to act natural. He couldn't show any outward signs that things were amiss. Slowly, he let out the breath. "How is the president, sir? Has there been any word?"

"He's holding his own right now, recovering from the surgery to remove the bullet from his abdomen."

"That's good news then." James headed to the counter against the wall at the far end of the room.

The oak countertop was slanted at a slight angle, with a narrow wooden lip running across it so one could place documents beside each other for examination—or in this case, photographs. A groove carved into the thin strip of wood kept papers from sliding off. The mullioned windows above the counter allowed for adequate lighting while items were viewed.

One by one, his heart thumping wildly in his chest, James placed twelve photographs next to each other on the counter—in order, in case the captain happened to notice the tiny numbers etched in the corner. They were small enough, and his eyes were old enough, that he hopefully wouldn't see them.

The guilt James felt at hiding the pictures of Czolgosz in the Nowak Hotel was more overwhelming than he thought it would be. And if anyone realized it, he'd be disgraced all over again. And this time, there would be no second chances. He prayed no one would notice, and if they did, that they wouldn't think anything of it.

Disgrace aside, protecting Clara was of utmost importance. If anyone had asked him a week ago if he'd ever put his career on the line again, he would have said no. But clearly, he'd do anything for those he cared about. And clearly he wasn't meant to work in law enforcement.

Captain Green picked up a photograph in the same clumsy manner James had, before Clara showed him how to hold them properly. The one he picked up was of the domed ceiling in the Temple of Music.

"That was one of Cl—Miss Lambert's—practice photos, sir. It was inside the Temple of Music while she was waiting to meet the president. She told me she was caught almost speechless at the stained glass that makes up the domed ceiling."

"Easy to do." The captain nodded. "It's an amazing piece of architecture." He reached for another photograph.

"Officer Brinton." Captain Green's voice was low and slow, and James cringed, knowing what was coming next. "Another practice shot?"

Was that amusement that tinged the edge of the captain's voice? Who was he kidding? Of course it was. Before long, he'd hear similar tones while his fellow officers ribbed him. Their ribbing likely wouldn't be as friendly as the captain's, though.

James's face grew hot, and he tugged his collar as he stepped closer and pretended to study the picture. "That, sir—um, yes. That is one of her practice shots."

"Of you? She practiced on you?"

"Yes, sir. That's what she told me. She wasn't far from the platform, and I was just there. It wasn't like she had a lot of options."

The captain made a humming sound before he pursed his lips and drew his bushy white eyebrows toward the bridge of his nose. "So what do you make of the rest of these?"

"As I said, most of them were practice shots of random sights before she even made it into the Temple of Music. But the pictures that she filmed after the shooting are right over here." Hopefully he could deflect the captain's interest toward the people in the photos taken at the president's reception.

"You can see here, sir, Miss Lambert was able to capture a fair amount of the people who were at the Temple of Music that evening."

Though James and Clara hadn't spotted anyone suspicious, he didn't want to make that observation to his boss. It was best to let the man form his own opinions.

The captain leaned over the photos, taking his time as he studied them. Then he pointed to the one where the president was standing in front of the patriotic bunting, with his hand extended toward one of the men who'd come to greet him.

"She does fine work."

"Yes, she does." James was happy to agree with the captain on that point—and in this case, it was the truth. Clara most assuredly had a way with the camera. "And over here, these are of the aftermath. Chaos was happening all over the place, and a gang of men knocked Czolgosz to the ground and jumped on top of him. But there was no one rushing in to offer him aid."

"That's one of the hallmarks of these anarchists, Brinton. They won't lift a finger to help their own. Rather, they pretend not to know each other. In fact, they encourage each other to declare they've acted alone."

James knew all of that, but the more Captain Green talked the less likely he was to take a closer look. Usually people focused in on what was right in front of them, not noticing the perimeter and the finer details.

"Good work getting these from the photographer. Did she give you any trouble?"

"None at all, sir. She's very pleasant." James couldn't help but smile. Clara was more than pleasant. She was charming, kind, and when her smile lit her eyes it was infectious.

He wouldn't trade the time he'd had with her for anything, and he hoped it wouldn't be long before he could see her again.

The captain made that humming sound again while he gave James a measured stare. "Any luck catching the person who attacked her?"

"No, sir. Not yet." He planned to do everything he could to find that man. "There was another incident the morning we left. We were assaulted on the way to the train station."

Captain Green raised an eyebrow. "Oh?"

"Yes, sir. We were attacked from behind."

"Obviously you weren't able to arrest the assailant, or I would have heard about it." There was a slight change in the captain's tone. It had an edge to it, and was more than effective in its mission to leave James feeling small and incompetent.

"No, sir. He got away."

"Did you recognize him at least?"

"I never got a look at his face, sir."

The captain's disapproval was evident, and James knew no explanation would meet with his approval now. James failed to apprehend a man who'd assaulted a police officer. That was considered incompetence in Captain Green's view. James's as well.

Once again, he had the overwhelming sense that perhaps he didn't have what it took to be a police officer.

"No matter," Captain Green finally said. "We have the pictures. I'm sure she's safe."

James clenched his jaw, not certain of anything of the sort. And he didn't particularly care for the captain's dismissive attitude.

"There was a lot of excitement while you were off in Rochester." The captain made it sound like he was off somewhere on pleasure while the others were here working the case.

Weren't you?

He clenched his jaw and felt his back teeth grind together. Maybe he had enjoyed Clara's—Miss Lambert's—company. Better to start thinking of her in a more formal manner and forget their time together. He'd never tell the captain. Besides, he was protecting both the evidence and Clara. Okay, mostly Clara. But the captain didn't have to know he would willingly put Clara's safety above little strips of celluloid.

"Oh?" James tried to sound interested, not panicked.

"Yes, Brinton. A lot of excitement." A slow smile spread across the captain's face, and James was certain he wouldn't like what he was about to hear.

"While you were gone, we made some arrests. It was a raid, actually. A very big raid."

"A raid, sir?"

A wide grin spread across the captain's face and he nodded. "We caught us a whole passel of anarchists."

James leaned forward. So he needn't have worried about Clara's photos after all. It was over. They could breathe easier. Whoever had been after her was likely locked up as well.

"Unfortunately, first thing this morning, we had to let them go."

"All?" Dread seized his heart.

Though he wasn't prone to feeling anxious, where Clara was concerned all of his normal reactions and emotions had fizzled away like a sputtering firecracker. And Clara was still in danger. In more ways than one if anyone were to catch on to Mr. Eastman's numbering system.

"Almost all of them. We've detained a few on suspicion of other activities." The captain's grin faded. "My hands were tied. As positive as I am that some of those men were involved, the judge was equally certain we didn't have enough evidence to keep them under lock and key."

James slowed his breathing, careful to temper his tone before he responded. "Do you know who they were, sir?"

"A group of men, and a few women, all known to be associated with Czolgosz in one way or another, and most of them were seen meeting together the same night the president was shot."

Any or all of them could be part of Czolgosz's rumored group of co-conspirators.

"We'll have to gather the evidence then." Though he wasn't due to start his shift until late this afternoon, James would willingly work day and night, as many hours as it would take to prove Clara innocent of any wrongdoing. Proving who really was part of the anarchist group would be a start. His hope started to pick back up. "Where should I begin?"

Before the captain could answer, a group of fellow officers burst into the room laughing over something James couldn't quite hear. James hoped he could go unnoticed, but it wasn't to be.

One of the officers, Bales, gave him a steely glare and uttered a derogatory remark.

Now that he was officially back to work at the precinct, James had hoped to be part of the so-called brotherhood that made up the close group of officers. But it was apparent it wouldn't happen anytime soon. Though he didn't like it, he understood their reluctance to openly welcome him back. The men who knew him were still angry. Those who joined the department while James was on suspension knew him by reputation only.

Despite the grief and heartache James suffered as a result, he would never be able to live down the disaster that led to his parents' murder. Nor should he have that luxury. There would never be a day where he didn't think about them, mourn their loss, and know it was his fault they weren't here.

"What do we have here?" Bales walked to the table and thumbed through the pictures.

James pulled in a long breath and concentrated on it, seeking its steadying effect, and yet still almost lost the battle against the urge to slap the man's beefy hands away from Clara's work. He hardened himself against reacting. *Feel nothing. Say nothing. Don't engage him in conflict.*

Bales dropped the pictures back on the counter. "Is there enough evidence here to convict Czolgosz?"

When Captain Green spoke, his voice dripped with sarcasm and he pinned Bales with a narrow-eyed stare. "Even without photographs, I don't think that will be a problem."

"You're right, of course. There's no denying he shot the president. Besides, he confessed." Bales studied the captain for another moment. "Is there any evidence here that he had an accomplice?"

A growing sense of unease gnawed at James. He didn't like the look on Bales's face and his gut told him not to trust the man. Before Captain Green could respond, James interrupted. "The captain and I were in the middle of a conversation, so if you'd excuse us?" He turned to his boss. "Sir, you were about to tell me what I can do to help the investigation."

"Was I? Oh, yes, I was." Captain Green watched Bales, clearly distracted.

Bales went and sat in a straight-backed chair behind a scarred wooden desk. He picked up a sheet of paper and a stubby pencil that was bumpy with teeth marks. He promptly stuck it in his mouth. When he did, his right shirt sleeve shifted just enough that James could see an angry red pucker of skin on his forearm slightly above his wrist. It was the result of a knife wound he'd received when apprehending a bank robbery suspect a few months ago. It had never healed right, and sometimes it still bled. Oftentimes, Bales picked at it. James suspected that was part of the reason it wasn't healing well.

What kind of assignment had Bales been on? Even though James was curious, he resisted asking. He had enough to worry about.

"I have a list of names here that I wanted you to start investigating.

I wanted to find out what they might have in common besides the saloons on Broadway."

"Great. I'll start checking right away."

From his place at the desk, Bales spoke up. "It's all circumstantial according to the judge. But I say there's more to it. A lot of those men appeared to be holding meetings in various saloons the night the president was shot. And as for the others, their names didn't come to our attention by accident."

What made Bales think that? Before he could question him, the captain cleared his throat.

"Actually, Brinton, that's what I *wanted* you to do. We already have to put that on hold. One of the hallmarks of the job— something always comes along that takes precedence."

"Really, sir?" What could possibly take precedence over the assassination attempt on the president of the United States? James kept his eyes fixed on his superior officer, well aware that Bales was watching.

"The raid and then having to turn so many people loose wasn't the only thing that happened while you were gone." The captain looked from Bales to James. "The body of a young woman was found by the river. We need to find out what happened. Brinton, I want you to lead the investigation."

Nothing could have surprised James more. Not even Bales throwing his pencil on the desk when he jumped up to protest.

"But Captain Green, the anarchists—"

"This takes precedence, Bales. Czolgosz is behind bars. McKinley's secret service agents are investigating every man we had to set free. In the meantime, we have a woman's murder to investigate."

Bales turned away, but not before James noticed the rosy hue bloom up the man's face. Was he angry that the captain assigned it to James?

"Are you sure it's murder, sir?"

Captain Green tilted his head toward James. "I'm sure."

"And do you know who she is?"

"We do. Her name was Patricia Mane. Miss Mane works—worked—at Nowak's Hotel."

James's stomach plummeted. Clara was there right now, telling Mr. Nowak she wouldn't be back to work. He had to stay calm, had to act normal. "Do you have any suspects, sir?"

"One. The man who owns the hotel. John Nowak. We brought him in to question him about Czolgosz—the man was staying at his hotel. But as I said before, we let most everyone go. The woman's body was found a few hours later. But she was last seen the day before the president was shot."

"What makes you think he's the murderer? Why not Czolgosz?"

"She worked for Nowak."

"But Czolgosz was staying there. Why wouldn't you look at him as a suspect?"

"She was last seen struggling with a man who matched Nowak's description."

"Which is what, sir?"

"Average height. Brown hair, brown eyes."

Just like Clara's assailant. Just like the three men in this room—James, Bales, and the captain. Although none of them were gaunt like the attacker. Was Nowak thin and gangly? What about the man who was seen struggling with Patricia Mane? But Clara would have recognized her employer, wouldn't she have?

"And Czolgosz doesn't fit that description?"

The captain pressed his lips into a straight line and tilted his head as if thinking hard. "No. Not really. Czolgosz's hair is too light. His eyes are blue, and he's not that tall." Captain Green lifted one corner of his mouth. "You were there, Brinton. You should know Czolgosz doesn't fit that description."

"Right, sir. Except I wasn't close enough to see the color of his eyes." He didn't add that it was because he was too busy looking at Clara. Better to get back to the matter at hand. "And you think Nowak kept the woman imprisoned and killed her shortly after you released him?"

The muscle beneath the captain's right eye twitched so slightly it was almost imperceptible.

"Or do you think he stashed her body and dumped her later?"

"I really don't know, Brinton. That's why I put *you* on the case instead of myself—so you can do the figuring."

James sighed. "Where is Nowak now, sir?"

"He's been brought back in for questioning. He's in a cell at the moment. We'll take him to the interview room as soon as you're ready."

If Nowak was the killer—and somehow James didn't think he was—then Clara was safe as long as the man was locked up.

But if he wasn't the killer....

Clearing his throat, James gave the captain a curt glance and prayed he would succeed in exerting authority over his new assignment.

"The suspect will have to wait in his cell until my shift starts this afternoon, sir. There's something important that I need to take care of first."

Only one thing topped James's priority list at the moment. Clara. He had to get to her. He had to be sure she was safe.

CHAPTER 16

The sun was bright, and it wasn't long before Clara turned onto Broadway and stood in front of the doorway with the numbers 1078 stenciled on the glass. Nowak's Saloon and Hotel.

Courage. She needed courage. She closed her eyes and whispered a prayer that Mr. Nowak wouldn't be angry and dismiss her from his employ.

When she opened her eyes again, she sucked in a deep breath and pushed open the door.

"Clara, I've been so worried about you!" Vivienne, Mr. Nowak's assistant, ran out from behind the counter and pulled Clara into a hug. She was a pretty young woman with jet black hair and equally dark eyes that burned brightly against her porcelain skin. "Where ever have you been? And how did you get that bruise on your face?"

"I've been—" Clara brushed her hand across her face. She'd tried to cover the bruise with rice powder—clearly she hadn't been successful. She shook her head. It would take too long to explain it, and then she'd have to repeat it to Mr. Nowak. "Is Mr. Nowak in? You can listen in while I tell him."

Vivie's face blanched, and her mouth dropped open. "You mean you haven't heard?"

"Heard what?"

When the other woman pressed her fist to her mouth, Clara's alarm increased.

"Vivie, what is it?"

Vivie's tone simmered with rage as she explained about Mr. Nowak's arrest and release. But when she finished, the blood drained from her face, creating a white contrast to her rosy red lipstick that was even paler and more extreme than usual.

Something else was wrong.

Unease prickled at the base of Clara's neck, growing in intensity like tiny spiders crawling across her skin. "Vivie, what is it?"

"Patricia has been missing since the other night."

"What? Has anyone contacted her family?" As soon as Clara said it, she was hammered with guilt. Mr. Nowak and Vivienne had been dealing with more than enough without having to pick up her share of the work. She had to figure out a way to make it up to them.

"Clara." Vivie's tone was a whisper, serious and unsettling. "They found her body near the river."

"No!"

"She's dead."

It was impossible to even imagine. Patricia was a mother to three small children. Clara couldn't begin to fathom what her family must be going through. "What happened? Did she fall in and drown?"

"It would be better than the alternative."

The alternative? The prickle of unease intensified, skittering across the back of her neck once again. "You can't possibly mean someone did this to her?"

Vivie chewed at her bottom lip and bent her head. "They don't think she fell in. And worse, they've taken Mr. Nowak to the police station for questioning—again."

For a moment, all Clara could do was stare at her friend. But as she did she pictured Patricia holding hands and laughing with her children as they walked down the sidewalk in front of the hotel. She brought them by occasionally, and it was clear the tots adored their mother. Pain sliced Clara's heart. How would those children ever begin to pick up the pieces of their now broken lives?

Finally, she blinked and cleared her throat. "I'm sure there's been a mistake, Vivie." Though in truth, could she really be sure of anything? It seemed unfathomable that someone could mortally wound another person. But she'd witnessed a man point a gun and shoot President McKinley. So to think Mr. Nowak might have killed Patricia for some unexplainable reason was no longer improbable. Still, she had to try and reassure her friend. "I'm sure he'll be released any minute."

A high pitched creaking caught her ear and she looked up, certain Mr. Nowak was coming through the door. She even turned and opened her mouth to greet him. But the words died in her throat.

James.

He filled the doorway, and his presence should have been warming. Instead, his eyes glinted with some unnamed emotion, and Clara could picture wisps of cold air swirling about him.

"James."

Instead of greeting her, he remained stone-faced and tilted his head toward the door.

Clara ignored it. She wasn't sure why he was being rude, but she wasn't about to indulge him.

"James," she repeated, keeping her tone steady. "This is my friend, Vivie."

Wide-eyed, Vivie cast a questioning glance toward Clara before turning to James with a smile. "I don't know where Clara has been hiding you, but it's so lovely to meet you, James."

"Pleased to meet you as well, Vivie." Though his greeting might sound warm to most, and hopefully it did to Vivie, Clara knew it was forced. But she knew now that he wasn't being intentionally rude. Something was very wrong. His next statement proved it. "Forgive my bad manners, Vivie. Clara, I'm sorry. We need to go."

"But what—"

"Now. We need to go now." In spite of his abruptness, she sensed urgency. Could this have something to do with the photographs? Or maybe Patricia?

"Bye, Vivie. I'll see you soon." She drew her friend close in a quick hug. "Everything will be all right," she whispered before following James to the door.

"Do you want me to give Mr. Nowak a message when he returns?"

She knew Vivie was really asking if Clara would be returning to work. She shared a quick glance with James. Uncertain of its meaning, she hesitated. "No. Thank you, though. I—just tell him I won't be able to come back. Please give him my apologies for not letting him know sooner."

James pulled her out the door before she could say more.

"I'll see you soon," she called over her shoulder as he bustled her along.

It was obvious James had some serious misgivings about her coming back here. And though she wouldn't change her actions based solely on what one person thought, James *was* a police officer and possessed instincts she didn't. These last few days with him had shown her she could trust him—even if it happened to be something she didn't understand.

"Really, James, I can tell there's something wrong, but are you certain it was necessary to pull me away before I could finish my conversation with Vivie?"

"Quite certain."

"What is it?"

"We'll discuss it soon. But we need to go somewhere we can speak privately."

"But why? Does this have to do with the arrests the other night?"

"We'll talk about it. Please, Clara. Come with me."

He tugged her by the hand, and his footsteps were so quick she had to run to keep up with him.

"James, I can't walk that fast."

"I'm sorry." He slowed his steps, and Clara only had to partly run. But she'd heard all she needed to in order to prove her hunch was right.

They'd walked almost two blocks with nothing but the sound of Clara's heels striking the hard-packed dirt and scraping an occasional pebble to break the silence. Unable to keep quiet any longer, James reached for Clara's hand and pulled her to a stop. A sweeping glance of the area assured him they were alone. "Listen, Clara. We need a place where we can talk privately."

"The Martins—"

"I don't think you should go back there tonight."

Surprised when she didn't argue, James held tight to her hand as she tugged him forward.

"My church is just around the corner. We can sit on the bench outside, or we can go inside."

"That will be good." James nodded. What kind of church was it? Perhaps it was someplace where she could take refuge. Didn't some churches do that?

When they approached the small building, James breathed a little easier. Two trees shaded one side like an umbrella. A small wooden bench sat between the trees. Golden-brown leaves danced across the ground. The bench was nicely shielded from the view of anyone walking down the street. Still he wouldn't feel better until Clara was safely away.

"Okay, James. Tell me what's wrong? You're scaring me."

The moment was so brief James had to wonder if he imagined the split second where anguish flashed across Clara's face. Surely he had. But he also knew Clara struggled constantly to keep up a front of strength and determination.

He couldn't meet her eyes. What would she think of him? After she let her guilty feelings take hold of her, she'd given him the pictures—to do the right thing. And he'd taken it upon himself to undermine that moment.

"I didn't give my captain the pictures of Czolgosz."

"James." Clara's tone was low, brimming with disbelief. "Go get them. You have to give them to him. You can't wait. Please don't wait."

They matched each other stare for stare. Then, surprising himself, James shook his head. "You don't understand, Clara. They've been arresting people just for being in Czolgosz's vicinity."

She expelled a breath. "I know. That's what Vivie and I were talking about before you came in."

"There's something else you need to know."

Pressing her lips together, Clara tilted her head in disgust. "I'm sure I already do. He was taken back to the police station to be questioned for the murder of a young mother who worked with me at the hotel."

"I know. I just learned about it. I'm really sorry, Clara." He reached out to catch her hand in his, and she clasped it tight. The look in her eyes told him how much she needed his reassurance.

"I appreciate that, James." Clara lowered her voice to an anguished whisper. "I hope the police—*you*—find whoever did this to her."

"I will." James pulled her close, and when she pressed her face to his chest, he brushed his cheek atop her head, not caring that her hat was stiff and scratched against his face. Because with that simple action his heart was flooded with strength, protectiveness, and something just a little bit more. He breathed a prayer that he wouldn't let her down. "I've been assigned to lead the investigation. I'll do the best I can to find the killer." *Even if it's Nowak.*

"Thank you, James." She looked up at him, eyes wide. "Your captain assigned it to you. That means he trusts you again."

Fairly certain of what she'd say next, James sighed.

"You need to make sure there's nothing standing between you and that trust. I can't let you protect me to the point of losing your job."

He tightened his hold on her and breathed in the scent of the fresh clean soap that perfumed her skin. It reminded him of the sprig of lavender he'd given her on their picnic. Her stubbornness, her eagerness to do the right thing, was one of the things that drew him to her. "The photos—if I turn them in—won't prove your innocence. If one didn't know you, they could very well decide you're part of Czolgosz's conspiracy."

"James, I'm innocent. Besides, God will protect me."

Though he wanted to contradict her, he kept silent. She looked up at him and he was lost. Her facial expression reflected a woman who'd been battered by life and come out strong. Who was he to say God *wouldn't* protect her? Besides, he had enough respect for the religious beliefs of others; he wouldn't say anything to cause her to doubt her own statement of faith.

"We have to find a safe place for you first. Just until I have everything sorted out."

The tough mask faded from her face and her expression softened. "Thank you for wanting to protect me. But I don't have anywhere to go."

Though he wanted to press her about her father, he didn't. He would just go with his next choice and pray it was a good one. "I might have a solution."

"So do I. I'll go with you to turn in the photos."

"No." Just the thought of her at the precinct had anxiety twisting his insides.

"But James, I'm innocent. I'll explain the situation to them. Everything will be all right. You have to believe me. God will keep me safe."

"If that's true, then why were you attacked? Why is your friend dead?"

"Because someone acted with evil intent. But as you can clearly see, *God* used *you* to protect me."

"Yeah, I was real successful." She was safe, but they'd both ended up with bruises. James looked away. Did she really believe God used him to protect her? "If you think that's the way He plans to keep you from harm—" He shook his head. "It won't work."

"That's just it. We don't know how—we just have to trust that He will."

For a moment, he had the urge to look heavenward and utter a prayer. He wanted to trust, he really did. But where Clara's safety was concerned, he wasn't certain that he could.

James sounded doubtful, and Clara wanted so desperately for him to put his faith in God. She wasn't willing to let him put his job on the line to keep her from being arrested—which was certain to happen once his captain saw the pictures.

"I can't have you losing your job over me, James. You barely know me."

If only she hadn't chosen that moment to notice his eyes. The expression reflected in their brown depths was one of hurt. Had she done that? He was the last person she wanted to hurt. "I'm sorry. I didn't mean that the way it sounded. It's just—" What should she say? She thought he cared beyond the job, but what if she was wrong? She felt like they'd grown close over the last few days. What if she told him she wanted to spend more time with him, wanted to get to know him more? Would she scare him away?

"Clara, once those pictures are turned in, you'll find yourself in a jail cell and there won't be a thing I can do to protect you."

It warmed her heart to know he wanted to protect her.

"You won't need to. I have the truth on my side. And the truth will eventually be known."

"Do you even realize innocent people go to jail, too?"

"Of course I do. And I'd be lying if I said I wasn't scared. But I also know that lying to protect myself is the wrong thing. God won't honor that. But He *will* honor me if I tell the truth. So if you don't take the photographs to your captain, I will."

"How did you get to be so stubborn, Clara Lambert? You know I'm not happy about this at all." His gaze was tender as he searched her face, and her eyes. She could see how deeply torn he was, and her heart went out to him.

"I know, James. But it's the right thing. You'll see."

Lips pressed into a line, he gave a slight shake of his head.

"I hope you're right. I really do."

"I am." Did she sound more sincere than she felt? She hoped so. Not that she didn't trust God to see her through. But she was certain she really would have to go to jail before God worked things out. Did that indicate a lack of faith? Was it a contradiction? She wasn't really sure, but she didn't think it was.

A slight tug on her fingers drew her attention as James clasped her hands in his. At the same time, a lilting whistle drifted down from the tree above her. She recognized the sweet birdsong and tried to focus on the branches until she spotted the red cardinal whose beak was parted in time with the precious trills.

"You amaze me, Clara. Do you know that?"

"I do?" Clara looked down at their clasped hands. As she did, James tightened his hold.

"I'm praying the pictures won't be an issue. But if they are, I'll do everything I can to make Captain Green see you're innocent. And then I'll bring you home."

At his words, Clara's heart warmed. Did he even realize he'd said he was praying? Had he meant it, or was it simply a figure of speech he repeated like others so often did? Platitudes didn't fit James. She was positive he was sincere.

And what about his statement to bring her home? Where would she go? And would he still be in her life then?

Finally, after a long silence, James spoke. "I know you said you won't consider going to your father's. Are you sure you won't change your mind?"

If only she could. But it was impossible. "I can't, James. I just can't."

"Not even if it means your own safety?"

Her heart plunged and she blinked several times. "Not even then."

Her father, she knew, would protect her in a heartbeat. And she longed to see him. But she wasn't ready to put aside the fact that he wasn't there when her mother lay dying, calling out for him even as she took her last few painful breaths. Was the pursuit of money really worth not being there when your family, when the wife you vowed to love forever, needed you most?

She bit her lip and shook her head. "I can't. I just can't." She freed her hands from his and fussed around in her camera bag until she withdrew a clean embroidered handkerchief. She used it to dab at her eyes, and then, discreetly, her nose.

"Remember I said I might have a solution?" James reached for her hands again, and she relished the secure sense it gave her. "I think it will work. Please hear me out before you say no."

Unable to help herself, but certain she'd say no, she nodded.

"My sister, Janine—no one at the police department knows about her."

"Really? But your father was an officer. Surely they know about your family?"

"Those who are still around, maybe. But she left her husband several years ago. He used to hurt her. And after her daughter was born, Janine left him in order to protect the baby from his abusive ways. She's been living in New York City. He finally gave up looking for her and actually remarried."

"How did he do that? Surely that can't be legal?"

"It's most definitely not legal. Not until enough years have passed to declare abandonment. But a man who beats his wife doesn't care about the law. And I'm just thankful he doesn't know where she is."

"And the new wife? Does she know about your sister?"

"I think she does. My mother always thought he was seeing her before Janine left."

"So this woman knew he was hurting your sister?"

"I'm positive of it."

Clara felt sick at the thought of a woman walking willfully into an adulterous relationship with a man whose temperament was volatile. What made the woman think he wouldn't do the same to her?

"At least your sister and her baby are away from him."

"That's so true. And I want you to be somewhere safe, too. Away from my police captain, who might not believe you're innocent, and away from the person who killed Patricia. Please, will you consider going to stay with her?"

How could she say no and cause him further worry? For surely he would worry. She could see it etched in his face. But at the same time, she didn't want to be responsible for causing him trouble at work. He'd suffered enough where his job was concerned. Her heart went out to him.

"Could I have the afternoon to think about it? While I take pictures at the fair?" She smiled up at him in spite of her sadness.

He reached out and stroked her cheek, then rubbed his thumb along the corner of her eye, catching a tear she hadn't realized was still there.

Then he drew close and tilted her face up toward his.

"You'll really consider it?"

"For you, James, yes. I'll consider it. I promise."

"Thank you, Clara. I can't focus on getting the captain to see that these pictures are totally innocent if I'm worried about you. Especially now with your friend's murder and while your boss is sitting in a jail cell waiting for me to question him."

"He didn't kill her. I know he didn't."

"I believe you." His tone was as soft as the look in his shiny brown eyes. He brought his face closer until their lips met with a gentle softness that felt so natural, so right.

When they drew apart he gazed at her a moment more, his eyes searching hers. "James, I—" What? *I love you?* How could she say that to him when she'd only known him a few short days? She'd had beaus before and never, ever had one made her even think about declaring her love. But there was something about James, something that made her heart warm as it spiraled in her chest. Was that love? Was it a hint of what her heart might eventually feel if her feelings deepened to love? Although she suspected her heart had already turned in that direction. And what about James? What did he feel?

Before she could ponder it further, he drew her into another kiss. This time deeper, more tenderly, and, as his fingers brushed at the curls that had escaped the confines of her hat, her heart lifted even higher than she thought possible. Finally, when they broke apart, he said, "I'll walk you to the fairgrounds so you can take your pictures. I intend to stay at your side. Then, before I go back to the precinct, I'll put you on the train to New York."

"I said I'd consider it. You're making plans as if I'd already agreed to go there. And if I do agree, don't you think you should give your sister some warning first?"

"You'll agree. I know you will. As for Janine, I'll send her a telegram, letting her know of your arrival."

"Does she have access to a telephone?" Even as she said it, she realized he'd take it as a victory.

"No, she doesn't. It's for her own protection. You know things said over the telephone can be heard by the switchboard operators. Not that I'm saying the operators aren't honest. I just can't be too careful where my sister is concerned." His brow furrowed as he glanced at her. "And we can't be too careful where you're concerned, either. I do wish I could accompany you."

"Me, too." Even though she'd yet to agree to go, there was nothing about traveling alone that appealed to her—especially since the man who'd attacked her was out there somewhere. Just because they hadn't seen him since they left for Rochester, it didn't mean he wasn't around.

"I doubt he'll come after you again."

"How did you know—"

Before he answered, he dropped a kiss on her forehead. "Your eyes, Clara. Your most beautiful, expressive eyes. They give your thoughts away."

He thought her eyes were beautiful? Her pulse quickened. "What makes you think he won't come after me again?"

"The pictures are developed. And as far as anyone knows, they've all been turned in to the police."

"But he won't know that."

James raised his eyebrows. "He'll know. Men like him—they have a way of finding things out. They always seem to know the right people to ask, *and* they ask the right questions."

A shiver raced through her. She prayed he was right and the man was out of her life for good.

CHAPTER 17

Clara and James walked along the banks of the river on their way to the fairgrounds, and she couldn't help but point out half-a-dozen people on bicycles. "I do hope you'll think about getting one, James."

"Once I make sure your photographs aren't going to make you an anarchy suspect and I get you back home from my sister's, I might just consider it."

Though she nodded, it was more a gesture of kindness rather than agreement. Clara had no intention of arguing with James, or of making him worry.

"There's one other thing I've been meaning to ask you, Clara."

There was a smile in his voice, if that was possible. Leastwise, he sounded more cheerful than he had since their bicycle ride.

"When it's safe to bring you home, and I come to New York to get you, what would you think about watching the New York Giants take on the Boston Beaneaters?"

They were words that sent excitement surging through her. Just the thought that James might want to attend a baseball game—the thought of attending one with him—made funny things happen to her heart. And then the reality crashed straight through the excitement like raindrops on a birthday cake.

She wasn't going to New York, so it would never happen. And while she'd like to think that there would be other baseball games they could attend together, James might not forgive her for allowing him to think she would go along with his plan.

There was no chance she would let him put his career on the line for her. None. She could only hope that when tomorrow came she'd be able to face the unknown with courage, knowing full well that God would see her through. Because she wasn't about to hide. That would make her seem guilty, and it would make James appear as an accomplice. She was touched by his intent, but she simply couldn't go along with it.

A sweaty man in a uniform similar to James's came running up to them before she could give him an answer about the baseball game.

"There you are, Brinton. I've been looking everywhere for you."

"Bales." James spoke the name with derision, and as Clara looked at the man, she could see why. Something about his eyes—they were cold as the Niagara River on a winter's day. Maybe even colder. Though she didn't know him, Clara had the strong sense she wouldn't like him.

"The captain needs to speak with you right away. You need to get back to the precinct."

When James glanced at Clara, she could see the concern pinching his face. "You go ahead, James. I'll be all right."

"Now, Brinton."

The other officer spoke in an ominous tone. But if he thought he could snap his fingers and James would jump, it didn't happen.

"I'm sure it can wait, Bales. I still have a couple of hours before my shift, and I told the captain I had to take care of something."

Bales was average in height, with brown hair and brown eyes— like James—once again proving there were a lot of men who fit that vague description. Clara knew Bales wasn't tall enough or thin enough to have been her attacker. Which was good, because the ice in his eyes assured her that he would have finished the job and walked away without a backward glance.

"The captain will be interested in knowing just what it is you had to take care of." Bales gave Clara a wink as he looked her over. She had an unmistakable urge to slap him.

Curling her fingers into her palm, she turned to James. "Please, James?" She leaned closer so she could whisper without the other man hearing. "I don't want you to get into trouble. Please go."

"I'll be back as soon as I can. Promise me you'll stay here?"

"I promise. I'm just going to walk around taking pictures. And maybe I'll stop in at the Japanese tea garden for a little while."

James left with her assurance she wouldn't wander off the perimeter. As Clara watched him disappear with Bales, she had a strong sense of unease.

Still, she shook it off and wandered around the fairgrounds with her camera. She noticed some of the luster seemed to have worn off. In spite of her promotion, there didn't seem to be a bright spot in her day, no hope or anticipation. It was the aftermath of the shooting, she knew. This was the first time she'd been back here since that awful afternoon.

Thankfully the president was on the mend.

It would have been so hard for people to run joyfully through the fairgrounds, to explore different cultures with anticipation, if the darkness of anarchy hovered at the edge.

In spite of her obligation to Mr. Eastman, news of the president's recovery was the only reason she could walk around the Exposition taking pictures. If President McKinley was anything less than recovering, the thought of enjoying herself at the fairground would be disgraceful as well as disgusting.

Still, it was hard to be here in the place where it happened. Feeling suddenly uncomfortable, Clara looked over her shoulder. No one was behind her, yet she felt as if someone were tracking her every move. Hopefully James would be back soon.

Odd though it may seem since she'd really only spent a few short days in his company, she couldn't imagine another day passing without him in it. Her mother had always believed in the love-at-first-sight cliché. Clara never had, and had in fact never listened when her mother espoused that nonsense. Well, maybe she had when she was younger, before the reality of her father forsaking his promise of *"in sickness and in health."*

The cliché hadn't done her mother any good at all. But in spite of that, something inside Clara ached for love-at-first-sight to be truth.

A memory of her mother filled her mind—she was laughing as they sipped tea and ate cookies. Clara ached for her mother, missed her so very much.

What would her mother have thought of James? This time another memory danced in her mind. James, laughter sparkling in his eyes as he pedaled a bicycle with wobbly tires—continuing to smile in spite of the possibility that he was about to crash.

Clara's heart missed a beat as she remembered their picnic—and their kiss. "Hey, lady." A child's shout drew her into the present. "Can you take our picture?"

Turning, Clara smiled and lifted her camera as she headed toward a little girl with a head full of red-gold curls. The girl held tight to a woman's hand, gazing up at her with a look of admiration. Clara remembered looking up at her own mother that way.

When she reached them, Clara drew a small manila card from the silver case she kept in her camera bag for this exact occasion and handed it to the woman.

"If you don't mind filling this out, we'll be sure to have the photograph delivered to you after it's been printed."

When the woman returned the card, Clara numbered it in the corner in order to ensure they would receive the correct photo then tucked it back in the bag. As she did, the other *numbered* photographs came to mind—unwelcome though they were.

"Gracie, honey, smile so your daddy can see your new front teeth." Gracie's mother tickled the girl's ribs to get the desired effect then bent to pose with her cheek against her daughter's curls. Clara pressed the button on the camera, listening for the now familiar sound of gears.

"Thank you so much," the woman said. "Her daddy's somewhere in Washington, at a place called Fort Casey, guarding the Puget Sound."

The Puget Sound? She wasn't sure she'd ever heard of it. "Is he in the army?"

Gracie's mother nodded. "He hasn't seen her in almost a year. I sure thank you for this. He'll be delighted to receive a picture."

Clara smiled. "It's my pleasure."

Standing right in front of her was the perfect customer for Mr. Eastman's camera. She completely fulfilled his vision of a woman recording her family's memories for future generations.

"The camera is simple to use." Clara held it out to her. "Would you like to try it? You can take a picture of your daughter yourself, and I'll make sure you receive it as well."

"Oh, no, I couldn't." Gracie's mother shook her head. "I don't want to break it."

"You won't. I promise. Just point this"—she indicated the lens—"at your daughter, and then when she's posed the way you like, press this button." She handed the camera over to Gracie's mother.

The woman practically beamed. "Hold still, Gracie. Mommy's going to take your picture."

After they walked away, Clara reminded herself to notate two photos on the card. Mr. Eastman wouldn't mind, and he'd be especially pleased if he sold a camera as a result.

For the next couple of hours, she walked the grounds of the fair taking photos for women and their children. She demonstrated the camera for happy people who seemed unaware of the circumstances that occurred here just a few days ago. But she was aware—just as she was aware that James hadn't returned and it was well past the time for him to start his scheduled shift.

Should she take that to mean he wasn't coming?

No.

James was a man of his word. He said he'd be here, and Clara trusted him.

"Were you with the Lambert woman when she went to Rochester?"

James had barely stepped through the doors of the precinct when Bales started questioning him.

"I was, yes."

"Did you run into any issues?"

"Such as…?" He wasn't about to volunteer any information. He'd never trusted the man.

"You know, any attempts on her life? Like the night of the shooting?"

"She—no. And how did you know about that?"

Bales blinked, his features flat and emotionless. But James could see right through him, and knew exactly what this little side conversation was about.

Leaning back, James tilted his head and eyed Bales in a way he hoped would make the man uncomfortable. He was aware of the captain's scrutiny throughout the entire exchange and hoped the man wouldn't interfere.

"Bales?" He dropped his tone and kept it steady, measured. And, he hoped, threatening. "How did you know about the attack on Miss Lambert?"

While Bales squirmed every which way, James was careful to retain his composure.

"I—" He swiveled to look at Captain Green. "He told me. The captain."

With a quick glance to James, the captain opened his mouth. But before he could speak, Bales hurried on. "I overheard you talking about it, sir."

"Lying isn't a very good trait in a police officer, Bales." James wished he could recall the words, but it was too late.

"You should know, Brinton. You should know."

He didn't defend himself. It would serve no purpose. And he wasn't about to engage in a schoolyard game of one-upmanship. James knew the truth and, he acknowledged, God knew the truth. He hadn't lied, but he had deceived—and his parents had paid the price.

"By the way," Bales said, dropping his voice to a smug tone that was too subtle for most of the men in the room to pick up on it. James did, and he pressed his lips together, waiting to see what Bales would say next. "Where are the rest of the pictures?"

James tensed. "What are you talking about? What pictures?" How could Bales possibly know about the other pictures?

He stepped toward Bales and the table where the captain had left the photographs.

"See here?" Bales pointed at the tiny numbers scrawled in the bottom left corner. James pretended to peer closer. Of all people, he couldn't believe Bales noticed.

"I'm sure this means nothing. It could be an identification that only means something to Mr. Eastman's company."

It sounded weak, even to his own ears. Still, he tried to appear nonchalant, as if nothing was wrong. The captain's sharp gaze burned into him as he struggled to keep from making eye contact.

"Brinton?" Low and deep, the captain's tone demanded he make eye contact.

"Sir?"

"Is there something you neglected to tell me?"

How did he answer? The last thing he wanted to do was incriminate Clara. She was innocent, but he knew exactly how the captain would interpret it. It would be worse with Bales's input. The only chance he had to keep the captain from hauling Clara in for interrogation was to speak to him in private and try to explain the situation to him.

"Sir, may I speak to you privately?"

The captain didn't speak. But he did walk out of the room. Before James followed, he turned to Bales.

"This is between the captain and me, Bales. Stay out of it."

Bales only smirked. Rather than give in to the urge to throw a swift jab to the man's upper jaw, James walked out of the room. By the time he made it to the captain's office, his boss was seated behind his desk. He glared at the door, a dark stern glare meant to intimidate. James, however, simply walked in, shut the door, and sat down. He knew better than to ask permission—the captain would eat him alive. He didn't like weakness. Nor did he like groveling. But if that's what it would take to protect Clara, then that's what he would do.

"You know I took a big risk bringing you back, Brinton."

"Yes, sir."

"Did you know pictures were missing?" The captain stared him down and he tried not to react.

"Yes, sir, I—"

"A simple yes will do. I don't need any explanations."

"Yes, I know, but the pictures were taken before McKinley ever arrived at the fair. They were taken by Cl—Miss Lambert—when she first started using the camera. They were practice shots, nothing more."

"If they're nothing more, then why aren't they here?"

The captain slammed his fist on the desk, and the lamp rattled. It was an intimidation tactic, James knew. Nothing more. And one the captain was well known for. Were the roles reversed, James wouldn't use that method. All it really accomplished was to make the person on the opposite side of the desk angry.

"Because they belong to Miss Lambert, and she wanted to keep them."

"She *wanted* to *keep* them? What kind of officer are you? You don't let a suspect keep evidence."

Suspect? This was going from bad to worse.

"I didn't know Miss Lambert was a suspect, sir. On what grounds? All she did was take photos at the fair. Photos that ended up getting her attacked."

"On the grounds that she didn't give you all the photos."

What could he do to stop the bleeding? James stifled a groan.

"It wasn't that she wouldn't give them to me. She tried. I didn't think they were pertinent to the investigation."

"Then that makes *you* a suspect as well. Or an imbecile. I'm not sure which is worse."

The attention was on him now. At least it was deflected off Clara.

"Now I want you to get out of here and go get those pictures. Either that or I'll have both of you arrested. Do I make myself clear?"

He'd rather go to jail than have them think Clara was involved with Czolgosz. But not Clara. She couldn't go to jail. Things kept getting deeper, with no one to blame but himself for making them worse. He was an abject failure at being a police officer. Probably at being a man, too, since he seemed unable to protect Clara.

"Now, Brinton." The captain brought his hand down on the desk again, and James flinched. "If you don't go get them this instant, I'll send Bales after them."

Not about to let Bales anywhere near Clara, James stood and nodded. He couldn't bring himself to answer. The image of Clara in jail nearly brought him to his knees. He couldn't let that happen. He had to figure out a way.

CHAPTER 18

"The president's taken a turn for the worse."

Clara overheard the horrible words while she sat on a wooden bench sipping a cold bottle of Coca-Cola. She held the drink in her mouth, unable to swallow for a moment for fear she might choke. The sweet flavor overwhelmed her, angered her even. How could she possibly be sitting here enjoying the fizzy beverage while President McKinley was fighting for his life?

She stood and began walking. Slowly at first, but in mere moments she broke into a run. Before long she stood staring up at the large dome that covered the Temple of Music.

Organ music wafted through one of the open windows, hitting a sour note as it did. Had it really only been a few days since she was here?

It seemed like a lifetime ago that the president had smiled at her as he shook her hand. Her pulse quickened and her chest constricted as she recalled the look on his face the moment he realized he'd been shot. She remembered his concern for both his wife and for Leon Czolgosz. President McKinley was a sweet and generous man. The salty sting of tears felt gritty to her eyes and she blinked rapidly. She forced herself to breathe in deep, slow, steadying breaths.

How was Mrs. McKinley coping? Clara could only imagine her concern, her fear. Were the president and his wife believers? She read somewhere that they were. And when the president gave his speech the day before the shooting, he'd knelt before an altar. She remembered that quite specifically, and she hadn't photographed it. The moment the president kneeled down and closed his eyes was too heartfelt, too real. To photograph him then would have been like intruding on a person in one of their most private moments.

"Please, God," she whispered. "Please heal him. Let him be all right. And please give comfort to his wife."

A shadow fell across the ground at her feet. Startled, Clara jumped. Then she turned to run. She wasn't about to let that man catch her again.

"Clara, it's me."

James. Relieved, she stopped and slowly turned. Her cheeks burned. "James. I'm sorry. For a minute I thought—" She broke off, feeling foolish.

"Hey. It's all right." He furrowed his brow. His dark eyes searched hers. "There aren't many people over this way. Why are you here by yourself?"

"I wanted to get away from the crowd and the noise for a few minutes so I could think." She clasped and unclasped her hands.

"Did something happen?"

"You haven't heard?" She thought for sure he'd have been one of the first to hear. She opened her mouth. Then, unable to speak, closed it again. She bit her lip.

"Clara?"

"I came here to pray. It's the president," she said finally. "I heard someone say he's taken a turn for the worse."

His whole demeanor seemed to crumble. "I hadn't heard. I thought he was making improvements every day."

"I know. I can't bear to think of what his wife is suffering."

When James held out his arms, Clara didn't even hesitate. She carefully let her camera slide to the soft grass. She stepped forward and his arms closed around her, enveloping her in a rush of strong warmth. Resting her head against his chest, she could hear the thrumming of his heart as it vibrated against her ear.

"Hopefully we'll hear something positive before long."

"I hope so. It feels like it's happening all over again."

"I'm sorry I took so long."

"It's all right." But even as she spoke the words she saw the grim lines flattening his mouth. Something else had happened. And it obviously wasn't good. "James, what is it?"

"They figured out there were photographs missing."

Her heart stuttered. There was no way around it now. Once they saw the pictures it would be hard to convince them she didn't know Czolgosz. She nodded once, not daring to raise her head lest James see disappointment in her eyes. "Let me just get my things and we can take the pictures to your captain."

She started to turn, but James pulled her back. Before she could even react she found herself in his arms, his lips pressing against hers. Closing her eyes, she let the dizzying sensation overtake her.

In spite of the dire circumstances, it felt to Clara as if she'd found her way home.

Moments later, when they drew apart, panic began to claw at Clara's throat, and even looking into James's liquid brown eyes couldn't calm her. She was about to go to jail.

"Let's get this over with." She bent down to pick up her camera, but it was gone.

"How could someone get that close to us without us even noticing?" Nothing rendered James quite as helpless as the sight of Clara's wide green eyes filled with tears. She'd been so brave through all of this. And now to see her crying—it ripped at his heart.

What kind of officer was he, that he hadn't been aware enough to realize someone had come so near to them?

"Gracie!"

James looked at Clara, puzzled. Her eyes glistened and she said the name again.

"For Gracie, James. We have to find it for Gracie."

"Who is Gracie?"

"She's a little girl whose daddy is gone. She wants to show him her new front teeth. We have to find the camera."

When she looked up at him like that, he found himself promising what might well be the impossible. "I'll find it, Clara."

What kind of husband would he ever be? What kind of father? He couldn't protect a rock. He couldn't protect his parents, and clearly he hadn't learned a thing from it. He looked at Clara and his heart sank. He'd let her down.

He didn't deserve to court her.

The thought surprised him, though it shouldn't. He supposed it had been in his subconscious for a while—maybe even since they shared the aerio-cycle when she was being chased by the fake secret service agent.

No.

If he was honest, it would be the moment he first set eyes on her. Eager. Hopeful. Watching for the president. Hoping for a great photograph of McKinley shaking hands with someone. Her expression tugged him and she sparked his interest—he just hadn't realized it yet.

"Why don't we split up?"

"To what purpose?" James tipped his head toward her, eyebrow raised. Surely she didn't think it was a good idea for them to be separated. What would she do if she encountered this man alone?

"We have a better chance since he could have gone any number of ways."

"No. Clara. We already have the pictures you took after the

shooting. There's nothing on that camera now that can't be replaced."

Her lip quivered in a way that had him longing to kiss her again.

"I know. But Gracie—" Her eyes glistened, bright with all the emotion that filled her tender heart.

"Film can be replaced." He pulled her to him and pressed a kiss to the top of her head "But you, Clara, you can't. Stay close to me, please?"

She looked torn, glancing one way and then the next before settling her gaze on him. Anxiety filled his chest. Finally, she nodded.

Then she held her hand out. He clasped it in his own. It nestled there. Small, warm, a perfect fit. He pulled her toward him and placed their clasped hands against his chest. Protectiveness flooded his being. "I think it would be best if I took you back to the Martins'. They can look out for you while I search for whoever did this."

"No. I—"

"I'll find him, Clara. I promise."

But would he really? Had he just lied to her?

CHAPTER 19

"Help!"

The shrill voice pierced his eardrum and James winced. As high pitched shrieking rent the air, Clara turned to James. "Go, hurry!"

For a split second, he hesitated. He didn't want to leave her. But the woman screamed again and he knew, as an officer of the law, he had no choice. As he ran, he whispered a prayer for God to watch over Clara.

A crowd had formed around the elderly woman by the time he approached. She clutched her chest. Her hat was askew and locks of silvery curls sprang from beneath it. A bright spot of pink stood in contrast with the stark white of her face.

"My handbag. He tore it from me. I tried to fight him, but he hit me in my face." Her voice faded to a near whisper. Tears sprang to her eyes. "I tried."

Beside him, James heard Clara gasp, and she hurried to the woman's side.

Warmth spread across his chest. In spite of the fact she needed to find her camera, she put compassion for this woman first and foremost.

"You go, James. Find her purse. I'll sit with her." Clara led the woman to one of the nearby benches, gently with her arm around her.

James took off in the direction the woman pointed, with witnesses calling the description of the woman's assailant.

It didn't take long before he spotted the youth on the Midway, trying to blend in with a crowd waiting in line for the same aeriocycle he'd ridden with Clara.

The foolish boy didn't even bother to hide the woman's white lacy bag.

"You there!" James reached out and grabbed the boy's arm before he could run off. "You're coming with me."

The boy's eyes widened in his face and his freckles popped out against his pale complexion.

"You have some explaining to do after we return the lady's purse."

"It weren't my idea, mister! The man—he gave me two whole dollars to take the lady's bag. My mother can pay her bill at the grocer with that two dollars. It's the only reason I done it. Honest."

James didn't answer, but he did loosen his grip on the boy's collar.

Empathy for the boy welled, and his mind churned through memories of his own parents struggling to put food on the table.

"Look, I can kind of understand why you might do what you can to earn some money. But you can't steal from other people to do it. And you sure can't hit them in the face."

"Are you going to put me in jail, mister?" The boy was looking up at him, eyes wide, brimming with tears.

Sure the boy was scared, and it tugged his heart. But it might do him some good to be scared. It might save him from a future spent in a small square room lined with iron bars.

"Unfortunately, son, it's not up to me. But if you return the lady's purse and apologize, I'll be sure to put in a good word."

"I will, mister. I will. I promise."

In spite of the sincerity James heard in the boy's tone, he didn't loosen his grip on the kid's shoulder. And as they drew close to the elderly woman and Clara, he saw that Clara stood with her arm around the woman's shoulder.

When the woman looked up James noticed the brightness of her cheek had darkened to an angry red welt. He pressed steely fingers into the boy's shoulder.

"Ow! Mister!"

James clenched his jaw as he spoke. "About that good word I promised you? I just changed my mind."

"I didn't mean to, mister. She wouldn't let go of the purse. I didn't know what else to do."

Though he didn't loosen his grip, James had to force himself not to tighten it. Much as he wanted to box the kid's ears, he couldn't trust himself not to do some serious damage.

"Get over there, now." None to gently, James pushed the boy toward the woman.

The boy stumbled but caught himself before he landed at Clara's feet. The woman looked up and her eyes widened.

"You!"

"I–I'm sorry, ma'am." Hand trembling, the boy held the white bag out to the woman.

She snatched it and immediately used it to smack him on the head.

Unable to help himself, James let out a laugh. He quickly reined himself in but still had to bite back a smile. Meanwhile Clara looked on, wide-eyed.

"Hey!" The boy glanced around, and his eyes filled with tears as he realized no one would be coming to his rescue.

"Clara."

Clara looked up and walked toward him.

"Did anyone bother you?"

She shook her head. "No, we were fine. But—" She stamped her foot, lips pressed together. He could tell she was irked. He had the urge to lean forward and kiss the sweetness back on to her face.

"Did you see what that—" Her face reddened and he had the

distinct impression she just stopped herself from saying something she found inappropriate.

He bit back a smile and raised one eyebrow. "Yes?"

"That boy!" She nodded over her shoulder. "Did you see what that boy did to Helen's face?"

"Helen, is it?"

"Why are you smiling?" When he didn't answer, she stamped her foot again. "James, I'm serious."

"I saw it. I could barely keep from doing the same back to him."

"I tried to talk her into letting me take her to the doctor, but she refused. Maybe you'll have better luck."

"He paid the boy to steal her purse."

"Who paid—" Her eyes widened. "The man who stole my camera?"

James nodded. "And now I need to get that young man to the station so I can question him."

"Helen doesn't want the boy arrested. She told me that as you were walking up with him. I tried to change her mind, but she refuses. Perhaps you can convince her."

James caught sight of Helen, her arms wrapped around the boy. "Something tells me that won't happen."

Clara turned to look over her shoulder. Her eyes reflected her disappointment as she glanced back up at him. "I'm sorry."

"For what?"

"You chased him down for nothing."

"Not for nothing." He studied her as she appeared to think over what he said. He could tell the moment she understood. Her eyes widened and a touch of that smile he'd looked for earlier made its appearance.

"He can give us a description!"

"I certainly hope so."

"What are we waiting for then? Let's get him to the precinct."

James nodded and turned back to Helen—who stood by herself, looking off into the distance as she watched the boy run off.

"Get back here," Clara shouted.

The boy didn't act like he even cared as he lifted his hand in a wave.

Unbelievably, Helen waved back.

James was so busy watching the boy disappear from sight, he forgot to look in front of him and nearly knocked Clara down as he smacked into her. He put his hands out to keep her from falling. "Clara, I'm so sorry."

"It's all right, James. I'm all right. Please get him. I'll stay here with Helen."

"Promise?" He was torn between leaving Clara and catching the boy who was the only link to the man after Clara. Leaving her for even a few minutes seemed risky, but it might be the only way he could ultimately keep her safe.

"I promise, James. I'll be right here when you return."

"I'm holding you to your word." James held her gaze, seeing she was sincere. He nodded to let her know he believed her and took off running.

Clara watched James chase after the boy. As he disappeared around a corner that led to the Midway, she knew it would be difficult for him to catch up to the little thief a second time. Still, she sent a prayer heavenward, asking for his success. Then she turned to Helen, who stood watching Clara.

"Why did you let him go?"

Helen dropped her hand and tipped her chin up. It was hard to miss the defiance in her stance. Clearly she'd underestimated the petite woman.

Helen was a woman used to getting her way.

"He didn't mean it, dear." The older woman pursed her lips and as she did, Clara noticed deep lines etched all around her mouth.

"How do you know?"

"Why, he apologized, of course."

"And you believed him?"

Helen's blue eyes flashed at her sharp tone. Clara held her hand up.

"I'm sorry, Helen. I just don't understand. He *hurt* you."

"Well…he said he didn't mean to hurt me." Helen sounded uncertain. "And he said he intended to bring my purse back as soon as the man was gone."

"How would he know when the man was gone? And how would he know you'd still be here?"

"I guess he—" Helen held her hand up, then dropped it to her side. Her expression fell. She closed her mouth, and then opened it again. "He lied. I know you think I'm just a gullible old woman. I believed him."

"Helen, you said yourself he didn't mean it. I'm sure you're a good judge of character." Clara hoped *she* sounded sincere. It wouldn't do for Helen to berate herself.

"No. No, I'm not. And I let the boy get away, and we don't even know why the man wanted him to steal my purse."

"Actually, we do."

"You do? Why?"

"Well, I don't know the exact reason, but I do know it was to distract James and me so he could get away with my camera."

"You're a photographer?" Helen sounded truly surprised. Clara nodded. She wanted to say more, but now wasn't the time for her photographer spiel.

"But why did he want your camera?"

"That's the part I don't know. I think I took a picture of something he didn't want me to see." Clara left out the part about Czolgosz. No need to cause Helen undo fear, thinking she'd been the target of someone involved in shooting the president.

"I hope you get it back, Clara. Really, I do." Helen reached out and clasped her hands. "And I'm sorry I let the boy go before your young man could question him."

Her young man? Clara quite liked the sound of that, though she wasn't sure how James would feel about it. How did she want him to feel about it? Just the thought made her face burn as if she spoke it aloud.

"And now, my dear, I really must be going."

"No, Helen, please don't leave. Wait until James gets back so we can see you safely home." Clara felt desperate to keep Helen there, so they could make sure she made it home without incident.

"I can see myself home, Clara, dear. Please don't worry about me." Helen patted her hand. "I promise. I'll be fine."

Clara felt an overwhelming sense of protectiveness for Helen. "I'll go with you, then. James will know where to find me."

"No, he won't. You need to wait here for him. He'll be expecting you to be here, not wherever else it is you think he'll eventually find you."

"I don't think he'd like it if you went alone. We don't know if the man is still somewhere nearby."

Helen shook her head, her fine white hair falling loose from under her hat to brush her cheeks. "I don't think he is. I think I was merely a decoy so he could get away." Helen was correct, of course.

Clara's heart sank. She opened her mouth and then closed it again. She couldn't argue. She studied the soft grass beneath her white ankle-high boots.

"Don't look so glum, Clara. Here." Helen dug into her bag and withdrew a small silver case, much like the one Clara used for her name cards.

And that only reminded her of Gracie and her mother.

"Hey." Helen chucked her under the chin. "You're going to give yourself wrinkles."

Clara gave her a half-hearted smile.

"Here's my address. You and James can drop by to check on me if that will keep you from worrying. I'll have a nice pot of tea waiting."

Not wanting to be any part of agreeing to Helen going off alone, Clara accepted the card but didn't nod in agreement.

"Really, if you accompany me now, your young officer will be worried. And you don't want to give him any more to worry about."

Finally, Clara nodded. She looked up and sighed as Helen started to walk away. "Be careful. We'll be there soon, Helen."

Just as soon as James returns with that little scoundrel.

Guilt settled over Clara as she watched Helen walk away. She promised James she'd keep watch over the elderly woman. She didn't keep her word. It hardly mattered that Helen was spry and sharp-witted. People half her age with twice her strength were mugged or taken advantage of every day. And besides, the man who wanted to misdirect James and Clara's attention could still be out there, intending full well to use Helen to his advantage again. She could hardly tell James that because Helen said she could take care of herself, Clara let her go.

No, that wasn't good enough. In fact, she could almost see the disappointment in James's brown eyes as she tried to explain.

Now she was just being silly. Her mother always did tell her she had an overactive imagination. The mugger was simply a distraction—he did his job. Helen wasn't in any further danger.

Still, the older woman had been shaken by the incident, and Clara felt compelled to see her home.

Hopefully James would understand if he arrived back here before she did.

Clara started walking the same direction Helen had. She strained to see her in the distance. If she hurried, she should be able to catch up with her.

But she found herself walking faster with each passing second until somewhere along the way, she realized that running wasn't enough to catch up with the spry woman. Helen had disappeared from sight.

Uncertain which way to go, Clara stopped to look at the card with Helen's address out of her pocket. She walked over to a nearby bench. Before she could sit down, she noticed something on the ground. At first she dismissed it as a piece of litter, but the she realized the paper had tiny writing that looked strangely familiar.

Heart pounding, she bent to pick it up and immediately recognized the writing. Gracie's mother—this was the card she'd filled out. At least a piece of it, anyway. Not enough to be able to find them. Her heart sank—again.

Could that mean her camera and bag were nearby?

A quick glance around told her it wasn't. Heart heavy, she looked down at Helen's card and started walking in the direction that would take her to Helen's house.

Still, she couldn't help but watch the ground as she walked, hoping she'd spot her camera. Or more pieces of the card that had Gracie's address.

The sights and smells of the fair faded away along with the music that played at the last bandstand she'd passed. The only thing she could hear were her thoughts and the only thing she noticed was the grass as she put one booted foot in front of the other.

Just when she was about to give up, she spotted something that made her heart fall.

A strip of something dark, like shiny paper, fluttered up against a boxwood. As Clara neared the shrub, her pulse pounded at the base of her throat. Tears pooled in her eyes as she reached for the piece of film.

Her film, she knew without question. Probably its dark depth obliterated the image of little Gracie and wide smile. She couldn't be unequivocally certain of course, but deep inside Clara knew. After all, how many other strips of film would be fluttering around the fairgrounds? It wasn't like there were scores of people walking around with cameras. And she knew it wasn't very likely that it had come from the photo booth on the Midway. Clara's camera was undoubtedly gone, and the film destroyed. And whether or not this torn piece of overexposed film would have been Gracie didn't really matter because Gracie's pictures and those of the other people she'd photographed were gone.

And how would she ever begin to tell Mr. Eastman about this?

She could bid farewell to her promotion.

When she contemplated each person and the way they'd smiled for her today, hope inspired her in spite of the fact her heart was breaking. She had a small piece of the card for Gracie. Thinking of Gracie and how much the little girl missed her father brought a sudden lump to her throat. She had to find the rest of that card and the cards of the others so she could track them down and redo their photos.

As she searched, an occasional scrap of film would turn up. Clara gathered each one—not that they would do any good as the film could no longer be processed. But it was the sentiment behind it. To not pick them up, to ignore or throw those bits of film in the rubbish bin would be like throwing away the people she'd photographed.

Pieces of the cards turned up as well, and she soon had both hands full. Eventually she even came across the winding spool. Swiping her eyes with the back of her hand, Clara shuffled through the cards. As she did, some of the film floated to the ground.

Just lovely. She needed to put these safely in her pocket before she lost them. She could look at them when she got back home.

Except she'd almost forgotten. She wouldn't be going home. She was going to jail.

CHAPTER 20

Panic rose when James returned to the garden and Clara and Helen were nowhere in sight. *Please, Lord, don't let anything have happened to her.*

They probably grew tired of waiting for him and went for a walk. Or more likely, Helen just decided to go home. The moment she let the boy go, James had pegged Helen as the strong-willed independent type. Clara, strong and independent in her own way, had a soft heart and would be no match for Helen once her mind was made up. Undoubtedly, Clara would feel obliged to see the woman safely home.

Since he didn't know which direction Helen lived, he decided it would be best to head back to the Martins and wait for Clara there. His pace was brisk, but not too fast to be observant in case the boy was somewhere nearby. The kid had too much of a head start, and James had been unable to catch up with him.

Halfway through the Garden of Lilies, he saw Clara standing at the edge of a row of boxwoods. Relieved, he started to call out to her. But something about the way she stood caused him to hold back.

Helen was nowhere to be seen.

James approached Clara slowly until he stood directly in front of her. He spoke her name gently, but she didn't look up. Instead, she stared down at her hands. She had something clenched in each one. Small bits of paper—cards maybe? And pieces of what looked kind of like film.

Slowly, he reached out and covered her hands with his own.

"Clara? Are you all right? Did you find your camera?"

He watched her carefully, expecting her to nod. But, still not looking up, she shook her head.

He reached out and gently touched her chin. When she looked up at him, tears shimmered in her eyes, and his heart clenched. He wished he could do something to ease her pain.

"Did you find the camera?"

"No." She swallowed hard. "Just a few of the cards and some of the film. It's ruined. He ripped it out of the camera. And then cut it up somehow."

Clara held her hand out, and James took a piece of the film. He studied the edges where it was cut. Angled instead of square, the hazy surface appeared as if it had been folded before it was cut.

"It shows you how little he knows about cameras. Once the film was exposed, it was ruined. He didn't need to cut it."

"I don't think he'll bother you again."

"Really?" Clara sounded hopeful.

He wished he felt the same. Just the fact that the man had a knife sent a chill through him. He studied the film again. This was the act of an angry person, and Clara should be aware of it. She deserved honesty from him. That was the best way for her to protect herself if he wasn't around.

Pressing his lips together, he shook his head. "I don't know, Clara. He has the camera. That's what he was after when he attacked you."

"But you don't think it's over." Clara stared at him, obviously waiting for his answer.

James took the rest of the film from her hands and stuffed the pieces in his pocket. Then he clasped her hands in his.

She met his gaze, and the corners of her mouth moved the

slightest bit. Not enough to be a smile, but he could tell she was trying. Something in the center of his chest softened.

"Hopefully he figures any evidence that could tie him to Czolgosz is destroyed and there's nothing more to worry about."

Clara squeezed his hands and then let go. "I hope you're right, James."

Closing his eyes, he breathed in as he nodded. He hoped so, too.

"James, I want to make sure Helen made it safely home. Will you go with me to check on her?" Clara nodded toward the east entrance. "We need to go this way. She lives on Pearl Street."

James was surprised Helen had given Clara her address. But he said nothing as he fell into step beside her. They walked side-by-side for about five minutes before he reached out and took her hand. Even though he knew it was impossible, he wished there was some way to protect her from ever being hurt again.

"So how did she get away from you?" He kept his tone light so she wouldn't think he was upset with her.

Clara smiled up at him. "She's determined."

"Yes, I think I realized that the instant she let the kid run off."

"She didn't want anything to happen to him in jail."

James thought about that for a moment. "I doubt the captain would put a kid that young in jail."

"And I wouldn't want him to. But I think it would be better for the boy to learn the consequences of his behavior now so he won't keep making the same mistakes."

"You're right about that." He'd arrested far too many young men, seen too many lives ruined. "I do hope the boy will learn from this and never does anything like this again."

"James, if we find him, I'd have some groceries delivered to his family. Or do you think that would be rewarding him for stealing?"

James thought back to his own childhood. How would he have seen such an act? As kindness? Or as a reward? "It's hard to say." He remembered long nights where his stomach ached from emptiness. "It's almost impossible to turn away from a family in need."

"I'm glad you feel that way." Her tone softened as she gazed up at him. He swallowed hard. "But how will we find him?"

"Your idea of having groceries delivered to him—perhaps we can check with nearby grocers. Someone may recognize his description. Especially with the mention of his family circumstances."

"Perfect." Clara beamed. "James, you're brilliant." Never letting go of his hand, she stood up on her tiptoes and kissed his cheek. "But let's check on Helen first. She invited us to tea."

"Oh." This surprised him. He'd never been invited to tea before. The breakfast with Mrs. Eastman was awkward enough. How did one act when invited to tea? "Should we bring her some little cakes or cookies, or whatever you ladies serve at tea?"

"Some flowers would be nice." Clara indicated a nearby flower vendor, and James stopped. He turned to Clara. "Would you like to pick them out?"

She pressed her lips together and shook her head. "A lady likes it when a gentleman picks out the flowers. I'm sure Helen is no exception."

Not the answer James hoped for since he knew next to nothing about flowers. Still, he acquiesced.

"So many choices." Picking out flowers had been so much easier when he was a boy running through a field picking dandelions for his mother. Lacing his fingers together behind his back, he walked the length of the vendor's stand, as if trying to choose between one or two different types of flowers.

After several agonizing moments, Clara mercifully came to his rescue and whispered in his ear. "The pink carnations would be nice."

This time he was the one to kiss her cheek. Only as he bent toward her, she turned and his lips caught hers. He felt more than heard her soft intake of breath, and he deepened the kiss. Did it affect her as much as it did him?

"Excuse me, sonny," he heard someone say. "Are you going to stand here all day, or are you buying these flowers?"

But it wasn't until Clara pushed him away that he realized the person was speaking to him.

Before James turned to the vendor, his gaze swept Clara's face. He was more than a little pleased to see the flush of her cheeks.

"More tea, dear?" Helen reached for the pot of tea, but Clara shook her head.

They were seated around a tiny table in Helen's sitting room. Next to her, James held one of the delicate teacups at an awkward angle. He was trying so hard to be proper, Clara felt obliged to rescue him.

"Thank you, Helen. But we'll have to be going soon." At the woman's crestfallen expression, Clara added, "Perhaps we can have tea again sometime."

Helen's face immediately brightened. "That would be lovely, dear." Then she turned to James. "Thank you for the beautiful carnations."

"You're welcome." James placed the cup on the table and stood before he gave Helen a smile that tugged at Clara's heart. Though she knew he was in a hurry to get her out of town, he was still kind to this elderly lady who was so obviously lonely.

"I'm sorry we have to leave so soon, Helen." Clara rose and went to stand next to James.

"I am too, dear." Helen hesitated as if debating her next words. Then she turned back to James. "Forgive a nosy old lady for asking, but where are you off to in such a hurry?"

"Clara has a train to catch. She—"

"Really?" Helen looked at Clara. "I love the train. Where are you going?"

"I—" Clara promptly closed her mouth. What could she say? She couldn't very well tell Helen James's plan for her. But neither could she lie.

"Clara's going to visit my sister for a few days."

Though she was relieved that James answered for her, Clara found she couldn't meet Helen's gaze.

"I see." Helen's tone grew cold, and it was obvious she didn't believe him. "I know something is wrong, dear. Perhaps I can help in some way."

James looked at Clara, clearly searching for a tactful way for them to leave without hurting Helen's feelings. Not knowing the answer and feeling helpless herself, Clara pressed her lips together and raised one shoulder. How was James going to answer this one?

"What are you two hiding?" Helen's sharp eyes clearly didn't miss a thing. "Does this have to do with the boy who took my purse?"

"No, not at all." The instant she spoke, Clara regretted not waiting for James to answer. Helen was quick to pin her focus in Clara's direction.

"Then what's wrong? You can trust me, Clara." The woman's bright blue stare didn't waver for a second. "Please let me help."

Uncertain what to say, Clara glanced at James. "Maybe she can help us."

He gave her a stern look, and her stomach clenched.

Feeling helpless, she pressed her lips together and turned back to Helen. She was caught somewhere between being rude, lying, and trusting Helen with the truth.

"James is trying to protect me." Perhaps if she gave her just a tiny bit of information, Helen would let it go.

"Protect you from what?" Helen's words came out sounding sharp, but Clara could hear the underlying concern. It was genuine, and she had the sudden overwhelming sense that they really could trust her.

"Clara." His tone was low, and it was clear he didn't want her to say anything more.

"We can trust her, James."

"I'm not saying we can't. It's just that we really shouldn't be speaking about this with anyone."

Helen watched them both with unwavering interest.

"If he doesn't get me out of town, he's going to have to arrest me."

Helen gasped. Clearly rattled, she picked up the teapot then set it down again. "Arrest you for what?"

James sighed and sat down. Relieved, Clara sat next to him and then turned to Helen. "His captain suspects I might be involved with the man who shot the president."

"How could he possibly think such a thing? You would never take up with someone like that." Though Helen's voice trembled as she spoke, she looked Clara in the eye. Clara knew her instinct to trust Helen had been the right one.

"There were some pictures in my camera when the film was processed. They're innocent, but they implicate me. James believes me, of course. But his captain isn't as certain. If James doesn't bring them the pictures, we'll both end up in jail." Clara swallowed hard as she looked at James. "For some reason, he's willing to ruin his career for me."

Helen's shrewd blue gaze went from Clara to James and back to Clara again. "I'm fairly certain I know the reason."

A flush crept over Clara's face and she grew still, not daring to turn in James's direction.

Next to her, James cleared his throat. "Hopefully the captain will realize the truth, but if he's the least suspicious of Clara, there won't be anyone who can talk him out of it."

"James wants me to go to his sister's until he can prove I'm not involved. But I'm afraid his sister could end up in danger."

"From the police?" Helen frowned, and her paper-thin skin creased into a dozen fine lines.

"No." Clara shook her head. "But if the police figure out where I'm at, they could lead the danger to her."

"Clara, no one knows where Janine is. Both of you will be perfectly safe, and I know she'd insist on helping you."

"Nonsense." Helen rose to her feet and stared at James. "There's no need for Clara to travel anywhere. No need to put your lovely sister in any kind of danger. Clara will stay here with me. I'll keep her hidden." She turned to Clara. "I insist, dear."

"Thank you, Helen, but I can't accept. The last thing I want to do is put you in danger as well."

"You won't. Unless someone followed you here, no one would ever think to look for you here."

Helen was right, of course. But Clara would never impose herself on this woman or anyone else.

Clara waited for James to explain to Helen all of the reasons why they couldn't accept. When he said nothing, she studied the highly polished wood floor beneath her feet. Then she studied the delicate flowers painted on the teapot and cups. Finally she heard him sigh. She braced herself for Helen's protests once he told her no.

"I think this could work."

"What?" Startled, Clara looked up at him.

"I think this could work," he repeated. Then he met her shocked look with a smile. "Think about it, Clara. This is a lot closer than New York City. When I'm not at work, I can keep an eye on things here."

"You mean in case the man who hired that boy to do his dirty work tries to come around?"

In spite of the seriousness of the situation, Clara couldn't help but laugh. "You don't miss a thing, do you, Helen?"

The woman pressed her lips together as if trying not to smile. "No. I don't."

Clara placed a hand over Helen's. "I just want you to know that if he finds me here you could be in more danger than just having your purse stolen. That would never have happened if not for me, and I don't want to be responsible for something happening that might be worse."

"Nonsense." Helen gripped her hand and gave her a stern look. "Things happen in this world, and what becomes of them is due in large part to how we respond. That young boy chose how he planned to respond. And unless he learns how to change his responses, he's in for a long and miserable life."

Almost exactly what Clara said to James earlier. She bit back a smile and then turned to him. "I still think it would be better if I went with you to the station and talked to your captain."

James swiped a hand over his face and sighed. "Under ordinary circumstances, I'd agree with you. But these aren't ordinary circumstances, and I just—I don't know if I can trust the captain to be reasonable."

"If you two will excuse me for a moment, I have some things to do in the other room." Helen hurried to make herself scarce. Clara couldn't believe they'd carried on like this in the woman's house. Shame filled her. What was she doing? It was bad enough that James was distressed, but now she'd gone and done the same thing to Helen. It had to end now. If saying she'd stay with Helen was the only way James would take those pictures to his captain then she had no choice but to agree. It would give them both peace of mind, although it meant she'd have to do a lot of praying for forgiveness.

"Clara—" James studied her face so intently, she didn't have the heart to make him wait a moment longer.

"I'll do it, James."

Clearly not expecting her response, he blinked. "You'll stay here?"

She couldn't meet his eyes as she nodded.

"Thank you." He pulled her hands into his.

"Don't thank me too quickly, James. I hope this works, but I'm positive your captain is going to order my arrest when he sees those photographs. And when I'm nowhere to be found, he'll accuse you of concealing evidence."

"If that happens, you'll be safe with Helen until I can make him understand what really happened."

She could only pray he was right.

CHAPTER 21

James hadn't been gone very long, but already Clara missed him in much the way she'd miss it if she could never have another taste of Coca-Cola—but deeper. And she was trying not to worry about him. Would his captain believe him? Or had he already dispatched an officer, maybe James himself, to come and arrest her?

Helen did her best to make Clara comfortable. In some ways, her graciousness and hospitality reminded Clara of her mother. She missed her terribly. And in truth, she missed her father as well. But that wasn't a longing she was willing to entertain. Her father was gone from her, just like her mother, in spite of the gifts he continuously sent her. Gifts she should return but couldn't bear to part with for reasons she wasn't ready to consider.

When an ample amount of time had passed for James to get to the station and show the photographs to his captain, Clara gathered her bag and went to kiss Helen on the cheek. "Helen, there's something I have to do."

After a heavy sigh, Helen put down the sweater she was knitting then looked at Clara through narrowed eyes.

"Arguing won't change my mind, Helen. I have to do this."

"I understand. But do be careful, dear. There are so many things

I could say to you at this moment, but it will be better if I put my efforts into saying a multitude of prayers."

Heart pounding, Clara slipped through the front door of the Martins'. She couldn't let fear hold her back. If she let love guide her, it would be so much easier to press forward.

Love? The thought stopped her. Could she really love someone she'd only known a few days? Or was it the heightened sense of danger that had her heart tipping toward James?

No. It wasn't the danger. It was love. And her heart sang because of it.

It really shouldn't surprise her. If she hadn't loved him since the moment he stepped on to the aerio-cycle, then it was for certain that she loved him from the moment he borrowed the bicycles for the picnic and then handed her a fizzy bottle of Coca-Cola.

And because of that love, she would press forward with God going before her as He did for the Israelites when He appeared before them as a pillar of cloud to guide them on their way. And by night—He stood over them as a pillar of fire to give them light. God would do the same for her. With Him going before her, she could do this.

"Has James been here?"

Mrs. Martin stood at the kitchen rolling out a doughy mixture. A bowl of apples sat beside her. Clara felt a prick of regret as she realized she wouldn't be there when the apfelstrudel was ready.

"Oh, Clara, dear. Do come in." Mrs. Martin brushed her hands on her apron and ushered Clara to her place at the kitchen table. "Let me put the tea on, dear."

"No, thank you. I've just had some."

"Oh?" Mrs. Martin waited expectantly but Clara didn't have it in her to give an explanation of where she'd been, how she came to have tea with someone Mrs. Martin didn't know, and what they'd talked about as they sipped their tea.

"Mrs. Martin, has James been here?" She hated to ask a second time, but needed to know if he'd already come and gone with his captain. Although surely she would have said something to Clara had they been here.

"No, I haven't seen James. I thought you were with him. Are you expecting him?"

"Yes, I'm expecting him, but neither of us will be able to have tea."

"I'll put some on anyway. If there's time, it won't hurt you to have another cup."

There won't be a later. Clara looked longingly at her friend and mother figure, wishing she could tell her what was about to happen.

Clara finally accepted a lemon cookie, knowing it would be the last sweet she'd have for a while. She savored it, though there was a moment where it stuck in her throat and threatened to choke her. It was the same moment she heard footsteps on the porch outside.

When the knock came at the door, she didn't flinch.

"I'll answer it," she said before Mrs. Martin could put her dough down and wipe her hands a second time.

To his credit, when she opened the door, James masked his expression expertly. Clara figured she only recognized his surprise because she'd spent so much time with him over the last several days.

Focusing her eyes only on him, she tried to send him a message by blinking slowly one time. *It will be all right.* She could only pray he would come to understand. *A small muscle beneath his right eye twitched ever so slightly.* When the captain clamped a strong but sweaty hand around her elbow, the twitch under James's eye grew larger.

"Clara Lambert?" The captain's tone was stern, and his fingers bit the tender skin on the underside of her arm.

"Yes." She kept her tone matter-of-fact. There was no sense acting indignant or even outraged. She was innocent, and she would be proven as such. And she wouldn't give the man the sense of satisfaction of knowing he hurt her. Besides, if she did, James might react negatively and that would defeat the purpose.

The captain tugged her by the arm, pinching deeper as he pulled her through the open doorway, and she almost lost her resolve not to cry out. He maneuvered her around until she stood in front of James.

"Go ahead, Brinton."

For a moment, James didn't say anything. He opened his mouth and closed it again.

Clara felt terrible about not warning him ahead of time that she was coming here. She bit the inside of her lips and tried to send him a silent apology, hoping he'd understand it had to be this way. But his expression was so stricken, her heart broke.

"Brinton, get on with it." The man who snarled the words stood to the left of the captain, glowering at her.

Bales. Why did he hate her so much? Prior to today, she'd never seen him. But the look he cast both her and James was nothing but pure venom.

In that moment, she realized this was about more than Czolgosz and his anarchy group. This was about James. The captain and this other officer were using her to make James prove his loyalty to the precinct and to the captain.

"Clara Lambert." James's voice faltered slightly, and the sound pricked at her already aching heart. "I'm arresting you on suspicion of conspiracy in a plot to kill the president of these United States."

"Hey there! What is this all about?" Mr. Martin's loud shout came from the sidewalk, and he stormed up the porch steps. Before anyone could respond, Bales and the captain quickly subdued him.

"Unhand me. You have no rights here." Mr. Martin struggled against the men. "This is my house. I've done nothing wrong. Neither has Clara. She is a model citizen. I insist you let her go."

"Please, Mr. Martin. We must let Ja—Officer Brinton—do his job."

Another round of protests and struggling were followed by a florid hue and a sheen of sweat that bathed Mr. Martin's face and alarmed Clara.

"Come, Emil." Mrs. Martin tugged at his arm. When Bales wouldn't release his grip on her husband, Mrs. Martin whirled on him. "He has done nothing but defend someone he loves. Let him go, or you will answer to me."

Bales appeared to think about this, and for a moment Clara thought he was going to laugh in Mrs. Martin's face. Instead, he let go of Mr. Martin's arm.

The man went immediately to his wife's side. "That wasn't necessary, Eulalie. I can defend my home just fine." Mr. Martin brushed at his sleeves, not meeting anyone's eye.

Even in this dark moment, warmth managed to bathe Clara's heart. "Thank you both." She whispered through the tightness that swelled in her throat, though she wasn't sure they heard her. Then she turned to James. She thought this was where he was supposed to elaborate on her supposed crimes and slap the shackles on her wrists. But he appeared to be having trouble doing his job.

Once again, he opened his mouth then shut it again. This time he swallowed hard, and the twitch beneath his eye was much more noticeable.

For the second time in a matter of seconds, warmth flooded Clara's chest. She felt a pull toward him deeper than any she'd ever felt. Tears pricked her eyes. Turning to the captain, she tried to use them to James's advantage lest the captain notice something amiss.

"Please, sir. I won't give you any trouble. Please don't let him put me in shackles."

In response, the other officer planted his hands in the center of her back and pushed her toward James. "Get on with you, then."

"Bales." James's tone was low and threatening.

Frantic to keep him out of trouble, Clara said, "It's all right, Officer Brinton. I'll come along quietly." *Please, James,* she willed. *Please don't say anything.*

The look he rewarded her with seemed to warn that she'd hear about this later.

"Men!" The captain's shout got the attention of both men and they quickly turned toward him. "Brinton, get her in the wagon. Sit next to her to make sure she doesn't try to escape. Bales, you sit across from them and keep your eye on the prisoner. Just in case."

Was the captain warning Bales against her, or against James?

The captain turned back to Clara. "Don't be giving them any trouble, or a set of chains will be the least of your concerns."

They ushered her through the door, heedless of a new round of threats from Mr. Martin. Behind her, Mrs. Martin sniffled loudly. "Don't worry, dear. We'll get you released. We'll send for your father if we have to. He'll have these imbeciles tripping over themselves to apologize."

Clara whirled. "No! I don't want him—he can't know."

Before she could say more, Bales gave her another push.

They led her to the wagon, and James helped her up the wooden step. She scooted down the plank seat until she sat flush against the other side. James slid in next to her. Bales climbed in behind James and sat on the opposite seat, glaring at both of them. The captain sat in front with a driver. She wished Bales would sit in front as well. She would have preferred it if she and James were alone so they could speak privately. She wanted to reassure him, as well as herself, that obeying his boss was the right thing. He'd been right earlier when he said he couldn't help her if he was in jail. This really was quite the predicament, and she didn't want James blaming himself. The steady clomp of horses' hooves sounded through the night air, but Clara's heartbeat sounded even louder. She glanced at James to see if he noticed. He didn't meet her eye.

The wagon rolled past each house lining Sycamore Street. Had the neighbors noticed her being hauled off to jail? What would they discuss over tea tomorrow?

Across from her, as though reading her thoughts, Bales watched her with a sneer. Willing herself not to wither, she stared back. And as she studied him, a prick of unease rippled through her. Earlier, she hadn't thought she recognized him. She still didn't, but there was

205

something that seemed familiar. Why hadn't she noticed it before?

Perhaps she met him at the fair. Perhaps she'd taken a picture of his wife or children. Although she couldn't imagine forgetting a man with a scowl so deep. If he did have a wife and children, she felt rather sorry for them.

The thought that she might have met him while taking pictures reminded her of Gracie. It saddened her, knowing Gracie would be watching for the photos to be delivered to her—photos that would never arrive.

As soon as she proved her innocence, she'd have to find the mother and daughter so she could take the pictures over again.

Of course, she'd have to get to Rochester first, to get another camera from Mr. Eastman. And she'd have to pray that he didn't terminate her employment, and that he would be willing to give her another camera.

Sounds from up ahead caught Clara's ear.

The fair. They'd be going right past the Midway and the aeriocycle. Had James noticed? She glanced over to see him studying her. She remembered their ride, the defensive way she held herself, all the while being grateful to be away from the fraudulent secret service agent. She remembered the way James described his stomach plummeting in much the way hers had also done. She wanted to smile at him, to reassure him, but felt Bales's gaze still upon her. So she kept her expression neutral.

At least, she hoped Bales would think it neutral.

As for James, she prayed he would see the love in her heart, the concern that she felt for him, and wouldn't blame himself.

When they reached the precinct, James helped her down from the wagon. He pulled her too hard, and she stumbled against him.

Only when he whispered in her ear did she realize he'd done it intentionally.

"I'm going to get you out of this. I promise."

She wanted to answer back but didn't dare risk being overheard.

CHAPTER 22

They led her to a small room where she was instructed to sit on a hard wooden chair. It wasn't until the door closed and she was left alone that she let her guard down. Almost immediately, fear began to battle against the trust she had in God. *No.* She shook her head. Lies and evil had no place here. She would not give in and allow them to win. Through Him, truth would overcome lies. Through Him, good would outdo evil.

Keys rattled on the other side of the door.

"Thank you for waiting ever so patiently." Bales appeared in the open doorway, still wearing his hateful sneer.

Where was James?

Clara angled her head to try to see past him, then took a deep breath to try and quell the panic pushing up into her throat when James was nowhere in sight.

Bales held up a large bulky camera that seemed antiquated compared to hers. "I'm going to photograph you for the police record and then escort you to your new home."

Home? "I don't understand."

"A steel cage, Miss Lambert. This is a jail, remember? Your new home is behind a set of iron bars, courtesy of the City of Buffalo.

Now smile for me. Smile really wide."

Bales laughed as he pointed the camera lens in her direction.

For a moment, Clara dared to believe they'd already realized their mistake and he'd come to let her go. She swallowed against the salty bitterness of tears and disappointment.

When he finished with the camera, Bales grabbed her by the elbow and steered her toward the door. When she hesitated, he shoved her roughly, and she banged her hip against the solid doorframe. "Come on with you now. Let's go."

Not willing to cry out or give this man the satisfaction of knowing he hurt her, Clara glanced around the room for a sign of anyone else.

"If you're looking for your boyfriend, he's gone."

"Gone?" Too late, she realized her mistake. Satisfaction spread across Bales's face. "He's not my—he helped me when I needed it, and—he's just an acquaintance." It sounded like a lie, even to her own ears.

"I know about the photos, and how he accompanied you to Rochester."

Something in his tone sent shivers across the back of her neck. "You do?"

"Of course I do. That's why you're here."

How could she be so stupid? Of course he knew about the pictures. Her mind was daft because as much as she didn't want to admit it, she was afraid. Especially knowing she was alone with Bales.

"Come on now. Don't make me knock you on the head and throw you over my shoulders like a sack of potatoes."

Clara could only stare. Surely he hadn't meant that.

"I'll drag you by the hair if I have to. Now quit your gawking and move your feet."

Never in her life had she ever come across a man with such a mean streak. "Where are we going, anyway?" If he said it before, she didn't remember.

"The women's floor."

"Oh." Relief coursed through her. She hadn't stopped to think about it at the time, but she was thankful to know she wouldn't be in the same area as the men. And she wouldn't have to see the monster that shot President McKinley—if he was even housed here. They might have taken him to Albany to the federal prison. She recalled James mentioning the possibility but couldn't remember if he'd said they'd actually moved him. The stress of this situation seemed to have altered her ability to clearly process her thoughts.

Pillar of fire, God. Pillar of fire. Please, please go before me. She wanted to whisper the words but didn't want Bales to hear her. It didn't matter, because she knew that whether they were whispered in a room or in her heart, God would hear them.

As she followed Bales up the staircase, the sound of their heels striking each step echoed around them. When they reached the women's floor, it was stone silent and empty as a tomb.

Alarmed, Clara looked around, but it was difficult to see in the dim light. Surely she wasn't the only woman here? It didn't seem likely. How was that even possible? Something definitely wasn't right.

Anger at James rose within her. She knew it was unwarranted. It wasn't his fault she was here. But how could he have left her to face Bales alone? And really, why was this man even escorting a female prisoner to the women's floor? Wasn't there a matron on the premises?

A shudder worked its way up her spine, and she couldn't suppress it. Had Bales noticed? She prayed he hadn't. She didn't want him to have one more thing to feel smug about.

But what would she do if he tried to hurt her?

"Put these on, Miss Lambert."

Bales had stepped toward a cupboard and now held out a gray dress and white apron.

A tingling sensation skittered up her neck and buzzed the back of her skull. "What?"

"This is what you wear in jail. We don't allow *prisoners*"—he practically spat the word—"the privilege of wearing their own clothes." He waved the dress at her. "Get undressed and put these on."

"In front of you? No." She stamped her feet for emphasis.

"You'll do it, or I'll do it for you."

"And you're just going to stand there and watch?"

His salacious grin said it all, and Clara fought back a wave of nausea.

"Get over here, Miss Lambert, and do as I say." He tried to pull her away from the staircase, but she planted her feet on the ground. "Remember what I said about dragging you by the hair? I meant it."

"Do it and I'll scream loud enough to break every window in this building."

"And you really think anyone in here would pay any attention? You'd be surprised at some of the screaming that goes on around here."

"Then I guess it won't matter if I go ahead and scream."

Before she could make good on her promise, Bales slapped a meaty hand over her mouth. Instinct made Clara bite down on his hand.

"Ouch! Why you—" He swung his fist at her. Before Clara could duck, light flashed in her head, somewhere behind her eyes. Quick tears followed, and she staggered to keep from collapsing at the pain.

"What's going on here, Bales?"

"Captain!" Bales caught Clara before she hit the floor, deftly slapping one arm across her chest. She pulled at it, trying to free herself from his grip, but he held her fast. As she struggled, she noticed a puckered red scar just above his wrist. Something about it struck an odd chord within her even as her head ached and adrenaline pulsed through her veins.

Had she seen it before? She didn't think so, and yet—

"Bales? I'm waiting for your answer. What's going on here?"

"Miss Lambert here, she's a scrapper, sir. She tried to get away and then bit me when I tried to restrain her."

The captain sighed. "No, Bales. I mean, what are you doing on this floor? You were supposed to be taking her to the women's floor."

"Right sir. I was doing that." He dug steely fingers into her arm as if in warning to keep her from crying out. Would there be more punishment for her if she did? Did she dare try? Yes. The captain seemed a lot fairer than Bales. She'd definitely try.

But Bales must have sensed her thoughts. "She got away, sir, and I chased her up here."

"Sir? Captain Green?"

"Yes, Miss Lambert?" For a moment she thought she saw a softening in his eyes before the man turned a swift scowl on Bales. "What are you doing, Bales? Why are you gripping her so tight?"

"You never can tell about these anarchists, sir. I'm just trying to keep her in line."

"That'll be enough from you tonight, Bales. You're dismissed."

Bales let go of her but didn't turn immediately away. The glare he flashed her was so cold and angry it gave her chills. A warning of what was to come if she didn't keep silent?

As he turned from the captain and made his way toward the door, the prickle of familiarity struck her again. Why? Where had she met him?

"My apologies, Miss Lambert." The captain distracted her before she could ponder it further. "Bales gets ahead of himself sometimes. He's somewhat of an eager chap. Here I promised young Brinton I'd keep you from harm, and now this."

The words were a surprise. "You did?" James had extracted a promise from his captain on her behalf?

"Yes, I did. Right before I sent him off to question another suspect."

So he hadn't abandoned her after all. He was simply following orders.

"Wait a minute." She looked up at the captain. "You believe I'm innocent, don't you?"

"It hardly matters what I believe. There's evidence. We have to examine every bit of it, turn over every rock—so to speak. We have to find out everything we can regarding Czolgosz, and anyone who may be involved with the dastardly crime he committed."

"I'm innocent." She stared the captain in the eye.

"Yes, so you say. And so does Brinton. I hope he can prove it. You seem like a nice young woman."

And yet he'd been rude and allowed Bales to treat her in a rough manner. And James—the captain had put him through unnecessary misery. "Then why—"

"I can't do anything that looks like favoritism. That wouldn't do you or Officer Brinton any good at all." He didn't explain himself further, but merely took her by the arm. "Come on, now, Miss Lambert. Let me get you up to the right floor. We've one more flight of stairs to go."

It was late when James finished questioning the suspect that Captain Green wanted him to interview. He wasn't sure where the captain heard about this particular man, but everything about it seemed bogus. This man wasn't involved in anarchy and certain had no ties to Czolgosz.

This particular man had caught one of his friends trying to steal a kiss from his wife. The man defended his wife's honor with a swift blow to the jaw, and out of spite the "friend" reported the man as having ties to Czolgosz.

It had taken longer than he'd expected to finish. But though it was late, James headed back to the precinct to see Clara. He needed to be certain she was comfortable, and not frightened.

Then he'd give her an earful. What was she thinking by going to the Martins' instead of staying at Helen's? She knew he'd likely be headed there under orders to bring her in for questioning once the captain saw the photos.

He knew her intent, and he appreciated it. But that didn't mean he had to like it. He'd let her know of his appreciation, too. As soon as he kissed her and told her what was in his heart.

And what exactly *was* in his heart? The thought that he was beginning to believe he was in love with her in spite of only knowing her a few days? That he thought love was what he felt every time he looked at her or even thought about her?

Lengthening his stride, he hurried toward the station.

The captain had left Clara with a matron who appeared much sterner than she really was. The woman saw Clara settled, if one could call it that, behind steel bars on a cold metal cot upon an even colder floor. Then she disappeared to find some blankets to keep her warm.

And she hadn't even tried to make Clara change into the gray dress and apron.

Now Clara sat upon the edge of the cot, trying not to let her skirt come in contact with the soiled ticking. It would be difficult because her face throbbed and her head swam. She feared she would pass out if she didn't sit down.

But she was also afraid of giving in to the urge to lay her head down. She couldn't. Not without something between herself and that soiled pad.

Forcing herself to think about something else, Clara tried to take in her surroundings. It was difficult with the throbbing pain, but she forced herself to concentrate. The cell was small, with bars on every side except a back wall.

In the cell next to hers, a woman lay in bed crying. Her face was turned away, her cries muffled under the blanket.

"Hello? Can you hear me?" She watched for some sign of movement, but the girl in the bed didn't move. The crying, however, had lessened. "Is there anything I can do? Hello? Can you—"

"I hear you." The woman's voice was faint with the choppy sort of shuddering that comes with a heart-wrenching cry.

That was something Clara wished she could indulge in. But there would be time for that later. "Are you all right?"

Another hiccupping sob echoed in the room, followed by a thin voice. "No."

Clara's heart welled with empathy. "I'm so sorry. I don't know if it helps, but I'm not all right, either."

"It doesn't." The woman sounded younger than Clara—too young to be in here.

"Oh." At least she tried to be friendly and kind.

"But it does help to know I'm not alone."

"I feel the same way. My name is Clara."

"I'm Sadie."

Clara wished Sadie would sit up so they could talk face-to-face. "How long have you been here, Sadie?"

"I don't know. I've lost track. Two, maybe three days."

"That's a long time." Clara resisted the urge to ask Sadie what she'd done. Perhaps, like herself, Sadie was innocent. Perhaps she smiled at Czolgosz as he was walking down the street.

"How long has it been since the president was shot?"

"Five days."

"Then I've been here four days." Sadie broke off in a sob and the crying began anew.

Clara swallowed hard and her heart pounded. Was Sadie involved in anarchy?

"They accused me of conspiring with the man who shot him. I didn't. I don't even know him. But I sell flowers on Broadway. Someone said the man bought flowers from me. Probably for his ma, or for his girl. I guess because of that, they think I'm guilty."

Clara sucked in a breath. James and Vivie were both right. They really were rounding up anyone Czolgosz had contact with, whether or not they knew him. "It's like the witch trials."

"What?" Sadie sounded alarmed. "I'm not a witch."

"No, of course you aren't. There is no such thing. But once, a long time ago, there were people who recklessly accused others of being witches. The outcome was tragic and horrible beyond belief. I just mean they're recklessly accusing people of conspiring with Czolgosz."

"Who?"

"Leon Czolgosz. The man who shot the president."

"Is he, you know...dead?"

"No. Thank the good Lord. President McKinley survived. He had surgery to remove a bullet from his abdomen. Now he's recovering at the home of his doctor."

"That's really good to hear. He's a good man."

"Yes, he is."

"What do you think they'll do to the man who shot him?"

"I'm sure he'll have a trial. Undoubtedly, he'll spend the rest of his days behind bars." Clara glanced around and shuddered at the thought of spending her life here.

"What about us?" Sniffles came from Sadie's side.

"We're innocent, Sadie. I'm sure they'll realize that and let us go."

"Here we are." The matron held two thin blankets through the bars. They wouldn't be nearly warm enough. Especially since she intended to use one to cover the pad on her cot.

Clara rose and took the blankets from the matron. "Thank you so much."

The matron nodded. "I'm going to turn the lights down. You two get some sleep. I'll be in my office, which is right over there. I expect some peace and quiet so I can do my work."

What kind of work was the matron doing that Clara and Sadie's conversation would disturb her? Still, she nodded so the matron would know she understood. Once the matron turned down the lights and disappeared, Clara waited for her eyes to adjust, and then hurried to make her bed. "Good night, Sadie."

"Good night, Clara. I hope I don't offend you by saying this, but I'm really glad you're here so I'm not alone. Thank you for talking to me."

Clara laughed. "I'm not offended. Tomorrow will be better. You'll see." If only she believed it herself. She did, of course. Any doubts she had were merely her thoughts getting out of hand.

For such a small voice, Sadie sure could snore, as Clara found out before much time had passed.

Sitting in the dark with only Sadie's snoring to listen to, Clara had too much time to think. And it was always quiet moments in the dark when her heart would betray her by thinking about her father—how much she missed him, how much she didn't want to miss him, how mad she was at herself for even thinking about him.

Tonight, those thoughts were stronger than ever.

What would he think if he knew where she was? Would he care? Would he come to see her?

Sorrow filled her, and finally, alone in the dark except for Sadie's snoring, Clara allowed herself to cry. And finally, when her tears dried up and her chest ached with emptiness and despair, she did the thing she should have done first. She prayed.

"Father, God," she whispered into the darkness. "Forgive me. Thank you for sending the captain to free me from Bales. I should have asked you this before I was sitting all alone. Will you continue to be my pillar of fire through this night? And tomorrow, in the daylight, will you be my pillar of cloud and shelter me from this fear? This is all much more frightening than I ever imagined."

But still, if her actions protected James, she would do it all over again.

CHAPTER 23

A soft tapping sound pulled Clara out of sleep. Her head was stuffy from crying, and it hurt when she moved. The skin around her eyes was tight and swollen.

When she sat up, the pounding in her head threatened to knock her back down. She shivered and reached for her blanket but it must have slid to the floor.

Inky darkness cloaked her, and she couldn't see her hand in front of her face. Panic welled in her chest. Had her lamp burned out? She put her hand out and touched cold stone. That was the reason the room was so chilled. Eulalie and Emil Martins' house was not made of stone. She wasn't in her room at their house.

An image of Bales's sneering face loomed in her thoughts, and she shivered again.

Jail. She was in jail.

"Please, God, keep him away from me."

The tapping sounded again, followed by a whisper.

"Clara?"

"James? Is that you?" She rose from the cot and moved toward the sound. A warm glow bobbed in her direction, and as it drew closer it grew brighter and there was James. Relief flooded her and she reached through the bars for his hand.

"Clara, are you all right?"

Aware of how she must look, she reached up to smooth her hair. Then she laughed. It wasn't like James could really see more than her faint outline in the shadows.

"I've had better days."

The jingle of keys followed the opening of the cell door, and James stepped inside. In his other hand, he held a stubby candle.

"What are you…? How did you—"

"Shh." James set the candle holder on the floor near the wall in the back corner. "It was all I could find. I didn't think it would be wise to turn on any lights." Before he even finished speaking, he took her in his arms.

"Ouch." Even though there was nowhere she'd rather be than in his arms, she couldn't help but wince when she pressed her head against his chest.

"What is it? What's wrong?"

How did she answer? If she told him of the treatment she'd received from Bales, he'd hunt him down. Then he'd end up in a cell, too.

"It's nothing really. I'm just uncomfortable from sleeping on that little cot." It was true. Her neck was sore and her hips screamed at her. But she didn't want to let that keep her from being close to him. She turned her face so that the side that wasn't sore rested against his chest. As she did, he wrapped his arms tighter around her. "But what about you, James? What are you doing here? How did you get the keys?"

"I wanted to check on you. I couldn't sleep. Clara, I can't tell you how sick this makes me. I'll never forgive myself if something happens to you, too."

She knew he was thinking about his parents. He carried such a heavy burden. And this only compounded the weight. "You can't keep blaming yourself. Let God do the forgiving for you, James."

"I'm not sure I can do that."

"You can if you try." Even before the words were out of her mouth, Clara laughed.

"What's so funny?"

"For a minute there, I sounded like my mother. She used to say that to me all the time." She swallowed hard, the memory bittersweet. "But she was always right. His grace is sufficient. He's already forgiven you. Once you ask Him for it, He'll give you peace. And you'll be forgiven."

"There's a lot that I need forgiveness for." His words rumbled up through his chest, vibrating against her ear. And if she was quiet enough, when he wasn't speaking, she could hear his heart thumping.

"We all have things that need forgiving. We're human. But the instant we ask, He forgives us."

Even as she spoke the words, Clara thought of her father. God had forgiven him, but she hadn't. She'd had an almost identical conversation with Mrs. Martin dozens of times. But she hadn't listened to Mrs. Martin and certainly hadn't bothered to listen to her father.

Why, then, did she expect James to listen to her?

I'm so sorry. She whispered the words in her heart, sending them heavenward to the Lord, with the hope that someday she'd have an opportunity to say those same words to her father. At the same time, she added a plea that James would find a way to turn his burden over to God and forgive himself.

She lifted her head from James's chest and tried to see his face in the dimness. "We just need to keep reminding ourselves of His forgiveness, James. It's the only hope we have. Ask Him to help you believe it, so you can forgive yourself."

Though he said nothing, she could feel him nodding against the top of her head.

"But I want you to know it's not your fault. None of it. What happened with your parents—it's a horrible thing. Your actions didn't cause that man to do what he did to your family. And it wasn't your actions that landed me here. Giving the photos to your captain was the right thing. Otherwise it would have looked like you were hiding evidence. And then we'd both be in here."

"If it means anything, the captain didn't want to do this. He doesn't think you're guilty. But Bales put on such a display over the pictures, he felt like he had no choice."

"Yes, that's what he told me when he—" She stopped herself when she realized she almost said the captain rescued her from Bales.

"That's odd. The captain doesn't usually escort prisoners—er, people—to the floor. He must like you, Clara."

"He was very kind. But I don't want to talk about that. I still can't believe you're here so late. It must be the middle of the night."

"It is. But I don't mind. I'm just sorry I couldn't get back here sooner. I wanted to be the one to escort you up here, but Bales managed to convince the captain that I'm too close to this, and the captain fell for his silver-tongued nonsense and sent me to question someone else."

"You mean you're *not* too close to this? Too close to me?"

"That's not what I meant."

"Even if you meant it, I'm still glad you're here."

He bent down and planted a quick kiss on her lips. "I'm going to have to leave in a few minutes, before Matron Penwick wakes up and finds her keys missing."

"Wakes up? She told me she had work to do. I wondered what kind of work she was doing." Clara laughed. "James, you really are going to end up in here because of me."

"No, I won't. I'm going to leave in just a minute. But first I have something for you."

"Really? What is it?" She barely had the words out when she felt a small box being pressed into her hand. Familiar with the size and shape, her heart quickened. This was the type of box one would bring home from a jewelry shop. "What is this, James?"

"Open it and see."

Eager, curious, Clara stepped deeper into the candle light where she opened the lid of the tiny box. "Oh. James."

It was the gold pin with the bird sitting on a branch. Somehow he'd managed to purchase it from the jewelers' shop in Rochester. She knew that because she was positive there wasn't another one like it. Joy lit her heart as she held the pin closer to the light so she could inspect every element.

"It's so exquisitely beautiful. Thank you. This means so much to me."

This time it was Clara who kissed James. Standing on her tiptoes, she raised her face to his until their lips met. She made sure this kiss lasted longer than the previous one.

Finally he said, "I want you to give me a list of everyone you know who can serve as a character witness and can help prove you aren't involved in some sort of conspiracy."

"There's no one." Clara shook her head. "Only the Martins." She'd been too busy since she came to Buffalo. There wasn't enough time for making friends—even at church.

"That's not true. There're your employers, Mr. Eastman, and Mr. Nowak. And don't forget Mr. Eastman's mother. She was quite taken with you. And now there's Helen."

"But Mr. Nowak won't count—especially now that he's a murder suspect."

"Of course. What was I thinking? How about the girl you work with there?"

"Vivie."

"How long have you known her?"

"I've worked with her since I came to Buffalo. I came here in February, after my mother died."

"Is there anyone from New York City who would come here to bear witness?"

She thought for a minute. "Not really. Most of my close friends are married and have moved away. None of us are very good at keeping in touch. There's a small journal in my room with their names and where they live. It would be wonderful if they were willing to help, but I just can't imagine them coming all the way here."

"Clara, I hate to ask this."

Dread rose inside her, and she knew what he was about to say.

"I know how you feel about it, but you really should let me contact your father."

"No!" Clara took a quick step away from James. "He can't know I'm here."

"But he might be able to help."

"I can't. I don't—" She started to say she didn't want him here, but that was no longer the truth. And now that she realized it, she found herself wanting to tell James everything. But she was too ashamed.

A rustling sound came from somewhere in the room. Sadie? Or the matron? If she found James here, there was sure to be trouble. She froze and held her breath.

"Clara, is that you?" The soft voice belonged to Sadie. Relieved, Clara let out the breath she'd been holding.

"Yes, Sadie. It's me. I'm sorry I woke you."

"It's all right. I've been awake off and on. It's so uncomfortable here."

"We'd better go back to sleep so we don't wake up the matron."

"You're right, of course. We don't want her to get angry. Did I just hear you talking to someone?"

Clara didn't want to lie, but Sadie couldn't know James was here. "I was just trying to figure out who can help me get out of here."

"Good luck with that. I've been trying to figure out the same thing."

"We can worry about it in the morning. Get some sleep, Sadie."

"Good night, Clara."

"Good night, Sadie." Clara leaned close to James and whispered, "As soon as she's asleep, you'd better go."

James responded by pulling her tight to his chest and leaning against the wall. Then he whispered in her ear. "I'm happy to wait."

Clara closed her eyes and nestled her head against him, listening to his heartbeat, drawing strength from his closeness.

It seemed way too soon that Sadie was snoring again. James bent and picked up the candle, but he didn't seem in any hurry to leave.

"I'll come by and see you in the morning. If Bales is around, I'll probably have to interrogate you."

"I understand." As long as she could see him, he could ask her anything.

"But please know I'll be doing everything I can to get you out of here as soon as possible."

"Thank you. And please promise me you won't contact my father."

"I promise, Clara. It's not a promise I want to make, but you have my word."

"I believe you. And James, I'm sorry I didn't stay at Helen's. I know it hurt you."

"I understand why you did it."

"Still, I'm sorry."

"What was that you told me a few minutes ago about God and forgiveness?" He bent forward and kissed her once more before he turned to leave.

After he slipped quietly from her cell without so much as a sound of bars rattling or keys jingling, Clara wrapped her hand around the delicate gold pin and settled back on the cot. She should be thinking about her plight and worrying about getting free.

Instead, all she could think of were James's soft kisses and the sound of his heart as it thrummed against her ear.

Instead of going home, James went to the Martins'. He needed them to know Clara was settled in for the night and was getting along fairly well. He also needed their help finding people who knew her.

It wasn't a surprise to see light coming from the windows, and

Mr. Martin answered on the first knock.

"I ought to beat the living tar out of you." Mr. Martin glared at him, shrugging only slightly as Mrs. Martin pulled him back.

"Listen, Mr. Martin. I'm sorry. You know I had no choice in the matter. Clara wasn't even supposed to be here."

"That's beside the point. You had no right arresting her."

"How is our girl?" Mrs. Martin pushed past her husband and motioned for James to come inside. He wiped his feet on the porch before he entered, all the while keeping a close watch on Mr. Martin, who glowered at him from the doorway.

Once inside, he followed the Martins to the kitchen and sat with them at the table. "She's doing better than I thought she would. There's another young woman under arrest, and Clara is looking out for her."

"I would expect nothing less," Mrs. Martin said.

"Neither would I. She's smart. That's how she ended up getting arrested."

James explained how he thought he had her settled at Helen's, knowing the captain would come looking for her at the Martins'. "They would have come here even without me. I didn't expect her to be here. I know she thought she was protecting me."

"How are we going to get her out?"

"They've already released most of the people they've arrested. It will be harder for Clara because she had pictures of the man who shot the president."

Mrs. Martin gasped.

"She didn't know him, of course," James was quick to add. "They were practice pictures she took at the hotel after Mr. Eastman gave her the camera. Czolgosz just happened to be there. If we can get enough people to swear before a judge that she's not involved in anarchy, we should be able to get her out fairly quickly. But I need your help contacting everyone who knows her."

"I've already wired her father." Mrs. Martin spoke the words without apology.

"Mrs. Martin, we need to wire him back and tell him not to come. Better yet, does he have a telephone?" James rose and headed toward the door.

"Where are you going?"

"Clara made me promise not to contact him. There's a telephone at the station. I'm going to call and tell him not to come."

Mrs. Martin waved her hand as if to dismiss a silly thought. "He needs to be here. She might not think so, but he can help. He knows people. His boss is a very rich man with powerful friends. Besides, he loves her."

"I don't doubt that." She was easy to love. "But she was very clear that she didn't want him here."

He'd have to tell her tomorrow. But would she believe him that he had nothing to do with it? Or would she think he broke the promise he'd made to her?

CHAPTER 24

"I'm going to tell him."

They were sitting in the small room where prisoners were interrogated. James paced the floor, furiously.

"James, sit down, please."

"I can't sit down. I'm too angry. I'm going to get the captain. He needs to see your face." The bruises on her face made him want to do the same—worse, really—to Bales. "Why didn't you tell me about this last night?"

"Because of this." She held her hand out as if demonstrating something at the fair. "Your reaction."

"Of course I'd react. What do you expect me to do? Bales has gone too far. He's the one who needs to be in a cell. Not you."

"James, calm down, please? Going after Bales right now won't do any good."

Before James could respond, the door opened and Matron Penwick appeared.

"You have a visitor, Miss Lambert. A man, and he's making quite a ruckus."

"Mr. Martin. He really shouldn't be here."

"They care about you, Clara."

She smiled. "I know. They're wonderful people, in spite of their hot tempers."

"Listen, Clara. Before you see Mr. Martin, there's something I need to tell you—"

"Where's my daughter? I demand that you take me to her right now."

Loud voices of protest filled the doorway just before the door burst open.

Clara gasped. "Father?" Instant tears filled her eyes, and she turned her back to the door as if afraid of what she'd see. But that didn't stop her from glaring up at James. "How could you?"

"But I—"

"I trusted you!"

"I know, and I—"

"Officer, take me back to my cell, please?"

The bewildered man acquiesced and led Clara from the room, leaving James frustrated and angry, while Mr. Lambert tried to follow them, only to be held back by two officers. His eyes were wide and the strain showed on his face as he struggled against them.

"Sir? Why don't you come with me and sit down? We need to talk."

Clara's father pushed his hands through his graying hair then shook his head. There was no mistaking the concern and distress filling both his green eyes and his heart. "I don't want to talk to anyone but my daughter."

"I'll do my best to arrange it. But judging by her reaction, it will be a while before she agrees. Now, let's talk."

Clara put the finishing touches on the letter she'd just written. She folded the paper in half and tucked it neatly in the envelope.

"There you go, Sadie." She smiled and handed the envelope to her new friend.

"Thank you so much." Sadie leaned into the cell and gave Clara a hug. Matron Penwick stood close, watching the entire exchange.

"You're very welcome, of course. And thank you, Matron Penwick, for the pen and stationery." The matron had kindly offered when she overheard Clara telling Sadie she'd write a letter of introduction and recommendation to both Mr. Nowak—presuming they could prove he didn't murder Patricia—as well as to the man at the gift shop she worked at before Mr. Eastman hired her.

And now Sadie was leaving. As kind as Matron Penwick had turned out to be, Clara would still be alone when she left.

Clara watched as Matron Penwick walked her toward the door. Sadie turned and waved over her shoulder. Clara waved back but knew the tears in her eyes weren't for her new friend.

Matron Penwick closed the door behind her, and Clara was alone.

All alone.

She didn't even have James. He'd betrayed her.

How could he go behind her back like that and contact her father?

Footsteps sounded on the stairs, and Clara brushed her eyes with her sleeve. It wouldn't do to have the matron catch her crying.

Not that she was really crying, of course. Still, she turned to face the wall in case the matron came back here instead of going to her office.

"Clara?"

James.

How was it possible for her heart to drop, and yet to pound at the same time?

"I'm not receiving visitors at this time."

"That's good, because I'm not a visitor. I just so happen to work here."

"Well, I just so happen to not wish to speak with *you* at this time. It's my right, I believe."

He was silent for so long, she thought he must have left.

Perhaps she missed the sound of his departing footsteps due to her continuously thumping heart. But just when she started to turn around, she heard his voice.

"Clara, please hear me out. I don't want to be ungentlemanly and point out that you're a captive audience. But I will if I have to."

It was a good thing she wasn't facing him, because her mouth betrayed her by trying to quirk up at the corners.

Only because she loved his sense of humor. No other reason. And she wasn't about to waste time pondering that *love* word even if she'd had such thoughts in the wee hours of last night. She needed to remind herself that she certainly hadn't known him long enough. It was possible to love someone's sense of humor without loving them, wasn't it? Of course she wasn't fooling herself one bit. She loved him. She was furious with him, and her heart ached over his deep betrayal.

She would just have to figure out how to *un*love him. But for now she was, as he said, his captive audience.

"Very well, then. Since you've put it so aptly. Say what you have to say and then leave, please."

"Clara."

His tone was lower than usual, and it rumbled its way to her ear. Almost as if he hurt as much as she did.

"I didn't betray you. I never would. I gave my word. You can trust me forever."

Her breath hitched in her throat. "Forever?"

"Yes, forever."

Her heartbeat faltered. At least she thought it did. It was the only way to describe the strange skittering sensation.

She turned slowly, and her gaze swept across James's face. Up, down, and up again. Stopping at his liquid brown eyes. Warm. Sincere. And he looked ever so handsome in his uniform.

"I love you, Clara. I would never betray you."

"You love me?" Tears flooded her eyes, but she didn't try to hold them back.

"You don't have to sound so surprised. You're quite lovable when you put your mind to it." His smile was a bit too saucy.

"Lucky for you, mister, I'm behind bars." She tried to match his smile, but all she could do was grin. *He loved her.* "James," she hesitated for only a moment, knowing she had to tell him. "We haven't known each other long enough for you to love me. But even so, I love you back."

James rattled the keys to her cell. "What was that? I didn't hear you."

"I said I love you back."

He put the key in the lock, and the door swung out.

"You're going to have to say it one more time. Never tell a man you love him when he can't hold you in his arms."

Clara met him halfway across the cell and launched herself into his arms.

"I love you, Clara."

"I love you, James."

"I'll never get tired of hearing you say that." He kissed her then, an intense kiss that left her light-headed.

"When did you know?"

"Remember that ride on the aerio-cycle?"

Clara drew her lip between her teeth. "We didn't even know each other yet."

"I knew all I needed to know."

"And what was that?"

"When I looked into your eyes, my heart did a somersault."

Kind of the way hers did whenever he was around. "I know that feeling well."

"I have to get back before Matron Penwick returns. But before I go, I have two really important things I need to ask you."

What could be more important than the conversation they were having? He'd just told her he loved her. And she loved him back. Even though she knew they hadn't known each other long enough to be considered proper.

"Have you ever traveled before, Clara?"

What an odd question. Clara looked up at James. "Yes, I went from Buffalo to Rochester and back again with you, on the train. That's traveling, don't you think?"

"No. Buffalo to Rochester doesn't count."

"All right, then, what about New York City to Buffalo?"

"I admit it's a long trip, but I meant someplace far away from here. Maybe London, or somewhere across the Mississippi. Someplace you'd go just for fun. You haven't done that, have you? Where would you go if you could go anywhere in the world?"

Back in time. Back before her mother got sick, back to that last happy night with her parents before everything changed. But she didn't really want to give a voice to a thought that would have too much power over her.

James was watching her closely, a look of expectation in his eyes. She didn't think he'd accept a pat answer of Paris or Rome. But those weren't at the top of her list anyway. Not that she never wanted to go there, but she didn't want to waste her one "anywhere in the world" on a place where everyone wanted to go.

"Avignon." She waited for him to laugh, or to say he'd never heard of it. But instead, he smiled.

"Nice choice. Rich history. The other Rome."

He surprised her. She hadn't expected him to know all of those details.

"Have you been there?"

He shook his head. "I love to read about new places. I keep a list of places I'd love to go. Believe it or not, Avignon was at the top of my list as well."

"This shouldn't come as any great revelation, but—I don't believe you."

He angled his head so he looked down at her. "I'm a police detective. How could you not believe me?" His eyes were so bright, engaging her, drawing her in. And though she tried to look away, her gaze kept wandering back to his, fascinated by the way they curled up toward his eyebrows when he opened them wide in his expressive way.

"It's too obscure," she finally said. "And really, what are the chances of us both having it at the top of our list?"

"I could show you my list, if you'd like."

"You actually have a hand-written list?" She didn't believe him.

If possible, his grin grew even wider. "When this is all over and I get you out of here, I'll show you."

"I'm going to hold you to it."

"And you'll find out that I'm a man of my word."

This time, Clara believed him.

"But wait," she said after a moment's thought. "You said, 'was.' It *was* at the top of your list. What did you mean? You've changed it?"

"It's still on my list, but it's moved down one spot."

"So what's your number one, now? Rémy? Aix-en-Provence? Marseille? So you can ride a newly purchased bicycle through the small country villages?"

"My number one is anywhere you are."

He said it so softly, she almost didn't hear him. She had to stop and process it through her mind, and when she did, she blushed furiously. But rather than let him see how it affected her, she acted nonchalant.

"What was the second thing you wanted to ask me?"

His face sobered, and she knew she wasn't going to like this question quite as much.

"I'd like to ask you to reconsider speaking with your father."

"But—"

"Please?" He held his hand up. "Hear me out. I didn't contact him. But I could have made a phone call to tell him not to come."

"Why didn't you?"

"Mrs. Martin talked me out of it. Besides, he'd obviously already left or he wouldn't be here yet. And now that I see the bruises on your face, I'm glad he's here. Perhaps the governor or Mr. Vanderbilt or whomever he knows can guarantee your freedom. So if you consider that a betrayal, I'm not going to apologize. Your safety is the most important thing here."

"It's Mr. Tiffany. My father works for him now, not Mr. Vanderbilt."

"So that's where all of that Tiffany glass came from."

"Wait. How did you know? I don't think I ever told you that."

James shrugged. "Mrs. Martin said something about it last night. She said he worked for a rich man with powerful friends. But she didn't say a name. I was just using Vanderbilt as an example."

Clara couldn't help but smile. "You're resourceful, Officer Brinton, aren't you?"

He answered with a smile, then turned serious. "Talk to me about your father, Clara."

The realization she'd come to last night about forgiveness wasn't one she wanted to discuss. It filled her with shame. But she just confessed her love to James. How could she not tell him? "My father used to work for a man who demanded nothing less than perfection. I guess that included traveling all over the world at his beck and call. That's why he didn't answer any of my letters when I told him my mother was sick. That's why he wasn't there when she died. He was off trying to please someone other than the woman he promised to love forever."

"I'm sorry, Clara."

She gave him a half-hearted smile. "I've held on to this anger toward him for months, in spite of the endless letters and gifts he sent. He was trying to buy my forgiveness. But last night, when I was talking to you about God and forgiveness, I realized what a hypocrite I've been."

"No." James spoke softly before he reached down and brushed his thumbs under her eyes to wipe at the tears she hadn't even known were there. "You're human, remember?"

"Even though I don't like what he did, I should have turned it over to God. And even as I'm saying it now, it's not easy. I don't want to do it."

"It's easier to hang on to the anger, isn't it?"

Clara nodded, surprised at James's perception. Although, of course, she shouldn't be surprised at all.

"Once you ask God to take it from you, you'll be able to let go of some of it."

"I don't want to, James. I know you're right. But I don't want to."

"I've spent the last couple of hours talking to him," James said. "He's deeply sorry about everything. He loves you. And he loved your mother, too. He still does. He's a man in mourning. If you would only hear him out, I think you'll understand. He's all broken up inside."

The thought twisted like a knife in a gaping wound. "I know it's not his fault my mother got sick. And even if he'd been there, she still would have died. But I just don't know if I can talk to him right now."

"Sure you can. And you have a great big heart, so I know you'll find a way to extend him grace and mercy."

Grace and mercy. Just as Jesus extended to her, so she should extend it to others. And most especially to her father. Deep down it was what she really did long to do. Her father had always loved her unconditionally, and he deserved the same from her in return.

She watched tears splash onto her hands as they rested in her lap.

She looked up to see James staring down at her, tenderly.

She nodded.

"I'll talk to him."

"I knew you would."

He kissed her soundly, then lifted her feet off the floor and whirled her around.

"I just need a few minutes to talk to God, first."

"Done." James set her back on the ground. "He'll be so happy. And now, speaking of grace, I really need to get that errand taken care of."

What an odd comment.

"James, wait!" She almost forgot about the pictures. "I meant to tell you something this morning, but then I heard my father's voice and here we are. Anyway, there's something about those pictures. I can't quite figure it out. It's eluding me, but if you can bring them to me so I can go over them again, maybe I can pinpoint whatever it is."

"I'll do that. And don't you worry. We're going to get you out of here. Whether or not your father is able to pull strings, I'm still going to make them see you're innocent. The captain will have no choice but to let you go."

"I know. I have faith, remember?"

"Yes, you do." His smile was wide, encouraging. "And I know you'll be able to apply it to this situation with your father. And guess what, Clara? I have faith, too."

Even though she suspected as much, her heart swelled to hear him say it. "How?"

"Listening to you talk about God, and the peace He gives us when we need it."

Even though she wasn't showing grace and mercy to her father? James was gone before she could respond. Which was just as well. She had a lot of thinking to do.

He wanted to travel to the same places she did. And he was talking to God. And he loved her!

CHAPTER 25

In spite of the cold, drafty cell that was her temporary home, in spite of the dire circumstances she found herself in, Clara knew that eventually everything was going to be just fine.

The door was unlocked. Clara tiptoed over and pulled it shut so Matron Penwick wouldn't know it was open. She didn't want James to get in trouble.

She barely had it closed when she heard footsteps on the stairs. Hopefully the matron would go to her office, and there really wouldn't be a chance of her noticing the lock.

Unfortunately, the footsteps drew closer to the cell until she heard the door creak open.

Clara sighed. She looked up, ready to apologize for the lock, and her breath caught. Her father stood in front of her. "Daddy." A lump formed in her throat so tight she didn't think she could get another word out.

His eyes, so like hers, were rimmed with red, a suspicious sheen making them glisten.

"Clara. My sweet girl. How could they ever think such a thing about you?"

When he held out his arms, she ran willingly to him. As he

held her close, she hugged him tight. He seemed thinner than she remembered, but as she breathed in his soapy scent she took comfort in that one familiar snippet from a past that would never be the same again.

She tried to swallow, but the lump still prevented her from speaking.

"I'm going to get you out of here, Clara. I promise."

Something about the way he said it made her believe him.

She was happy just to rest in his hugs, and for a moment it was as if he'd never left and her mother was still alive. Oh how she wished it were so.

"I've missed you, Daddy."

He pulled her closer, and she felt him trembling. She couldn't help but wonder if his face was as wet as hers.

"Oh Clara, I've missed you, too. More than you'll ever know."

"Daddy, can you ever forgive me?"

"There's nothing to forgive, my sweet girl. Nothing at all."

"Yes, there is. Even if you don't want to admit it, there's a lot to forgive. I never listened to you when you tried to explain why you didn't come home. I know you tried." She swallowed hard. "I let you deal with your grief all on your own. I'm sorrier than I can ever say."

"That means the world to me, honey. What changed your mind?"

"James reminded me of my faith. I'm ashamed to admit that while I proclaimed my faith, I forgot the most important thing that Jesus taught. Grace and mercy. It was the one thing I didn't focus on when Mother died. I mean, I never forgot my faith in other areas. Just that one. I forgot to extend grace and mercy to you. I'm so sorry, Daddy."

"You don't need to apologize, Clara."

"Yes, I do. I've thought about this a lot while I've been here. I just never liked the thought very much, so I continuously shoved it away. I know you had a good reason for not coming home when I wired you. I know you would have been there if you could have."

"Do you mean that?"

She looked at her father, at his tear-filled eyes and red nose, at the sweet face she'd loved her entire life. "I do."

Even as he rubbed his eyes with the back of one hand, a small smile lifted his expression. "I tried to get home to you, honey. I really did."

It was the truth. She could tell by his tone, by the sincerity shining from his eyes. "Where were you?"

"I was ill, too, Clara."

"I don't understand."

"While your mother was fighting scarlet fever, I was also fighting the same disease."

"What?" Clara straightened and studied her father. She'd noticed he lost weight. He looked older, too. She hadn't considered it more than the passage of time. But now she realized it was much more than that.

"How did you both get the same disease while you were so far apart?"

"I must have had it before I got on the ship. Your mother and I had to have been exposed at the same time. But there's an incubation period. You can have the disease for several days before you have symptoms."

She had no words. She could barely look her father in the eye. He'd been sick. Alone. He could have died.

"I'm so grateful you didn't get sick, too, Clara. I don't think I could withstand losing both of you."

"What about your boss? Did he get sick, too?"

"No. At least, I don't think he did. He took off the minute I showed signs of sickness."

"So that's the reason no one wired to let me know you were ill. I would have come, had I known." Though even as she spoke it, she knew it wasn't true. Nothing could have torn her from caring for her mother.

Her father must have read her expression. "It's all right, Clara. You were so busy tending to your mother. And possibly sick yourself for all I knew."

"But when you came back to find me at the Martins', why didn't you tell me then?"

"You were so angry. It didn't matter what I said, you wouldn't listen to me."

He was right about that. Even when he told her he quit the job that had constantly kept him from them, and that he had a job with regular hours working for Mr. Tiffany, she wouldn't listen. She studied a spot on the floor. Shame seeped through her, spreading its cold chill over her. She fought to keep from retching. It was the grace and mercy thing again. Or lack thereof. She had an enormous lesson to learn. That much was glaringly obvious.

"I'm sorry," she whispered.

"I know you are. I am as well. I should have explained it in my letters."

"I wouldn't have believed you." She didn't want to tell him she never read any of his letters. She still had them, but she'd never read them. It was easier to hold on to her anger. How stupid she was. The minute she got out of here, if she got out of here, she was going to devour every single one of his letters.

He nodded. "After you wouldn't see me, my pride got in the way. Though I wrote and repeatedly asked forgiveness, I never told you the reason."

"Did the Martins know?"

"Yes, but before you get angry, I made them promise not to tell you."

"All of these wasted months. It's my fault for being so stubborn."

"Hey, enough of that. We've forgiven each other, remember?"

Clara nodded.

"Now before we get down to the business of getting you out of here, why don't you tell me how you came by that pin?"

"It's your work, isn't it?" Clara touched the pin that was fastened to her blouse.

"I designed it especially for your mother. I'd hoped to give it to her when I came home. Then when I learned she was gone, I wanted to give it to you." Moisture gleamed from her father's eyes.

"I recognized it when I saw it in the shop in Rochester. James must have seen me looking at it. He gave it to me after I was arrested."

"Ever since I sold it to the merchandiser, I've regretted it. So I'm glad James purchased it for you. Now then." He reached in his jacket pocket and withdrew some photos. "James asked me to give you these."

"These are the photos that incriminated me. How did he get them?"

"I'm not certain, but he handed them to me before he sent me up."

"There's something that's been nagging at me about one of the pictures. I can't seem to figure it out. I asked James if I could look at them again. But I hope I didn't cause him more trouble for sneaking them out."

"He's man enough to accept the responsibility if he does. I like him, Clara."

"I like him, too." She tucked away her wild instinct to take the pictures and run. There was no chance of her doing anything to get James into trouble. "And yes, he is. Oh, and by the way…he loves me." Her heart nearly burst with joy at the thought.

Her father returned her smile. "I know that, too."

"You do?" Clara looked at her father with surprise. "He told you?"

"Honey, he didn't have to. I could tell."

Clara beamed from the inside out.

"He's willing to do whatever it takes to get you out of here. Any man willing to do that for my daughter is the man I want in her life."

James loved her, her father was here, and she had the gift of mercy and forgiveness from her Heavenly Father. What more could she ask for?

Other than her freedom, of course.

"Let's take a look, then, shall we?" Her father held out one of the pictures, and she took it from him. Then they sat together on the small cot, studying the pictures.

But it was no good. Whatever it was she thought she might identify in the pictures eluded her.

Until she started thinking.

"Daddy, you have to get James. I have it figured out." Clara held the picture up so he could see it.

"Certainly, my dear. But tell me. What is it?"

"This man and woman in this picture. What do you see?"

"I see a gentleman leaning a woman back for a—" Her father broke off and his cheeks reddened. "Ahem. He's leaning her back for a rather passionate kiss."

"There's nothing passionate about it. At least not on her part."

Her father peered closer then gazed back at Clara. "I don't see it."

"She's struggling. See how her foot is twisted? And her hands on his lapel? They aren't clenching him to her. She's trying to get away from him."

"Let me see that."

Clara handed the picture to her father. He held it at arm's length, all the while squinting his eyes.

"I think I see what you're talking about, but I can't quite tell. These old eyes of mine, you know."

In spite of the seriousness of what she'd just discovered, Clara found herself amused by her father's manner. But when she reached for the picture again, her heart filled with dread.

"Daddy, there's more. A lady that I worked with at the hotel went missing not long ago. And she was found dead. I think this is her. Why didn't I see this sooner?"

"What do you mean, dear?"

"Not only do I think this is her, I think I know exactly who that man is. And if I'm right and he's the killer, it all makes sense."

"You think she was killed right after you took that photograph?" Her father's eyebrows knit together at a sharp angle.

"Yes. And it makes me sick to think this was happening right in front of me and I was so caught up in the camera that I didn't even realize it." Clara's heart grieved over what Patricia must have suffered. She rubbed her thumb over the image. "Patricia, I'm so sorry."

"But wait a minute. You said you think you know who it is?"

"I didn't realize it before. I thought there was something familiar about him the first time I met him, but I didn't know why."

"Who? Clara, you've lost me. Who was familiar?"

"She means me, Mr. Lambert."

The sneering tone was followed by the jingle of keys, and an icy dread traced its way down Clara's spine.

Bales.

"Why don't you tell your father what you've figured out? Let's see how smart you are. And if you have it right?"

Just looking at his hateful grin made the skin under Clara's eye ache.

"This is you in the picture. There's a little bit of something metal on the man's jacket, just over his heart. You can't quite make it out because of his—your—angle. But right here, you can see a fancy braid on the jacket's cuff. And that flash of metal is a police badge." She stared up into Bales's face, not at all surprised that he continued to smirk.

"And the way your sleeve lifts up past your wrist—there's a mark there. The same mark I saw on your arm when—" She broke off, not wanting to upset her father unnecessarily.

She turned back to Bales. "You attacked Patricia, and then you killed her."

"Now why ever would I do that?" His tone was badgering now, and even though she watched him, Clara was aware that her father had stepped closer to her side.

"Because she wouldn't give you what you wanted. She's trying to get away from you here, but you wouldn't let her go. If I'd been paying attention, I might have realized it."

Forgive me, Lord.

"After I left the hallway, you probably dragged her into a room." She glared at Bales, and anger sharpened her tone. "Just like you threatened to do to me." The words spilled out before she could stop them.

"What? You *touched* my daughter?" Before Clara could even react, her father had Bales pushed up against the bars. But he was no match for the younger man, and Bales knocked him backward. Before he hit the ground, he struck his head against the metal frame of Clara's cot.

"Daddy!" Clara knelt beside her father. "Are you all right?"

Blood oozed from her father's temple.

"He's better than he's going to be. So are you. You shouldn't have thought so hard about all of this."

"And you shouldn't have attacked a defenseless woman. A woman with small children, by the way. Not that you care."

"You're right." Bales smirked. "I don't. She'd been flirting with me all evening. Let me think things were going somewhere they weren't." He had the audacity to wink at her. "If you know what I mean."

"Why you—" Her father struggled to sit up.

Clara gently cradled his head in her lap. "Be still, Daddy. Please?"

If the way he twirled the keys was any indication, Bales seemed to be growing more agitated by the second. Because she'd guessed the truth? She didn't want him to hurt her father.

Hopefully James or one of the other officers would check on them before Bales actually tried to hurt them. If not, she planned to scream long and loud.

When her father clutched at her hand, she patted his arm to reassure him. She leaned close to his ear so Bales wouldn't know what she was saying. "It's all right, Daddy. We'll be all right."

"James." It was barely a whisper, but Bales seemed to know what her father said.

"He can't help you now. The captain sent him on an errand. By the time he gets here, it will be too late."

"Too late for what?" Clara was afraid she knew the answer, but she needed to keep him talking.

"You know exactly what. The same thing that Patricia woman got. Just what's coming to you."

"You needed my camera, so that you could destroy the evidence. But it didn't work."

"No matter." Bales shrugged. "I have the picture now."

Apparently the man who'd taken her picture for the police log didn't really know anything about film and prints. She wasn't about to enlighten him. "So why did you destroy the camera if you knew the film had been processed?"

"Because that stupid beau of yours didn't turn over all of the pictures when he first came back to the precinct, and I thought—"

Surely he didn't think it would still be in the camera when the photographs she'd taken after that one had already been processed? But he did. She could tell by the way he wouldn't meet her gaze.

"So who is the man that attacked me? Is he your brother? Did you send him to do your dirty work for you?"

"What makes you think that?"

"It just seems like something a person like you would do."

"And what kind of person is that?"

"The kind that hurts innocent women. It's probably the reason you seemed familiar when I first came across you."

"And that's exactly why I couldn't leave you to make the connection."

So she was right. The man was Bales's brother. "He looks like you. But he's taller. Thinner." She narrowed her gaze on his face. "But the eyes are the same. Pure evil."

Stepping close, Bales reached down and gripped Clara by the elbow. "So they are. And they'll be the last thing you see." In one swift move, he yanked her to her feet. She struggled to hold on to her father, to protect his head, but when Bales pulled her off the floor her father fell back to the ground.

Clara winced at the loud thud, certain he'd just hit his already injured head. "Let go of me!"

She tried to struggle free of Bales's grasp, but he answered by shoving her down on the cot.

"Touch her, and you're dead."

Bales whirled around at the sound of James's voice. He stood just outside the cell, with his gun pointed directly at the cowardly police officer.

Clara took advantage of the moment. She jumped up from the cot and plowed into Bales like a baseball player trying to score a run for the team. Caught off guard, he lost his balance, and she struck him again. He fell against the steel bars, and this time it was his head that thudded against the hard floor.

"I guess you didn't need my help after all."

"James." Clara scrambled to scoop the keys off the ground where they lay next to Bales. "My father needs a doctor."

Frantically, she maneuvered the long slender key into the lock. But she couldn't get it to engage the mechanism.

"Here, Clara, let me." James reached through the bars and took the key. "This lock has always been kind of tricky."

As soon as the door was open, James ran to Clara's father. But not before he pulled her to his side.

"Here. Hold this." He pushed his gun into her hands. It was heavy, and she didn't like anything about it. Not the way it looked, and not the damage she knew it could do. "Keep it pointed directly at Bales. If he so much as moves an eyelash, pull the trigger."

The gun wavered in her hands. "I don't know if I can." She eyed the man who was beginning to stir. Whatever happened, she couldn't let him move until her father was safely out of the cell.

"You can. Believe me. Just think about Patricia Mane and what he did to her. Think about the little children who have to grow up without a mother."

That was all she needed to hear. Her stomach clenched at the thought of any woman suffering at the hands of an angry man. And most especially at the hands of a police officer—charged with protecting victims, not creating them. She tightened her grip on the gun and trained it at Bales's forehead. "Don't even blink."

"That's my girl." Though it was weak, the sound of her father's voice was a welcome relief.

"Clara, I think your father is going to be all right."

She didn't dare take her eyes off of Bales long enough to find out. She'd just have to take James at his word.

"That's more than I can say for Bales." Clara recognized the sound of Captain Green's voice.

"Captain." She heard James greet his boss, but she still didn't shift her gaze. Not until James stood at her side and gently pried the gun from her hands.

"I'll take it from here, Brinton."

Captain Green reached for the gun. When it was safely in his hands, Clara leaned against James's chest for the briefest of seconds before running to her father's side.

"Thank you, Miss Lambert." The captain turned to her, but he still managed to keep the gun trained on Bales.

She held her breath, waiting for the man to make a move against the captain. He didn't, but she still didn't breathe easy until the captain turned back around. "I didn't do anything, sir."

"Yes, you did, Clara." Her father spoke up, his voice sounding stronger now. "You figured out Bales was the killer. *And* you managed to knock him unconscious."

Was that a touch of pride she heard in her father's voice? His praise brought a flush to her cheeks.

"Good work, Miss Lambert. Now why don't the two of you help your father down the stairs so we can get him seen by a doctor?"

"I'll be fine, sir. But thank you just the same." Her father could protest all he wanted, but he was going to see a doctor.

"Brinton, before you leave with Miss Lambert and her father, could you send someone to Bales's residence to round up his brother?"

"Yes, sir. I sure will."

"If I remember the last time we had to arrest the man, we found him holed up there like the coward that he is." The captain shook his head and sighed. "I guess it runs in the family."

While James listened to instructions from the captain, he absently pulled Clara's hand to his chest. Beneath it, she could feel his heart thumping. He tugged her toward him, and she went willingly.

"You're such a good person, James."

He blinked in surprise and a slow smile spread across his face.

And Clara was happy to be the one to have put it there.

EPILOGUE

Niagara Falls, New York

Just over a month later, Clara stood near the precipice of Niagara Falls with her camera at the ready. She was flanked by her father and James as they waited for Annie Edson Taylor to make the one hundred and seventy-four foot drop over the Falls in a barrel that Clara was certain wouldn't hold together. Emil and Eulalie Martin were also there, standing just behind them.

She took a moment to whisper a prayer for Mrs. Taylor's safety, and when she finished she took an extra moment to pray for the comfort of Ida McKinley.

In spite of the doctors' best efforts, the president had taken a turn for the worse and slipped quietly away. It was rumored that he knew he was dying, and he called his wife to his side to assure her he was at peace. He was even said to have sung "Nearer My God to Thee" before he died.

Clara had waited a couple of weeks after the funeral before she wrapped up the photograph she'd taken of the McKinleys and had it sent to the former first lady at her home in Canton, Ohio. She prayed that it would bring the woman a small bit of comfort to look at the photo and see how happy she and her husband had been.

"Clara?" She looked up when James reached for her hand.

"There's someone here to see you."

Joy welled inside her as she followed James's line of sight. "Gracie!" She let go of his hand and raced toward the little girl and her mother. "I can't believe it. I've looked everywhere for you."

"I know," Gracie declared. "Mr. James told us. He told us how that bad man took your camera and broke the film. We're here so you can take a new picture for my daddy."

With her heart overflowing, Clara scooped Gracie into a hug. "How do you think he'd like a picture of you with Niagara Falls in the background?"

"I think he'll love it!"

Behind her, James cleared his throat.

"James, you found them for me. Thank you so much."

"I knew how important it was for you." Even as he said it, a bloom of pink appeared on his cheeks.

Somehow she thought it had to do with something other than his bashfulness over her thanking him for a kind deed. But whatever it was would have to wait until she took little Gracie's picture.

When she finished, Gracie wrapped her arms around Clara's legs. "Thank you so much, Clara. My daddy is going to love getting a picture in the mail."

"Yes, thank you," Gracie's mother said. "And James, thank you for waiting so patiently while Clara took the photos."

"You're welcome, ma'am." Even as he said it, his eyes were focused only on Clara, and her heart picked up an extra beat.

"James?"

"Clara, I've told you I loved you almost from the moment the aerio-cycle lifted us from the ground. But I waited because I didn't want to seem like I was in a rush."

Waited? A rush? "James, what are you talking about?" But as his face grew bright, she knew. Her heart lifted, and her vision blurred.

"Mr. Lambert, may I request the honor of your daughter's hand in marriage?"

Before she could protest, her father said almost the exact thing she was about to say. "As much as I like you, Brinton, my daughter can speak for herself."

"Thank you, Daddy. Yes, I can. And James, just for that, I should make you beg. Or better yet, you should accompany Mrs. Taylor over the Falls."

Even as she saw the mischief form on James's face, Clara knew she would say yes. She also knew that if she didn't grab his arm, he may just take her up on the challenge to go over Niagara Falls. So she did the only thing she could.

She kissed him.

ACKNOWLEDGMENTS

The origins of this book started with what appeared to be a miniature silver fluted vase. My father said it belonged to his grandmother. As I sat looking at it in a hotel room, I realized it had an etching on it. Buffalo 1901. That made me curious. I emailed a picture of the vase to my Inkwell Inspirations email loop, and Barbara Early got back to me and said it was a souvenir from the Pan American Exposition in 1901. As happens to most writers, my creative thoughts started spinning. How had my great-grandmother come across this? Had she gone to the fair? She was alone in New York with her two children. Was she working? Might she have worked at the fair? I was already working on a book set in Seattle at the Alaska Yukon Pacific Exposition in 1909. Could I write another book set at the Pan American Exposition? Could I write a series? I started researching different fairs, and decided that yes, I could. And it proved to me once again, that it only takes one item to spark and idea that becomes a book. Thank you to my father, Bill Smith, for inspiring yet another of my historical novels.

A huge thank you wrapped up with a hug to my sister, Pamela Mynatt, for being my first reader on this book. Your enormous encouragement and support means so much to me. I love you always.

Barbara Early, thank you so much for answering all of my questions about Buffalo – and for finding details about the Pan-American Exposition. You've been a great help to me.

Narelle Atkins, Marti Bodley, Stacy Monson, and Heather Steiner, my wonderful critique partners, thank you so much for reading, critiquing, and giving me your moral support along the way.

Always and forever, to my son, Kirk Johnson, and my mother, Barbara Smith, thank you so much for your love and support along the way.

Dina Sleiman and Roseanna White, your editorial input is the absolute best. Thank you for helping to make my words flow. Thank you for believing in me and this series. I can never say how much it means to me.

Suzie

ALSO BY SUZIE JOHNSON

They're on the hunt for something BIG...

Sweet Mountain Music

OTHER TITLES

You may also enjoy these other titles from WhiteFire Publishing

The Sound of Silver
Steadfast Love Series ~ 2
By Rachelle Rea

Journey back to Elizabethan England and into the hearts of a Catholic maiden out for justice…and a reformed rogue out to clear his name.

Soul's Prisoner
By Cara Luecht

In 1890s Chicago, the powers of redemption clash with society's failings in a sweeping tale of one woman fighting for her future… while another fights for her freedom.